To those people who read
this book.
— Best Wishes!
Carl P. "Buster" Hitt

SARAH

SARAH

A Young Girl's Struggle to Reunite Her Family

Carl P. "Buster" Hitt

MILL CITY PRESS

Mill City Press, Inc.
2301 Lucien Way #415
Maitland, FL 32751
407.339.4217
www.millcitypress.net

Note from the author:

This story is totally fiction. All of its characters and character names, locations and location names, happenings, and events are either from the author's imagination or are fictional representations created by the author. Any similarities or resemblances to actual persons, alive or dead; real places and locations, current or historical; or actual happenings and events, present or past, are entirely coincidental.

Library of Congress Control Number: 2023908096

Paperback ISBN-13: 978-1-66287-836-7
Ebook ISBN-13: 978-1-66287-837-4

DEDICATION

To my friend, Steve White, who was the first person to call me "A Writer" and mean it.

To my late friend, Patricia May, who was the first person to read this story, and who encouraged me to finish it.

To my high school English teachers, who didn't think I was paying attention.

To those who have devoted their lives to writing and are still unpublished. Never give up!

To all those whose works would have been written and published had they lived long enough.

Chapter 1

THE ABANDONMENT

AT THREE, THE Mickey Mouse alarm clock rang on Miss Gibson's desk at Austin School, four miles east of Piggott. She tapped its shutoff button and Xed off Wednesday, July 14, 1954, on her calendar with a red pencil.

Twelve-year-old Sarah Jane Skaggs opened the lid of her desk and stowed her school kit. Across the room, her brothers, nine-year-old Johnny and five-year-old Mark did the same.

"Don't forget now," Miss Gibson said, above the screech of chairs and the shuffle of feet, "there's a spelling test tomorrow for grades two through eight." She looked at her grade book, ran her finger down the list of thirty-three names, and peered up at Johnny. "Some of you really need to study."

Miss Gibson hadn't called Johnny by name, but she may as well have. Everyone saw her look at him. Sarah hated it when their teacher humiliated students that way, but they would show her. Tonight she would drill Johnny until he could spell every word on that list every time.

Sarah bounced to her feet, jerked her books from her desk, and strutted to the cloakroom. She dragged her lunch pail off the shelf and joined her brothers outside, where they threw rocks at turtles in Middle Slough while the rest of the eastbound cluster of kids assembled.

As the group stepped onto the shoulder of the highway, a pickup truck approached, loaded with teenage baseball players from Piggott.

"Hey, you split-term losers!" a boy in the truck yelled. "Too bad ya can't go to a *real* school!"

One of the Austin boys scooped up a rock and flung it at the truck. "Get outta here, you jackasses!"

Johnny looked at his sister and frowned. "How come 'em Piggott kids don't hafta go to school in the summertime like we do?"

"'Cause they don't hafta chop and pick cotton," Sarah said.

"That ain't fair," Johnny said. "We don't ever get no time off. We're always either workin' in the fields or goin' to school."

A half mile east of the schoolhouse, where the gravel road branched off to the north, the Skaggs kids split from the group and headed to their little house beside the Saint Francis River.

Sarah plopped down on an old tree stump, removed her brown Oxfords, and tied their laces together. Then she slung them over her shoulder and caught up with her brothers. A reader and a speller dangled from the leather book belt that coiled around her right hand like a chicken snake. And her lunch pail, an old lard bucket with a wire handle, danced beneath her left hand as she skipped along and sang, "Old Dan Tucker."

When a dust devil spun up in the road just in front of the kids, Sarah ran straight into it. "Hey, look at me!" she shouted as her dress flew up around her head. "I'm a hollyhock!"

While the boys stopped and poked at a dead possum, Sarah kept walking. As she approached home, she saw their old car sitting backed up to the front porch with a mattress tied on its top. Her feet froze to the ground, her eyes bulged, and her mouth flew open.

"Oh boy! We're movin'!" she mumbled. Then her long, lean legs whirled her to the house with her red braided pigtails bouncing on her shoulders.

As she ran through the gate into the yard, her stepfather, Hank, stepped out the front door. His dirty arms hugged two paper sacks that he carried to the car and loaded into the back seat. When he stood back up, a gust of wind blew open his shirt, and hot cigarette ashes fell into the sweaty hair above his belly. "Dammit!" he shouted and brushed away the sparks.

Sarah chuckled. It served him right for how he treated them. "So we're finally leavin' this broke-down, old place, huh Hank?"

He squinted at her and took a long drag on his cigarette. "Me and 'Lizabeth are," he said as smoke billowed from his mouth and streamed from his nose. "We're movin' to St. Louie, but you kids ain't."

Sarah's smile fell away to straight lips. "Whatcha mean, us 'kids ain't?'"

"Just that. Y'all are stayin' here."

"Who we stayin' with?"

Hank took another drag on his cigarette. "Go inside and ask your maw."

Sarah tried to look into Hank's eyes, but he turned away. She had learned that tongues lie, but eyes don't.

As Sarah entered the kitchen, her mother turned and faced the wall. She was sitting on the floor, packing dishes into a paper sack. Her shoulder-length red hair framed her sunken eyes and bony cheeks, and her floral-print dress hung on her skinny frame.

"Mama, you ain't really movin' away and leavin' us kids behind, are ya?"

Her mother's entire body shook as she tried to speak, but nothing came out. She cleared her throat and tried again. "I ain't got no choice. Hank's makin' me do it. He got fired at the shoe factory today because of his drankin'. We're movin' to St. Louie, whur nobody knows he's a drunk, so he can find work. Besides, there ain't room in the car for all of us. He says y'all can stay here with the church people till we come back to get ya. And he's right."

"But, Mama, we don't go to church."

"That don't matter. Church folks always help people that's in need. Hank was aimed to already be gone by the time y'all got home—said it'd be easier on ever'body thataway. He told me to leave ya a note, but I couldn't go without sayin' g'bye. So I punched a hole in one of the tires, and he had to patch it."

Sarah took hold of her mother's hand. "Please don't leave us, Mama. Just tell him you ain't goin', and stay here with us."

"I done tried that," she said and sniffled. "He says I gotta go to cook and do housework."

Then Sarah peered at her mother's face. Bruises—fresh ones—still red with a bit of purple. "Oh, Mama!" She reached toward them, but her mother shoved her hand away.

"Ah, it's all right. It's for what I done to the tire."

"No, it ain't all right!" Sarah said. "Let's run away, so he cain't ever hurt any of us again!"

"We cain't. We need him to take care of us."

"I wouldn't call knockin' us around, 'takin' care of us.' We'd be a whole lot better off takin' care of ourselves. Come on, Mama," Sarah whispered. "Let's slip out the backdoor and run to the woods. We can make it. I know we can. I'll tell Johnny and Mark to stall Hank, then meet us at the old cabin."

Sarah jumped up to go tell the boys, but her mother pulled her back down. "I ain't got the strength." She picked up the last dish, wrapped it, and put it in the bag. "Here, set this up on the counter for me."

Sarah picked up the bag, set it beside the other one, and sat back down. "He beat ya up really good this time, didn't he?"

Her mother didn't answer.

"Ya know, Mama? One of these days, he's gonna kill one of us."

Hank suddenly sprang into the room and glared down at the women. "What's goin' on here?"

"I's just tellin' Sarah how she's gonna hafta take care of her brothers while we're gone."

"Whatcha talkin' 'bout? *She* ain't gonna hafta take care of nobody. 'Em church people'll do that." Hank picked up the last two sacks and headed back outside.

Sarah jumped up, flung her shoes across the room, and hit him in the back. "You dirty old devil!"

Hank whirled around, plopped the sacks on a chair, and slapped her.

"No, Hank! She didn't mean it!" her mother screamed and pulled Sarah back to the floor.

Hank sneered, picked up the sacks, and stomped out the front door.

"Don't you go causin' no trouble, Sarah!" her mother said and frowned. "I got enough to worry 'bout without tryin' to keep him from hurtin' you kids!"

"Just let him try it," Sarah said. "Me and Johnny'll knock his head off."

From the front yard, laughter floated into the room.

"Hey, Hank, what's up?" Johnny said.

"Go ask your sis."

"What's goin' on, Sarah?" Johnny said as he and Mark bolted into the kitchen.

Deep inside, Sarah's soul trembled. She wanted to cry but stiffened instead. She could handle this without falling apart. "Hank lost his job today, so him and Mama's movin' to St. Louie to find work, but don't worry, it's okay. We're stayin' here with the church people."

"And once we're settled up there," their mother said, "we'll come back and get ya."

Sarah peered at her mother. "What if somethin' happens, and ya cain't come back?"

"There ain't nothin' gonna stop me from comin' back to get y'all."

"Come on, 'Lizabeth!" Hank shouted from the car. "Let's go!"

"I'm comin'!" she hollered back. As she stood up and hugged her kids, tears filled her eyes. "I love y'all more'n you'll ever know. You boys, mind Sarah. She'll watch out after ya, and y'all watch out after her too, okay?"

"Okay," Johnny said.

They walked to the front porch, and their mother kissed each of them a final time.

"Quit makin' such a fuss, and let's go!" Hank yelled. "All you're doin' is makin' it worse!" He started the car and revved its engine.

The tangled group shuffled to the old jalopy, untangled, and their mother got in the car. Tears streamed down Sarah and Mark's cheeks, while Johnny looked on with a blank stare.

"G'bye, Mama!" Sarah said.

"Bye-bye, Mama!" Mark said.

Johnny stayed quiet.

"Bye-bye, babies. I'll send ya a letter as soon as we get there."

"No, ya won't," Hank said in a low, spiteful voice.

Their mother shot a hateful look at him. "Oh, yes, I will!" Then she looked back at her kids. "So have them church people brang ya by here ever day to check the mail."

Sarah glared at Hank. He wasn't coming back for them. She knew it, but her mother didn't.

Hank tromped the clutch and shoved the shift toward first gear. The cogs ground, then caught, and the car lurched forward. As it groaned away from the house, the kids followed. At the edge of the yard, they lined up in front of the mailbox–Sarah, Mark, and Johnny.

Sarah draped her arm around Mark's shoulder and hugged him against her side. Then they stood motionless and watched until the car disappeared behind a cloud of dust.

"Whur they goin' to?" Mark said as he peered up at his sister through his tears.

"St. Louie."

"When they comin' back?"

Sarah smiled. She wasn't going to tell him the truth. "I don't know. Soon, I hope."

The kids wandered to the front porch and sat down.

"I'm hungry," Mark said.

"You're always hungry," Johnny said.

Sarah rubbed Mark's head. "Okay, I'll go to the garden and see what I can find. Y'all go draw us some water so's we can warsh our hands."

As Sarah walked away, Johnny headed to the tile well beside the house, and Mark followed. "Johnny, whur's St. Louie?"

"I don't know," Johnny said. "It's a big town somewhur."

"Why's Hank goin' 'ere to find work?"

"'Cause 'ere's lotsa good jobs in cities," Johnny said. "They ain't like the lousy ones here that don't pay nothin'."

As the boys set the wash pan on the back porch, Sarah called to them from the garden. "Hey! One of ya, come here and help me get this thang."

Johnny ran to her, and they lugged the watermelon to the house.

"How we gonna cut it?" Johnny said.

"We'll hafta bust it," Sarah said. "Get back, and I'll roll it off the porch."

The three-foot drop split the melon but didn't break it in two, so Sarah got on one side, and Johnny got on the other, and they pulled at the cracked rind until it split open.

Mark reached out to dig into the melon's ripe heart, but Sarah grabbed his arm. "Oh no, ya don't! Not with 'em nasty hands!"

After they washed, Sarah peeled off Mark's shirt while Johnny broke a melon half into smaller bits. Then they each took a piece.

When Mark bit into his melon, juice streamed from his chin and elbows.

"Well, dang it, Marky," Sarah said. "We'll hafta take off your pants too." And while he ate, she stripped him to his underpants.

7

As Sarah hiked up her dress tail to sit down and eat, Johnny spat a seed at a nearby washtub. When it dinged, they all laughed. And for a while, life returned to normal as supper became a seed-spitting contest.

Then Mark yelled, "Hey, Mama, come out here and look at this!" And they all froze.

"I'm 'bout to pop!" Johnny said when the trance broke, and he set his rind on the porch.

"Me too!" Sarah said, and she also laid down her rind.

Mark continued to eat as though he had just started.

"How can you eat so much, Marky?" Sarah said.

"'Cause I'm hungry."

"You're always hungry," Johnny said. "That's why you're fat."

Mark glared at his brother. "I ain't fat! I'm just round!"

"Yeah, you're so round ya cain't fit into none of the hand-me-downs I give ya."

"You had enough, Marky," Sarah said and took his melon away.

As the kids threw the rinds over the back fence, Sarah pondered what all needed to be done. It was too late for them to go to the church people, so they would do that tomorrow. And since they didn't know anyone at church, she would ask Miss Gibson to go with them.

Then Sarah shivered. What if the church people tried to separate them? That had happened to some other kids they knew. She wasn't going to risk that, so she called the boys to the porch. "Do y'all remember Chucky and Donna, who lived by the schoolhouse, and how they got split up when their mother died?"

The boys nodded.

"Well, if we ain't careful, the same thang could happen to us. So we ain't goin' to the church people, and we ain't tellin' nobody that Mama and Hank's gone." Sarah cupped Mark's face in her hands and stared into his eyes. "Do ya hear me, Marky? We cain't tell nobody, not even Sammy and Timmy. Ya wouldn't wonna be split up from Johnny and me, would ya?"

Tears welled up in Mark's eyes, and he broke free from Sarah's grip.

"Well, that's why we cain't tell nobody. They might do that to us."

"So what we gonna do?" Johnny said.

"Just what we always do," Sarah said. "We'll get up ever mornin', go to school, and come home just like we do ever day."

"What we gonna do for lunch?" Johnny said.

"Well, there's part of a loaf of bread left in the kitchen," Sarah said. "I'll carry three slices to school in my lard bucket. Then at noon, we'll meet at the lunch table. I'll fold 'em to look like sandwiches, and nobody'll ever know the difference."

"Ya mean all we're havin' for lunch is bread?" Mark said.

"Yeah. I'm sorry, Marky, but that's all we got."

"What we gonna do for supper tomorra?" Johnny said. "We gotta have somethin' more'n watermelon."

"Why? What's wrong with watermelon?" Mark said.

"For one thang, it makes ya go to the toilet a lot," Johnny said.

"Well, maybe I can get a job at Mr. Zimmerman's store," Sarah said. "We'll worry 'bout that tomorra. Right now, we gotta get ready for bed. If ya gotta go to the outhouse, do it now. Hank took the slop jar with him, and once we're inside, we ain't comin' back out till mornin'. Skunks, snakes, and other varmints prowl 'round at night."

They each visited the outhouse, then washed and went inside. Sarah latched the doors, and they crawled onto their mattresses.

As twilight faded into darkness, the calls of Chuck-will's-widows echoed from the woods, the bullfrogs droned from the river, and the cicadas sang from the trees.

"G'night, Sissy," Mark said. "I sure wish Mama was here."

"G'night, Marky. Yeah, I wish Mama was here, too," Sarah said, "but ever'thang's okay. So go to sleep now and have sweet dreams."

"Sweet dreams," Mark said.

Soon the light snores of her brother filled the room, but Sarah couldn't sleep. What were they going to do? How were they going to eat? They had no money, no kinfolks, and no close friends to ask for help.

Sarah got up, slid the wallboard from her secret hiding place, took out the locket her mother had given her, and opened it. In the dim light, she could barely see the picture of her parents. For a moment, she stared at them. Then she closed the gold case, kissed it, and put it back inside the wall. As she laid back down, a tear tumbled from her eye and trickled down her cheek onto the pillow.

Sarah hadn't prayed since September 28, 1950, the day God had let her daddy get killed. She was mad at *Him* for that, and since then, she had let her mother do all the praying. But now their mother was gone, and they needed help.

"Dear God, please take care of Mama whurever she is, and help me take care of my brothers. Keep us safe and together. Amen."

Sarah buried her face in her pillow and let go of a torrent of tears that swept her into a sleep that covered her like a thin blanket.

Chapter 2

ADAPTING

IN THE DISTANCE, a rooster crowed, and Sarah opened her eyes. She sat up, stretched, and glanced around the room. Everything looked okay, but something wasn't quite right. Then she looked at her sleeping brothers, and her world came clear. She rolled out of bed, dressed, and hurried to the outhouse.

As Sarah emerged from the privy, she glanced at the cloudless, pale blue sky. But as pretty as the day was, she didn't stop and listen to the songbirds or run her hands over the colorful flower petals as usual. Instead, she drew water from the well, and washed, then looked at the world around her. *Okay, you can do this. Take it one thang at a time, and the first thang is breakfast.*

Sarah picked two cantaloupes, broke them into pieces, and set them along the edge of the back porch. Then she walked back to the bedroom. "Johnny–Marky–Time to get up."

Johnny shifted. Then his eyes popped open, and he flung himself to his feet. "Dang it, Marky! Ya wet the bed! Ya shouldn'ta et so much watermelon!"

"Stop yellin' at me!" Mark said. "I couldn't help it!"

"Yes, ya coulda!" Johnny said as he peeled off his damp underwear and flung them into the corner. "Ya shouldn'ta et so much!" he yelled, and Sarah giggled.

"Stop laughin', Sarah! It ain't funny!" Johnny said as he opened the chest of drawers and put on a clean pair of briefs. "How'd you like it if he peed on you?"

"Oh, quit whinin'," Sarah said. "It ain't gonna kill ya. Let's carry that mattress out to the back porch and lay it in the sun."

"I ain't doin' nothin' till I go to the outhouse," Johnny said. "I'm 'bout to bust."

Sarah giggled again. "Well, ya shouldn'ta et so much watermelon."

Johnny glared at his sister and pushed past her.

"I'm hungry," Mark said. "What's for breakfast?"

"You don't get no breakfast!" Johnny said.

"Oh, yes, I do!" Mark whined.

"Quit bein' so hateful, Johnny," Sarah said.

"Well, what *is* for breakfast?" Mark said.

"Cantaloupe," Sarah Said.

"Cantaloupe? Biscuits is for breakfast–not cantaloupe."

"Well, cantaloupe's good for ya. Besides, it's all we got. Take off 'em wet underpants. They'll hafta be warshed," she said as she opened the chest and handed Mark a clean pair. Then she helped him dress, and they joined Johnny on the back porch to eat.

Mark gobbled down his portion of the melon and asked for more.

"There ain't no more," Sarah said.

"But I'm still hungry," Mark said.

"I cain't help it. You'll just hafta wait till supper."

Mark frowned. "You just don't wonna fix no more. 'Ere's lots left in the garden."

"Yeah, you're right, but we ain't got time right now. We gotta getta school, so help clean up this mess, and let's go."

Mark puffed out his jaws, picked up some rind pieces, and tossed them over the fence. Then, while Sarah went to the kitchen and put three slices of bread in her lard bucket, the boys wrestled the mattress outside onto the back porch.

Since Johnny and Mark always got to school before Sarah, they left home first. As they walked out the front door, Sarah reminded them to keep their secret, and they both crossed their hearts.

When Sarah picked up her book belt, she remembered the spelling test. She caught up with the boys and made Johnny spell words the rest of the way to school.

Sarah worried about their mother and how to keep their secret all day. The distraction caused her to answer two questions incorrectly in class–something she had never done before. But in general, the day went well. Mark hadn't even complained about his bread lunch.

On the way home, the kids hung back from the cluster.

"Ya both done real good today 'bout keepin' our secret," Sarah said. "I'm proud of ya."

"Well, I almost slipped, talkin' to Brewster, but I caught myself," Johnny said.

"Thank goodness!" Sarah said.

As they walked, Mark rubbed his stomach. "My belly hurts."

"Mine too," Johnny said.

"Yeah, so's mine," Sarah said. "We'll stop at Mr. Zimmerman's store. Maybe we can find somethin' there to eat."

At the store, the kids eased past an old pickup truck, parked out front, and tiptoed onto the porch. As they peeked through the bread advertisement painted on the screen door, a man set two full shopping baskets on the counter, and Mr. Zimmerman popped open some paper sacks.

"Lookee at all that stuff," Mark whispered.

"Yeah!" Johnny said.

As Mr. Zimmerman took each thing out of a basket, he punched numbers into his adding machine and placed the item into one of the bags. Then he opened a book and wrote in it. When the men picked up the bags and headed outside, the kids scampered down the steps and hid behind the corner of the building. While the men set the bags in the truck bed against the driver's side of the cab, the kids watched. Then the customer reached into his shirt pocket and pulled out a pack of cigarettes. "That reminds me. I need a carton of smokes," he said, and the men strolled back inside the store.

"Look at that! 'Em sacks is just sittin' 'ere!" Johnny said, and he bolted to the truck.

When Mark jumped up to follow, Sarah pulled him back.

"But I can help!" Mark said.

"No, let Johnny do it! You might get caught!"

Mark fought to break loose, but Sarah wrapped herself around him like a spider around its prey.

Johnny darted back with three cans, and Sarah stared at him. "I never thought we'd be stealin' to survive. It just ain't right."

"Maybe not, but we're gonna eat tonight!" Johnny said, and they dashed toward home.

Out of breath, the trio collapsed on the front porch.

Johnny rolled around and laughed as he hugged the cans to his stomach. "That was fun. Let's do it again tomorra."

They caught their breath, then Sarah picked up the cans and read the labels. "Hominy! Spinach! Pork and beans!"

Tears gushed from Mark's eyes. "We still ain't got nothin' to eat."

"Why, Marky, you like pork and beans," Sarah said. "Don't ya remember how ya like soppin' up the juice with bread?"

"But we ain't got no more bread."

"Well, ya can just drank the juice outta the can."

"Now we gotta find somethin' to open 'em with," Johnny said.

Sarah ran to the kitchen and jerked open the silverware drawer–Nothing but a fork, a spoon, and a butter knife–She grabbed all three. Then she dashed to the back porch and looked at the nail in the post where Hank's beer can opener always hung. There it was. She grabbed it, ran back to the front porch, and opened the cans.

"Here, Marky," Sarah said and handed him the can of pork and beans. "You can have this. Johnny and me'll share the other two."

"This spinach is wet and stringy," Johnny said.

"And this hominy is like soggy corn," Sarah said. "I wish we had some salt."

But after a couple of hesitant bites, they dug in.

"I didn't know cold hominy and spinach could taste so good," Johnny said.

With their bellies full, they lay on the porch in the warm sun and occasionally burst into spontaneous laughter.

Then Mark said, "I wonder whur Mama is?" And their laughter stopped.

"Let's go see if we got a letter from her," Sarah said, and they hurried to the mailbox. They stared into its emptiness momentarily as if hoping something would appear. When it didn't, they returned to the porch.

At sunset, they each visited the outhouse. Then they washed and went inside.

While Johnny and Mark carried the mattress back into the bedroom, Sarah locked the doors.

"Marky, if ya gotta pee tonight, get up and go do it out the windor," Johnny said as he crawled into bed.

"Oh, get over it, Johnny," Sarah said. "He don't usually wet the bed."

"Well, I just wonna make sure he don't."

In the blue moonlight, Sarah helped Mark get undressed. "Sleep tight," she said as he slid onto the mattress beside Johnny.

"Yeah, Sissy, sleep tight," Mark said.

"G'night, Johnny," Sarah said, but he had already fallen asleep.

As Sarah crossed the room to her bed, she rubbed her belly. *Dang! Supper ain't agreein' with me.*

She lay down on the cool sheet and closed her eyes. The sound of the cicadas, bullfrogs, Chuck-will's-widows, and her brothers' snoring blended into weird, rhythmic music, and she smiled.

Then her mother's face drifted into view. *"Whur are ya tonight, Mama? Are ya thankin' 'bout us? We're thankin' 'bout you."*

While Sarah concentrated on the picture in her head, a car roared around the four-mile turn on the highway. Through the window, its headlights cast tree shadows onto the wall. When she was little, Sarah pretended those shadows were a moving picture show. She curled into a ball and watched the images, wishing she were still a little girl listening to her mother hum songs while mending her daddy's shirts by lamplight in the next room. *Why did he hafta die so young? Why did You let that happen, God? How could You let somebody so loved and so needed get killed like that?*

Tears filled Sarah's eyes and trickled down her cheeks. She sobbed until the strange music lulled her to sleep.

Chapter 3

MR. JAKE

BELLY CRAMPS PUSHED Sarah awake at dawn. From the feel of it, she had wet her pants. She sent a hand to investigate and screamed when it came back bloody.

Johnny and Mark bounced out of bed.

"What's wrong?" Johnny said.

Sarah clenched her bloody hand and buried it in the sheet. Her chest heaved, and her thoughts bounced from one horrible idea to another as she sat glassy-eyed and stunned.

Johnny nudged her. "Hey, Sarah, what's wrong?"

She gasped and peered at the boys. She couldn't tell them. It was too private, and besides, it would scare them. "Oh, I just had a bad dream. Y'all go draw a pan of warsh water and pick us a couple of cantaloupes for breakfast. I'll be out in a minute."

Johnny shook his head. "Humm! Girls!" Then he and Mark dressed and headed outside.

Sarah eased out of bed and rechecked herself. Yes–It really was blood! Her heart pounded, and she trembled. Why was she bleeding down there? Had she hurt herself? She couldn't think of how or when. She closed her eyes. *God, please make it stop! Make me well! Don't make me die young like Daddy!*

In the corner of the room lay a pile of dirty laundry. Sarah pulled a washcloth from it, wiped the blood off her hand, then folded it and placed it inside her underpants.

What was she going to do? She couldn't go to school bleeding like this. She had to think of a reason to stay home, but what?

She dressed and stared at herself in the dresser mirror. She was shaky but looked okay.

When the boys' voices drifted into the room from the garden, Sarah's eyebrows shot up. Food! That was it! She would tell them she had to skip school to find food. She hurried outside and washed her hands.

"Lookee, Sissy," Mark said as he and Johnny carried cantaloupes to the back porch. "We got two big uns."

Sarah nodded and smiled but didn't really look at the melons. "Yeah, 'em's nice."

Mark frowned. "No, Sissy, lookee!" He waved his melon in her face.

She looked at it and smiled. "Yeah, that's really big. Set it down over yonder, and I'll break it up while you and Johnny warsh your hands."

As Sarah broke the melon into chunks, her cheeks quivered. She handed a piece to each brother and then took one for herself. Suddenly, tears gushed from her eyes.

Johnny grimaced. "Whatsamatter now?"

"I gotta find somethin' for us to eat. We cain't live on just watermelon and cantaloupe. We'll get sick. We gotta have meat once in a while to stay healthy."

"Okay," Johnny said. "Today after school, we'll go out again like we done yesterdee. Only this time, we'll go after meat. Mr. Greeson's got lotsa chickens. He won't miss one ole hen. We can build a fare in the backyard and roast it."

"No!" Sarah said. "No more stealin'! It ain't right! And if we's to get caught, we'd go to jail. What'd happen to us then? That's why I ain't goin' to school today. I gotta fig're out somehow to get food without stealin' it."

"How's not goin' to school gonna help ya do that?" Johnny said.

"I'll hafta do a lotta thankin', and I cain't do that at school with ever'thang else that'll be goin' on," Sarah said.

Johnny squinted. "That's dumb when all we gotta do is snatch one of old man Greeson's chickens. What am I gonna tell Miss Gibson when she asks why ya ain't there?"

"Tell her I got a bellyache. But don't tell her if she don't ask."

Johnny laughed. "You ain't got no bellyache."

"Yes, I do so have a bellyache. I had it all night."

Johnny sneered. "Oh, I see? It's okay to lie, but it ain't okay to steal."

"Dang it, Johnny! I ain't lyin'! But if I was, they wouldn't throw us in jail for tellin' a little fib."

"Well, since we're gettin' back our spellin' test today, maybe I'll just stay home, too. I know I flunked it."

Sarah stared at him. She hadn't thought of that. She felt sorry for him but not enough to let him stay home. "That's great! We'll just send Marky to school by hisself. Then we'll have all sortsa people snoopin' 'round here to see what's goin' on."

Mark puffed out his jaws and frowned. "I'm too sceared to go to school by myself."

Sarah knelt in front of Mark. "Well, you ain't gonna have to. Johnny's just bein' silly. He'll be right there with ya." She glared at Johnny. "Ain't that right?"

"Yeah, that's right," Johnny said.

As Mark headed to the front yard, Johnny peered at Sarah. "So what's Marky and me gonna do for lunch?"

"I don't know," Sarah said. "Ya might hafta do without lunch today."

"You know Marky cain't do that," Johnny said. "He's gotta have somethin' to eat."

"Well then, see if ya can get Brewster Holland to give ya some of his. He always brangs more'n he can eat. Tell him ya left your lunch at home. Or maybe ya can trade him somethin'. Catch a turtle at the slough. He's always a sucker for turtles, even snappin' turtles."

Johnny laughed. "I'd druther trade him a water moccasin."

"Well, he may be kinda dumb, but he'll help ya."

Johnny reached into his pocket and fondled the agate his real daddy gave him. He always had that to bargain with if he needed it. "Oh well, I'll fig're out somethin'."

"You take good care of Marky today," Sarah said.

"Don't worry. I will," Johnny said. Then he glared at his sister. "Whatsamatter? Don't ya trust me? Ya know, he's my little brother, too."

Sarah smiled. "Yeah, I trust ya."

"Come on, Marky. Let's go," Johnny said and headed out the gate.

Mark trotted to his brother's side. "Bye-bye, Sissy."

"G'bye, Marky. Don't forget to keep our secret."

"I won't forget."

As the boys disappeared from view, something wet fell on Sarah's foot: blood.

She checked herself and found more blood–A lot more.

She burst into tears, dashed to the river, and washed herself. Then she rinsed her underwear and washcloth, hung them on a bush to dry, and sat down on a submerged rock.

As the cool current carried away her blood, a flock of pigeons launched from the barn loft. Mesmerized by the birds sweeping across the sky above her, Sarah relaxed. Once, they even dipped so low that she ducked as they swished past.

Near midmorning, the trees along the riverbank shaded Sarah, and a school of minnows stopped to nibble at her toes. When a big catfish swam by, her mind returned to finding food. If they begged, people would find out their secret. If they stole, they would end up in jail. If she got a job, she would have to quit school. Nothing seemed possible.

Sarah sat in the river all day and only got up a few times to stretch and walk around. When voices sounded from the lane in the late afternoon, she stood up and checked herself–Just a trace of blood. She splashed out of the river, pulled on her underwear, and ran to the house.

"You still sick?" Johnny said as Sarah checked the empty mailbox.

"I'm better," she said.

"Why's your dress wet?"

"I fell in the river tryin' to catch a catfish."

"Is that what we're havin' for supper?" Mark said.

"No. I didn't catch it."

"Did ya fig're out somehow to get food," Johnny said.

"No, I didn't," Sarah said.

"Well then, what good did it do for ya to stay home?"

Sarah frowned and ignored his question. "Did Marky get lunch?"

"Yeah, we et good. I traded my marble to Brewster for some cheese and crackers and–"

"You traded your marble? The one Daddy give ya?" Her voice rose with every word. "The only thang ya had left of him?"

Johnny hunched up like a cornered raccoon. "Yeah, but don't worry. I'll get it back."

"Well, you better 'fore somethin' happens to it." She loved that marble almost as much as her brother did.

Then Johnny grinned. "Guess what? I got a C+ on my spellin' test."

"See there? What'd I tell ya?" Sarah said and smiled. "All it takes is a little bitta studyin'."

"Here, I brung ya somethin'," Johnny said and pulled a yellow apple from his pocket. He tossed it to Sarah, and she caught it.

"Gee, thanks!" she said. Then she looked at it, and tears filled her eyes.

"Whatsamatter now?" Johnny said. "Don't ya wont it?"

"Sure I do. I's just thankin'. We really are takin' care of each other like Mama told us to."

Johnny put his arm around her. "Ahh, don't worry. Ever'thang'll be okay. Eat your apple. It'll make ya feel better."

By the time Sarah finished the apple, she really did feel better. She tossed its core to the ground, ran to the bedroom, and checked her washcloth—only a spot of blood—she felt even better.

As Sarah stepped back onto the front porch, she squinted at the red-orange glow of the late afternoon sun and wrinkled her nose. The air smelled scorched. She wandered to the backyard, picked some large catalpa-leaf fans, and carried them to the porch.

"Gimme one with worms on it," Mark said as he ran to her.

Sarah picked out a leaf with two of the giant black yellow-striped worms on it and handed it to him. "Goody! I like playin' with 'ese worms 'cause they got horns on their tails."

As Sarah climbed the porch steps, movement down the hazy lane caught her attention. She shaded her eyes and gazed at the silhouettes of a man and a small dog. "Who's that?" she said, and Johnny and Mark also peered at the duo.

"I don't know," Johnny said, "but I hope he's friendly."

"Quick, go find a club or somethin' to fight with in case he makes trouble," Sarah said.

While the boys hurried away, Sarah kept an eye on the stranger. He didn't look dangerous in his railroad engineer's cap and faded blue denim overalls with his knapsack slung over his shoulder. In fact, his long, lanky stride and slight wobble made him look funny—like he was drunk. But maybe that was from the heat.

A moment later, the boys ran back into the yard with an old table leg.

"Y'all wait by the door while I talk to him," Sarah said. "If any-thang bad happens, come runnin' with that club."

Johnny held the table leg at his side while he and Mark looked on from inside the front door. Sarah sauntered to the fence and rested her hands on top of it.

As the stranger and the dog stopped beside the mailbox, he smiled and lifted the brim of his cap. "Howdy, ma'am. Reckon I could talk to your Pa or Ma for a minute? I wonna ask 'em if'n we can spend the night in your barn."

"Well, sir, they ain't here right now," Sarah said. "They gone to Aunt Maggie's to get buttermilk and cured ham, but they'll be back after while. There ain't nothin' better'n buttermilk and cured ham for breakfast."

"No, ma'am. 'Ere shore ain't," the stranger said and mopped his sweaty face with a bandanna he pulled from his hip pocket. "Ya sufose we could get a drank of water and rest a spell under one of your shade trees? It's awful hot out here."

Sarah peered at the tall, skinny, sandy-haired man. She suspected he was a good person from his honest eyes and kind manners. And his little dog looked okay, too. Mean people don't have happy dogs, and this one was smiling.

"Well . . . yes, sir . . . I reckon that'd be okay. But just for a little while."

"Thank ya, ma'am. That's mighty neighborly."

He walked through the gate, and his dog followed. With every step, the man's heavy shoes clunked on the hard-packed ground like they were too big for his feet. He swung his knapsack to the ground, sat down on the grass in the shade of the big oak tree, and his dog sat down beside him.

Always her brothers' protector, Sarah moved in-between the visitor and the boys.

Johnny set the club down, and he and Mark eased onto the porch.

Then, Mark launched down the steps and ran to the dog. The rat terrier bounced to its feet, wagged his bobbed tail, and licked the boy's face.

Mark giggled. "Lookee, Sissy. The doggie's kissin' me."

"Did ya ask the man if ya could pet his dog?" Sarah said.

Mark frowned at his sister, then looked at the man. "Is it okay, Mister?"

"You go right ahead 'ere, young feller. Houdini likes bein' petted."

Mark wrinkled his nose. "Houdini? That's a funny name."

The man scratched the dog's back. "Yep, this here's Houdini. I named him that after I seen him escape from the dog catcher in Poplar Bluff, Missouri. He's been with me ever since."

Sarah eased over to Johnny. "Go get the drankin' water."

Johnny hurried into the house and returned with the bucket. As he ran across the yard, the dipper handle slid violently from side to side, and a large wave hurtled the container's rim.

"Be careful, Johnny! The man wonts a drank, not a empty bucket!" Sarah said, and the stranger laughed.

"I can't help it, Sarah," Johnny said. "This dang thang's heavy."

"Our well's got good, sweet water, Mister, and you can have all ya wont," Sarah said.

Johnny set the bucket on the grass where the man could reach the dipper, then sat down beside Mark.

The stranger filled the dipper, leaned forward, and raised it to his lips. As he drank, a small stream dribbled onto the ground between his feet. Houdini walked over and licked the wet grass.

"Ummm! You're right, ma'am," the man said. "This is mighty fine water."

He finished his drink and tossed the last few drops onto the ground. Then he refilled the dipper, poured the water into his hand, and Houdini drank. Two dippers full later, the dog laid back down beside Mark.

The man filled the dipper again, poured the water on his bandanna, and wiped his face. "Ahh, that shore feels good," he said as he leaned back against the tree.

Sarah grinned. "Yeah, I bet it does. Today's been a hot one."

"So, your name's Sarah, is it, Missy?" the man said.

"Yes, sir."

"My name's Buford Dooley. But ever'body just calls me, 'Jake.' Ain't shore why."

"Do ya live 'round here, Mr. Jake?" Sarah said.

"Well, ma'am, I live whurever I am. So, yes'm, right now, I do live here."

"Ain't ya got no folks?" Johnny said.

Jake chuckled. "No, all I got is Houdini."

While Mark sat beside Jake's knapsack, he played with its drawstrings.

"Stop that, Marky," Sarah said. "That ain't yours to mess with."

Mark glared at his sister and continued playing with the strings.

"Ahh, he ain't hurtin' nothin', ma'am," Jake said. "That's just my clothes, a fryin' pan, a soap bar, and a little beef jerky."

"You got somethin' to eat in 'ere?" Mark said.

Jake didn't answer. He refilled the dipper and sipped it. "So your name's Mark, is it?"

"Yeah," Mark said. "But ever'body just calls me, 'Marky.' Ain't shore why."

"He's five," Johnny said, "but he's already in school."

"Well, he's almost six. His birthday's next week," Sarah said. Then her eyes watered. She hadn't thought of that, and their mother wouldn't be there for it.

Jake peered at Johnny. "And what's your name, young feller?"

"John Hubert Skaggs, but ever'body calls me, 'Johnny.' I'm nine. Sarah over yonder's twelve. How old are you, Jake?"

"Well, sir, I don't rightly know," Jake said as he rubbed his chin stubble. "But I thank I'm forty-seven. I been on my own ever since my sis died when I's 'bout twelve. I lost track of how many birthdays I had, and I ain't shore what year I's born."

Jake reached into his pants pocket and pulled out a tobacco plug and a knife. He sliced off a piece, raised both hands to his lips, and slid the tobacco from the blade into his mouth with his right thumb. Sarah stared at Jake's lips and teeth as they worked the plug like a mare nibbling an ear of corn. Neither she nor the boys had ever seen anybody take a chaw before.

"What's that taste like?" Johnny said.

"Oh, I don't know," Jake said. "I s'pect it's kinda like a mix of tar and horse manure."

"Horse manure!" Johnny said as he wrinkled his nose, and everyone laughed. "Ahh, it don't neither. You're just kiddin' me."

Jake reached over and ruffled Johnny's red hair. "Yeah, I'm just kiddin' ya."

"Hey! Ain't we gonna have no supper? I sure hope we ain't havin' hominy and spinach again," Mark said and grimaced.

"Oh hush, Marky," Sarah said. "Ya sound like you're starvin' to death."

Mark puffed out his cheeks and looked at his sister. "Well, I'm hungry."

"Okay, Johnny, you and Marky go brang us a watermelon," Sarah said, and the boys scampered away to the garden.

While they were gone, Sarah studied Jake some more. His long, skinny nose wiggled as he talked, and he spoke with a whistle. Sweat glistened on his scalp, and his skin color matched his short, straight sandy-red hair. Forked lines fanned out from the outside corners of his crystal blue eyes, and expression lines framed his face. As he chewed the tobacco, his teeth clicked, and small streams of tobacco juice flowed from the corners of his mouth that always bore the hint of a smile. Now and then, he brushed off the juice with the butt of his palm and wiped it on his pants leg.

As Sarah checked out Jake, he did the same to her. Her red hair reflected bronze in the late afternoon sunlight, and her green eyes sparkled. Freckles peppered her nose and cheeks, and a slight gap separated her front teeth. Tiny sweat beads covered her forehead, and she swung her legs as she sat on the porch.

Something about her quiet, assertive nature was familiar to Jake, but he couldn't quite figure out what it was.

These kids looked okay, but something wasn't right about them. They were in some kind of trouble and needed help, and Jake was determined to find out what it was.

Johnny and Mark returned with a big striped watermelon and set it on the porch.

"That's a right smart melon," Jake said.

"Yeah, they grow big 'round here," Johnny said.

"Now, while I bust this thang up, you boys go draw us a pan of warsh water," Sarah said.

"Bust it up?" Jake said. "Ain't ya got no knife?"

"No, sir. We ain't allowed to handle knives."

"Well, then, I'll cut it with mine."

The boys returned with the pan of water, and Jake rinsed his knife. As the blade punctured the rind, the ripe melon popped and split open. While Jake cut it in two and quartered one of the halves, Sarah had the boys remove their shirts. Then they all washed, took a piece of melon, and sat down to eat.

Jake broke off a small chunk of his melon and laid it in front of Houdini's nose. The dog sniffed it and licked it, then turned away from it.

"Don't guess he likes it," Mark said.

"This is the first watermelon I've et in quite a spell," Jake said. "But it's a good'n. Do ya grow 'em ever year?"

"Yeah, Mama always grows watermelons and cantaloupes," Sarah said. "Strawberries too. She plants a big garden ever spring, and we always have lotsa good stuff to eat. But this year's been so darn hot ever'thang's 'bout burnt up."

Mark finished his piece and asked for another one, so Jake cut the other melon half into quarters. Sarah and Johnny also ate another piece, but Jake didn't.

After supper, Sarah and Jake talked some more. She enjoyed visiting with him so much that she didn't notice twilight had set in until a lightning bug flew past her.

While Mark chased the bugs around the front yard, Houdini followed and watched, tilting his head from side to side.

Sarah laughed. "I don't thank your dog can fig're out what Mark's doin.'"

The terrier trotted back to the porch and laid his head on Jake's leg.

"Ain't your folks kinda late gettin' back?" Jake said.

"Oh well, they're prob'ly listenin' to the *Grand Ole Opry*," Sarah said. "Sometimes they do that since Aunt Maggie and Uncle Harvey has a radio, and we don't."

"Ain't y'all scared, bein' here by yourselves at night like this?" Jake said.

"Ain't nothin' to be scared of," Sarah said. "Nothin' bad ever happens 'round here. Besides, we got a emergency plan."

"What kind of emergency plan?" Jake said.

Johnny laughed. "Daddy useta say his 'mergency plan was to 'hit 'em hard and run like hell.'"

"Joohh-nnny Huu-bert!" Sarah said. "You oughta have your mouth warshed out with lye soap." Then she laughed, and Jake laughed too. Between laughs, he snorted. And every time he did, the kids and Jake laughed even harder.

On the highway, a half-mile across the cotton and soybean fields, a car's engine roared, and its lights flickered through the trees.

"Maybe that's your folks," Jake said.

"Could be," Sarah said without looking up as she poked the ground with a stick she had picked up in the yard.

The car drove past the turnoff to the lane, and Sarah peeked at Jake. She didn't want to lie to him, but she wasn't sure how much she could trust him. She liked his company but didn't want him hanging around long enough to find out they were alone.

As night fell, the music of the cicadas, Chuck-will's-widows, and the bullfrogs echoed across the countryside. While Sarah, Johnny, and Jake sat on the porch and talked, Mark caught more lightning bugs. Now and then, a bug escaped through his fingers that served as a lid for the jar. By the time he caught a dozen bugs, the cool night air had broken the day's heat.

Jake pulled a battered watch from the bib of his overalls and strained to see its hands. "Nine fifty," he muttered as he shook his head and put the timepiece back in his pocket. "Wonder why your folks ain't back yet?"

"Well, maybe Pa and Uncle Harvey's sippin' corn liquor and don't know what time it is," Sarah said. "They'll come draggin' in here after while. They always do."

Mark caught a half-dozen more fireflies, but as he tired, escapes outnumbered captures.

Houdini got up, walked into the yard, and checked on Mark again. Still bored by the game, he shuffled back to the porch and laid his head on Jake's leg.

Sarah and Jake's talk wandered from one subject to another until it ended up on the stars. They even saw one shooting star.

While they talked, Johnny fell asleep. Suddenly, he rolled off the porch and hit the ground with a thud. Before anyone could help him, he jumped back onto the porch and acted like nothing had happened.

Mark gave up on the lightning bugs, trudged to the porch, and sat down beside Sarah. Droopy-eyed, he peered at his bugs in the jar and yawned. "One, two, three," he said as he slid his finger from one shadow to another. Then he removed his hand from the jar's mouth, shook the container, and his prisoners flew away. Mark tossed the jar to the ground, leaned against Sarah, and put his arms around her. "I'm sleepy."

"Why don't y'all go on to bed," Jake said. "I'll wait here for your folks so's I can ask to sleep in your barn."

"Well, I don't know 'bout that," Sarah said. "Pa might get mad if he's to come home and find a stranger sittin' on our porch. He can get riled up perty easy when he's had a few."

Deep down, Sarah didn't want Jake to leave. She just felt better having a grownup around. But she was afraid of what might happen if he discovered their secret. For a moment, she wondered where Jake and Houdini would spend the night. But they were used to living on the road, so she knew they would be all right.

"Well, Mr. Jake, I reckon we'd better call it a night," Sarah said.

"Yes'm," Jake said and stood up. "Much obliged for your hospitality, ma'am. Maybe we'll drop back by tomorra and say, 'howdy.'"

"Well, I ain't sure we'll be here tomorra, but thanks for your comp'ny tonight."

"Yes'm, and thank y'all for yours."

As Jake picked up his knapsack and slung it over his shoulder, Houdini stood up and stretched. Jake put on his cap and tipped it to Sarah. "G'night, ma'am."

"G'night, Mr. Jake," Sarah said.

"G'night, Mark," Jake said. "Be shore'n tell Johnny g'night for me when he wakes up."

"Okay, I will," Mark said. Then he jumped off the porch, hugged Houdini, and got some doggie kisses. "G'night, Houdini. Come back and see me sometime."

Jake and Houdini strolled out the gate and eased down the lane until Sarah closed the front door. Then they doubled back to the barn, and Jake checked out the loft. It looked good, so he tossed his knapsack into the straw and carried Houdini up. Jake found a spot where he could see the house through a wall crack, and they lay down. Over the years, he had become a very light sleeper, so he knew it would wake him if anyone came around the house during the night.

The other loft residents, a chicken snake, a family of mice, a flock of pigeons, and a garden spider the size of a silver dollar, fidgeted until Jake and Houdini bedded down for the night. Then they all went to sleep.

Chapter 4

SURPRISE BREAKFAST

ON SATURDAY, DAWN'S sunbeam crept along the barn wall, fell through a crack onto Jake's eyelids, and woke him. Since he had slept undisturbed, he knew the kids' folks hadn't come home. He carried his knapsack and Houdini down the ladder, eased to the house, and peeked through the bedroom window. Sure enough, there lay the kids, still alone and fast asleep.

When Jake's stomach rumbled, his attention shifted to breakfast. During his decades of wandering, he had honed his food-finding skills into a science. But today would test those skills since he had three extra mouths to feed. Jake didn't know yet what breakfast would be, but he did know it wouldn't be cantaloupe. He shouldered his knapsack and headed to the river.

As Jake and Houdini approached the levee, a young rabbit sprang from its cover, and the dog pounced on it. With the prey in his mouth, the pooch strutted past Jake and glanced up at him.

"Well, King of the Mountain, how 'bout sharin' some of your luck with me?" Jake said.

While Houdini laid down to eat in the shade of a giant sycamore tree, Jake slid down the river bank. A water moccasin, a half-dozen turtles, and several frogs slipped into the sluggish algae-covered pool between him and the main river channel. He had heard of people eating all three, but he wasn't ready to try them yet.

As Jake eased to the river's edge, a large carp swirled the water in front of him. He set his knapsack on the ground, pulled out a fishing line wrapped around an ice cream stick, and stuck it into his hip pocket. Then he climbed back up the bank, pulled off his cap, and crept through the weeds. When a cricket scampered across the ground, Jake tossed his hat over the bug and seized it. Then he slid back down the bank, pulled the line from his pocket, and hooked the cricket so it would kick. He unspooled several feet of string, whirled the baited hook above his head, and cast it toward the water. It was a good toss, fifteen feet, maybe more.

For a moment, the cricket lay still on the surface. Then it started kicking.

As the cord waterlogged, it pulled the bug under. The line jerked, then fell limp again—just a nibble. The next tug would be the real one.

A moment later, the fish struck, and Jake set the hook. While the carp ran, first to the right and then to the left, water beads popped from the taut line as it ripped the river's surface. If he could land this big fish, there would be plenty of breakfast for everyone, even Mark.

For ten long minutes, the carp fought for its life. Then it made one last savage run and gave up.

Jake's fingers ached as he pulled the fish from the water and held it up. Two-feet long. It would make a fine meal.

Jake unhooked the carp and stuck the line back into his knapsack. Then he pulled out his knife and laid the fish on the ground. As the blade sliced into the flesh behind the carp's head, its tail curled upward. When the knife severed the fish's spinal cord, its tail fell flat again.

While Jake scraped the sides of the carp, nickel-sized scales flew into the air exposing the soft silvery flesh beneath them. After cleaning the fish, he tossed its head and entrails to Houdini. The dog sniffed them, then sneezed and backed away.

"I don't blame ya," Jake said. "It'd be hard to eat that after feastin' on a rabbit."

Jake cut several finger-width willow branches and wove them into a grill. Then he carried everything to the house and built a fire between two concrete blocks in the backyard.

While the blaze burned to coals, Jake filleted the fish and rinsed them at the well. Then he laid the halves on the grill over the fire and sprinkled them with salt.

As the fish cooked, its aroma drifted into the bedroom.

Sarah's eyes popped open, and she sniffed the air. "Ummm! I smell somethin' good!"

"Me too!" Mark said.

"Yeah! What is that?" Johnny said.

They all jumped out of bed, ran outside, and lined up on the back porch–Sarah in her nightshirt and the boys in their underpants.

As they gawked at the cooking fillets, Jake peeled off a piece of fish and tasted it.

"Mornin', Mr. Jake," Sarah said. Then she squinted. "I thought y'all left?"

"Yes'm, we did, but when I caught this big fish this mornin', I decided to come back by and fix us all some breakfast."

"How'd ya catch it?" Johnny said.

"With a big ole cricket," Jake said.

"What kinda fish is it?" Sarah said.

"Carp," Jake said.

"Carp?" Sarah wrinkled her nose. "Ain't that a dirty fish?"

"No, ma'am. Carp's a good fish. A little bony maybe, but good." Jake sliced off a couple of pieces and handed them to the boys. "Be careful now. This has some little bones in it you'll hafta spit out."

Mark popped his piece into his mouth. "Yum! This is really good."

Then Jake held out a piece to Sarah. "Here, Missy, wonna try it?"

She scrunched up her face. "Eww, I don't know. Daddy always said carp was a poor man's fish. But I reckon we are poor now. It sure smells good."

"Go ahead, Sissy," Mark said. "You'll love it."

Sarah took the piece, stuck her tongue to it, then took a small bite. "It really ain't bad, is it? It's just the idy of eatin' a dirty fish."

"Well, it come outta the clean river, so I fig're it's clean," Jake said.

With that comment, talk stopped, and breakfast began. A few minutes later, all that was left of the fish were its bones.

"Go catch another'n," Mark said. "I wont some more."

"Oh, Marky! You're a bottomless pit!" Sarah said. "Sorry, Mr. Jake. Marky never gets full, and he ain't shy 'bout askin' for more. He ain't got no manners."

"Well, growin' boys need lots to eat."

They washed their hands. Then Jake dumped the water on the fire.

"It was mighty nice of ya to fix breakfast for us," Sarah said.

"Ahh, it wudn't nothin'," Jake said. "That big ole carp was too much for me to eat by myself, so all I done was share it with ya. Cookin' for four's 'bout as easy as cookin' for one."

"Well, it ain't for me," Sarah said. Then she covered her mouth and looked at Jake. "I mean, Mama has me so spoilt that doin' any cookin' at all is hard for me."

"Are they here?" Jake said. "We shoulda give them some fish."

Sarah squirmed. "No, they left early this mornin' to go do some thangs in town."

"What time did they finally get in last night?"

"I s'pect 'round midnight," Sarah said. "If ya spent the night any-whur near here, I'm sure ya heard 'em. Our old car backfares like the 4th of July fireworks. And Pa was drunker'n the man in the moon— carryin' on and sangin' to high heaven. Lordy! Lordy! Ya never heard a awfuler sound in your life. I thought he's gonna knock the stars right outta the sky."

Jake laughed. "Yeah, I know what it's like to be fallin' down drunk."

"Mama and me had a heck of a time gettin' him in the house and puttin' him to bed."

"Seems to me, a feller that drunk would need lotsa sleep to sober up," Jake said.

"Maybe most fellers would," Sarah said and peered at Jake, wondering if he believed her. "But our Pa ain't most fellers. No matter what, he's already up and gone 'fore the rest of us even thanks 'bout gettin' up.'"

"You know, Missy," Jake said, "I's a orphan myself when I's your age."

Sarah's eyes shot to Jake's, and her jaw dropped. He hadn't believed her.

"I been a orphan just 'bout all my life. I never knowed my Ma or Pa, but I knowed my sister, 'Bessie Bug.' She was your age when I's born, and after our folks died, she took care of me. I's four or five when she got married. But her husband didn't like me, and after she died of pneumonia, he started knockin' me around, so I run away, and I been on my own ever since. Yep, I'm glad I had Bessie Bug. Sisters and brothers is good thangs to have."

"How'd ya know we's alone?" Sarah said.

"Ah, that ain't hard to know when you're alone yourself."

"So now I reckon you're gonna tell somebody 'bout us, ain't ya?"

Jake shook his head. "Nah, Missy, I ain't gonna tell nobody nothin'. It ain't none of my bidness 'cept'n maybe to hep ya out a little here and 'ere."

Sarah gazed deep into Jake's eyes. They were soft, kind, and true.

"'Sides," Jake said as he looked at her and smiled. "Us orphans gotta stick together. That's the orphan's code."

"If we ask for help, we're afraid they'll split us up," Sarah said. "We know some kids they done that to."

"Yeah, that happens sometimes, but y'all don't hafta worry 'bout that right now. If'n you'll lemme stay in your barn, maybe I can hep ya fig're somethin' out."

Sarah leaned over, pecked Jake on the cheek, and his red face turned even redder. "Thank ya, Mr. Jake!" Maybe now she could return to being a little girl for a while. She jumped up and ran inside the house.

Chapter 5

GERTIE GLEASON

SUNDAY MORNING, JAKE and Houdini got up before dawn and strolled down the lane searching for food. At the house of the kids' nearest neighbor, a mongrel dog, wagging its tail, shuffled out to greet them. In the backyard sat a chicken pen with a hen house. As the sun glinted over the horizon, a rooster flew up onto a fence post and crowed.

Jake squinted at the faded, hand-painted name on the mailbox. "Gertrude Gleason." He squinted even harder at the chalk drawing on the mailbox post–a cat–the hobo sign for a kind lady lives here.

Suddenly, the screen door banged open, and a woman carrying a broom stepped onto the front porch. When she saw Jake, she gasped and slapped her chest. "Lordy mercy!" her raspy voice said as she frowned. "You pert'near seared me to death!"

Jake tipped the brim of his hat. "Mornin', ma'am. Sorry! Didn't mean to startle ya."

"Well, whether ya meant to or not, ya shore-nuff did."

She rested one hand on top of the broom handle, propped the other one on her hip, and Jake chuckled. She looked like the teapot from the children's song.

"Well, I'm perty shore ya ain't just standin' 'ere for ya health. What ya wont?"

Jake took off his cap and folded it in his hands. "I's just wonderin', ma'am, if'n maybe ya got some chores a feller might do to earn a couple-a-dozen eggs? I can do just 'bout anythang."

"A couple-a-dozen eggs?" The woman squinted and pursed her lips. "Why two dozen? Your dog a egg sucker?"

Jake laughed and shook his head. "No, ma'am, he ain't. I got some folks back down the road there a piece that's needin' breakfast. And I fig're two dozen'll feed ever'body."

"Well, I don't cotton to bums."

"Well, ma'am, we ain't bums. We're just reg'lar folks tryin' to get along."

"If'n I give ya work, when it's done, I wont ya to clear out. I don't ever wonna see ya 'round here beggin' no more. Understand?"

"Yes'm," Jake said.

"Well, all right then. Ya see 'em warsh kettles sittin' back yonder? I need farewood for 'em. Ya split me enough for three months, and you'll get your two dozen eggs."

"Yes'm. I'll do 'er," Jake said.

Gertrude led him to a woodpile in the backyard, where an ax with its handle in the air was stuck in the big chopping block. Jake levered the tool from the block and ran his thumb along its blade. "Ya got a file, Ma'am? This thang's a mite dull."

"Yeah, 'ere's one hangin' on a nail over yonder in the woodshed. I got thangs to do. I'll come back out when I thank your pile's big enough."

Jake sat down on the chopping block and filed a sharp, glistening edge onto the ax. Then he chopped. As he worked, the dogs played around him in the yard, and Gertrude watched him through the kitchen window while she washed dishes.

An hour later, she came back out and examined the size of the woodpile. "Okay, I reckon that'll do," she said and handed Jake a wire basket. "Go gather the eggs, and don't break none. Whatever ya break comes outta your share, not mine."

Jake took the basket and stepped into the hen house. A hen, proud of the gem she had just laid, clucked and strutted past him. Jake gathered the eggs and returned to Gertrude in the yard. "How many'd ya get?"

"Twenty-eight."

"That's a mite short. Ya shore ya didn't break none?"

"Yes'm, I'm shore."

"How ya gonna carry 'em?"

Jake took off his cap and held it out to her. One by one, she placed all twenty-eight eggs into it. A kind woman indeed. Jake thanked her. Then he and Houdini headed back to the kids' house. The mongrel followed them for a short distance, then turned back toward home.

At the barn, Jake wrapped half the eggs in an old burlap feed bag and stashed it in the loft. Then he carried his knapsack and the rest of the eggs to the backyard and built a fire.

When Jake heard the kids stirring in the bedroom, he cracked the eggs into his frying pan and scrambled them.

"G'mornin', Mr. Jake," Sarah said as she and the boys stepped onto the back porch.

"Mornin'," Jake said.

"What's cookin'?" Johnny said.

"Eggs," Jake said.

"Oh boy! I like eggs!" Mark said.

"Whur'd ya get 'em?" Johnny said.

"Down the road a ways," Jake said. "I chopped farewood for Miss Gertrude Gleason, and she paid me with 'em."

"You chopped wood for old Dirty Gertie Gleason?" Sarah said and squinted. "Did she bite your head off?"

Jake grinned. "Nah, she wudn't too rough on me. I got out alive without much trouble."

"She's got a dog, too," Mark said. "His name's 'Tick.' Did ya see him?"

"Yeah, him and Houdini played while I worked."

"Too bad old Dirty Gertie ain't as friendly as Tick," Sarah said.

"Well, friendly or not, she give us our eggs," Jake said. "Got any plates, Missy?"

"No," Sarah said. "All we got is a fork, a spoon, and a butter knife."

"Well then, we'll just hafta eat 'em outta the skillet," Jake said.

He wrapped his bandana around the pan's hot handle and carried it to the stump. While the kids washed, Jake divided the eggs into four equal portions. Then Sarah fetched the flatware, and they gathered around to eat.

"Eat slow, Marky," Sarah said as she handed him the spoon. "When your share's gone, you ain't gettin' none of ours."

Sure enough, Mark finished before everyone else. "Sissy, can I have just a tiny bite of yours?" he whined.

"No, ya cain't. I already told ya you couldn't."

"Johnny, can I have a bite of yours?"

Johnny covered his eggs with his hand. "Nope, 'ese is mine."

"Here, young feller," Jake said. "Ya can have the rest of mine. I ain't very hungry this mornin.'"

"No, sir, Mr. Jake," Sarah said and pushed her little brother away from the stump. "He's had his share, and you gotta eat just like the rest of us. Hold your horses, Marky, and I'll go pick a cantaloupe."

When that pacified Mark, Jake ate the rest of his eggs. Now he understood what was so familiar about her. How she handled these boys reminded him of how his sister had treated him. She was raising them right.

Sarah finished eating, picked a cantaloupe, and they each ate a piece. While Mark finished the melon, the others washed dishes and cleaned the area. Then Jake doused the fire, and they all strolled to the front porch to relax.

At noon, Sarah walked into the house and returned with a towel around her neck and her only other dress draped over her shoulder. "I'm goin' to the river to take a bath."

"And I'm goin', too," Mark said as he jumped up beside her.

"No, Marky, I hafta go by myself. You guys can go when I get back."

"Just a minute, Missy," Jake said. He reached into his knapsack, took out a small brown soap bar, and handed it to her.

She sniffed it and wrinkled her nose. "This don't smell perty like the soap I'm used to."

"No, ma'am, it's ole lye soap, but it'll getcha clean. Just don't get it in your eyes. It burns like the devil."

While Sarah was gone, the guys lay on the porch and talked about this and that with several long, comfortable gaps in the conversation.

Then Mark asked, "Jake, you ever been to St. Louie?"

"Yeah, a few times. It's a big city," he said. Then he peered at Mark. "Why ya askin'?"

"'Cause that's whur Hank has took our Mama."

There was Jake's answer.

Johnny swung his legs off of the porch and sat up. "Dang it, Marky! You ain't supposed to talk 'bout that!"

"'Ey went 'ere to find work," Mark said.

"When 'ey comin' back to get ya?" Jake said.

"We don't know," Johnny said. "Our stepdaddy's like yours was— He don't like us. He forced Mama to leave us here and go with him. She said they'd be back, but so far, we ain't seen 'em."

"When did that happen?" Jake said.

"Five days ago," Johnny said.

"Who all knows you're livin' like this?"

"Just you, so far. We ain't told nobody else. Sarah made us promise not to."

Now the story was piecing together. Jake wanted to know more, but he didn't push the boys. He figured the rest would come with time. And until then, he would keep quiet about what they had told him. He didn't want to get them into trouble with their sister.

Sarah returned and hung her washed dress on the clothesline beside the house. Then she rejoined the guys on the front porch and handed Jake's soap back to him. "Dang, that felt good."

Mark looked at her and laughed. "You look funny with wet hair."

"I don't care. It feels good and clean."

"Okay, fellers," Jake said as he stood up. "Looks like it's our turn."

Sarah ran inside and returned with two clean towels. "Here, Mr. Jake. You can use this'n, and Johnny and Mark can share the other'n."

"I ain't takin' no bath," Mark said. "I'm just goin' swimmin.'"

Jake laughed. "Well, be careful there, Mark. Swimmin' might just get ya clean."

"Then, swim with your clothes on," Sarah said. "They gotta be warshed whether you warsh or not."

At the river, the boys plunged straight into the water while Jake emptied his pockets into his knapsack and set it on the bank beside his shoes. Then as Mark swam, Jake and Johnny washed their clothes and bathed.

When the trio arrived back at the porch, Sarah stepped out of the house carrying the bed sheets. "These hafta be warshed, too," she said, and they all hiked back to the river.

When the job was done, they hung the wet sheets beside Sarah's dress on the clothesline, then settled back onto the front porch to rest.

A couple of hours later, Sarah carried the dry laundry into the bedroom. While she made the beds, she smiled. With Mr. Jake's help, maybe they could do this after all.

As she stepped back outside onto the porch, the familiar rattle of an old truck drifted up the lane. "Oh no! It's Mr. Crockett!"

"Who's Mr. Crockett?" Jake said.

"Our landlord. We gotta skedaddle!" Sarah said.

Jake scooped up Houdini and his knapsack, and they all dashed to the backyard.

As Mr. Crockett's truck bounced to a stop in a cloud of dust at the front gate, the kids and Jake watched from behind the outhouse. He gunned the engine, and the truck backfired. When no one came out of the house, he hurried to the porch and knocked on the open door. "Hey, Hank, I need your rent money!"

Still, no one answered, so he stepped inside the house. A moment later, he ran back into the yard and screamed. "Hank, you lousy son of a dog!" he hollered. "I'll get your sorry ass for this!" Then he climbed back into the truck and sped away.

When the truck disappeared from view, Sarah led the group back into the yard. "Well, dang it! Now, he knows somethin's wrong, and before long, somebody else'll be snoopin' 'round here."

"Yeah, prob'ly so," Jake said. "But 'ere ain't nothin' we can do 'bout it right now."

"I shoulda knowed Hank didn't pay the rent," Sarah said.

She picked a catalpa leaf and headed back to the front porch, but Mark stopped her. "Get me one with worms on it."

"Do you wont one, Mr. Jake?" Sarah said as she picked a leaf and handed it to Mark.

"Nah, thanks, Missy."

Sarah had Johnny draw a bucket of fresh drinking water, then they settled back down on the front porch.

At suppertime, they ate another watermelon. Then, that evening, Sarah, Jake, and Johnny sat on the front porch and talked again while Mark caught more lightning bugs.

At bedtime, Jake and Houdini strolled to the barn, and the kids sauntered into the house.

"'Ese sheets is scratchy," Mark said as he crawled onto the mattress.

"That's 'cause they're clean," Sarah said. "They'll be soft by mornin'. Now go to sleep."

Chapter 6

THE LANDLORD

ON MONDAY, THE hoot of an owl woke Jake just before dawn. He eased to the hay door, pushed it open, and peered outside. A red fox, carrying a dead rabbit, was trekking across the lot between the house and the barn. It stopped, peered up at him, then continued toward the river.

Jake carried Houdini down the ladder and set him on the ground. Then he fetched his knapsack and the rest of the eggs. As they strolled to the house, the dog paused and sniffed the ground where the fox had passed.

At the back porch, Jake set everything down. Then, while he gathered firewood, Houdini hunted in the pasture. As Jake lit the fire, the dog sauntered past him, carrying a mouse, and lay down underneath the porch to eat it.

When the smell of smoke drifted into the bedroom, Sarah opened her eyes. "Get up, boys. Mr. Jake's cookin' breakfast."

They rolled out of bed, dressed, and walked outside. On the edge of the porch sat slices of cantaloupe. Mark reached for one, but Sarah pulled him back. "Hold on, Marky. We ain't hogs runnin' to the trough."

"Mornin', kids! How're y'all today?" Jake said as he set the skillet of eggs over the fire.

"Fine," Sarah said. "How 'bout you?"

"Couldn't be much better, don't reckon. Y'all hep yourselves to that melon. I'll have 'ese eggs ready in a minute."

While Jake scrambled the eggs, Mark devoured three pieces of fruit.

"Okay, come and get 'em," Jake said, and they gathered around the stump.

Sarah glared at Mark and handed him the spoon. "Eat s-l-o-w this time, Marky."

He frowned and puffed out his cheeks.

Then Sarah cocked her head and stared at Mark. "Hey, Marky! Ya know what today is?"

"Nope, what?"

"It's your birthday."

Mark chuckled. "Oh boy! I'm finally six!"

"Well, happy birthday there, young feller," Jake said. "Then this is your birthday breakfast. Sorry, there ain't no cake."

"Hap-py Birth-day to you. . ." Sarah sang, and Johnny and Jake joined in. Mark blushed, ran his tongue over the inside of his jaws, and wrung his hands behind his back until the song ended.

"Okay, let's eat," Sarah said, and they dug into the eggs.

After eating, the boys tossed the melon rinds over the fence while Sarah washed the skillet and Jake put out the fire.

"Have y'all got lunch?" Jake said.

"No, we ain't," Sarah said.

"Whur's the schoolhouse from here?"

"Thataway," Sarah said and pointed to the southwest. "Why?"

"Is 'ey a store 'tween here and 'ere?"

"Yeah, Mr. Zimmerman's is on the curve just 'fore ya get to the schoolhouse."

"Okay, then at lunchtime, look for me. I'll try'n brang ya somethin.'"

"Ahh, ya don't needta do that. We're gettin' useta not havin' no lunch."

"Well, look for me anyhow. I cain't promise nothin', but I'll see what I can do."

"Okay, I'll be on the schoolhouse steps."

Sarah leaned over, pecked Jake on the cheek, then ran inside to get ready for school.

Jake and Houdini strolled to the front porch and sat down. As Sarah ordered her brothers about inside the house, Jake smiled. More and more, she reminded him of his sister.

When the kids came outside, Mark ran to Houdini and got some doggy kisses.

"G'bye, Mr. Jake," Sarah said as they walked through the gate.

"G'bye, Missy," Jake said. "Remember to look for me at noon."

"Okay, I will."

While Jake watched the kids march down the lane, he pulled out his bandanna and wiped the sweat from his face. Johnny took long, deliberate steps while Mark trotted along beside him, a little brother to the core. Sarah set a slow pace that would put her several yards behind the boys by the time they got to school.

Jake smiled and rubbed the rat terrier's head. "Kinda nice bein' needed, ain't it, ole boy?"

After getting a drink of water and visiting the outhouse, Jake slung his knapsack over his shoulder, and the duo headed out for the day.

At the store, Houdini lay down on the porch beside the front door, and Jake stepped inside. "Mornin', sir," he said and removed his hat as Mr. Zimmerman approached him. "My name's Jake Dooley. I's wonderin' if'n ya got some chores a feller might do to earn some baloney, cheese, and crackers?"

"Why bologna, cheese, and crackers in particular?" Mr. Zimmerman said.

"Well, sir, I got lotsa mouths to feed, and that seems like a good way of doin' 'er."

"Oh, I see," Mr. Zimmerman said and smiled. "Yes, Mr. Dooley, I'm stocking shelves this morning, and I can always use help doing that."

"Much obliged," Jake said. "Ya got somewhurs I can put my bag?"

"Just set it behind the counter," Mr. Zimmerman said. "Nobody'll bother it there."

Jake stowed his knapsack and followed Mr. Zimmerman down the aisle to several open boxes of canned goods.

"It's pretty easy," Mr. Zimmerman said. "Just pull the older cans to the front, put the newer ones behind them, and make sure the labels face forward. Think you can do that?"

Jake nodded. "Yes, sir, I shore can."

"When you finish, let me know, and we'll bring out some more. I'll be working over on the next aisle."

Jake got down on his knees and went to work. Every few minutes, he glanced at the soda pop wall clock.

At eleven-thirty, Jake stood up. He wasn't sure what time the kids ate lunch, but he wanted to be on time, so he walked over to Mr. Zimmerman.

"Sorry for stoppin' when the job ain't quite done, sir, but I need to be goin'. Some folks is waitin' on me to brang 'em their lunch, and I don't wonna be late. I'll be glad to come back later and finish the job, but right now, I need to be gettin' along."

Mr. Zimmerman walked over and surveyed Jake's work. He had emptied all but one box. "Well done, Mr. Dooley. No, you won't need to come back. I can finish the rest myself." Then he looked at Jake. "So, how much bologna and cheese do you want?"

Jake rubbed his chin whiskers and peered at Mr. Zimmerman. "Well, sir, whatever you'll gimme, I reckon."

"How many people do you need to feed?"

"Well, 'ere's three kids. And it's the littlest boy's birthday."

"And how many adults?"

"Just me, but I don't need nothin'."

"Why not? Aren't you hungry?"

"Yes, sir, but I can do without if'n I hafta."

"Well, you don't have to."

"I just don't wonna put ya out none."

Mr. Zimmerman smiled. "Mr. Dooley, you're not putting me out at all. It's my pleasure. How about four bologna and cheese sandwiches?"

Jake nodded and smiled. "Yes, sir! That'll do fine!"

Mr. Zimmerman made the sandwiches and put them into a paper bag. "How many kids did you say there are?"

"Three."

Mr. Zimmerman opened two candy jars, took a scoopful from each, and dumped them into the sack. Then he opened the cash register and took out some money.

"Here you go." He handed the bag plus a dollar and sixty cents to Jake. "Enjoy your lunch. I threw in some free birthday candy for the kids."

"Thank ya," Jake said, "but what's the money for?"

"Well, you worked two hours. At a dollar an hour, that's two dollars minus the price of four sandwiches at a dime apiece."

"Yes, sir!" Jake said and smiled as he stuffed the money into his pocket. "Thank ya kindly!" He put on his cap, picked up his knapsack, and rushed outside. As he headed down the highway toward school, Houdini bounced into step alongside him.

When they arrived at the schoolhouse, Sarah was standing on the steps holding her lard bucket, and she dashed to them.

"Do y'all like baloney and cheese?" Jake said.

"Yes, sir, we sure do," Sarah said.

"Well, here's four sandwiches and some birthday candy."

"Four? Why four?"

"I fig'red Mark needed two."

"What 'bout you, Mr. Jake? Have you et?"

"No, but that's okay."

"No, it ain't okay. You brung these to us, so one of 'em's yours." Sarah pulled a sandwich from the bag and handed it to Jake. "You take this and eat it! What're we gonna do if you get sick?"

Jake smiled and took the sandwich. She was just like Bessie Bug. "Thanks, Missy. Now I'll go see what I can rustle up for our supper."

Sarah waved to Jake and smiled as she watched him give half his sandwich to Houdini. He was such a kind man. Hopefully, their worries about food were over. He was taking better care of them than Hank ever had.

She called her brothers to a lunch table, handed them each a sandwich and a piece of candy, then took one of each for herself.

Mark unwrapped the candy and popped it into his mouth. "Whur'd this come from?"

"Mr. Jake brung it to us," Sarah said.

Mark held out his hand. "Give me another'n."

"No," Sarah said. "If the other kids find out we got it, they'll all wont some. Then we won't have none left for later."

The boys wolfed down their lunches and hurried back to the playground. Sarah sat and savored her sandwich one mouthful at a time until it was gone. Then she stuffed the bag of sweets into her lunch pail, strolled to the schoolhouse, and stowed it on the cloakroom shelf. As she turned to leave, Miss Gibson stepped into the room. "Who was that you were talking to?"

Sarah's mouth gaped. "Oh, that was Uncle Jake. He brung us some sandwiches."

"Is he your mother's brother?"

"Yes'm. He's just here viztin."

Miss Gibson returned to the classroom, and Sarah ran back outside. Her eyes burned as she fought back the tears. Even with Mr. Jake's help, she still couldn't ever relax.

On the way home, Jake noticed a peach tree full of ripe fruit in the yard of an abandoned house. He walked over to it, picked a dozen peaches, and tucked them into his knapsack. Besides being a good dessert, they would also be good bait for the rabbit snares he planned to set that afternoon.

When Jake turned to leave, he saw a tow sack half-full of potatoes sitting on the back porch. He picked it up and started to walk away with it, but somehow that felt like stealing, so he set it back down and only took a few of the best spuds.

As Jake and Houdini strolled up the lane toward home, voices echoed from the yard. When the house came into view, he saw Mr. Crockett's old truck sitting backed up to the front porch. Jake picked up Houdini, sneaked across the corral, and ducked into the barn. With the dog in his arms, he knelt inside the door and watched as Crockett and two other men carried everything out of the house and loaded it onto the truck.

Jake's first inclination was to grab a hayfork and stop Crockett. But that would land him in jail. Then he wouldn't be able to help the kids. So he just watched as the men hauled everything to the pasture, piled it into a heap, and set it ablaze.

Jake cursed as the kids' possessions disintegrated into a pillar of smoke that billowed high into the air. Now they were like him—all they had were the clothes on their backs—except he was used to it. They deserved better, and he was determined to help them get it.

When Mr. Crockett and his men drove away, Jake released Houdini. Then he stowed his knapsack in the loft, walked to the pasture, and kicked through the ashes. The only things left were the wash pan, the bucket, the water dipper, and the three pieces of flat-ware. He gathered the items and carried them to the back porch.

While there, something else caught Jake's eye. On a rusty nail in the porch post hung a shiny can opener. He unhooked it and dropped it into the bucket with the other things. But then, a strange feeling swept over Jake. He fished out the church key and hung it back up. For some reason, it seemed to belong right where it was.

Jake took a deep breath and peered toward the river. No matter what, the kids still had to eat, so he fetched his knapsack and headed to the levee. With luck, he could at least give them a good supper. And maybe that would comfort them some.

With the snares set, Jake and Houdini returned to the house and lay down on the front porch. When the kids' voices drifted up the lane, he and the dog walked out to meet them.

"What's wrong?" Sarah said as she peered into Jake's eyes.

"Somethin' bad happened this afternoon," Jake said. "Mr. Crockett cleaned out the house and burnt ever'thang."

The kids dashed home and ran inside. As Sarah walked through the empty rooms, she cried. "Why'd he do this?"

"I fig're he wonted to clear it out so's he could rent it to somebody else. 'Ey's here when we got back from brangin' y'all's lunch to ya."

"Now, whur we gonna sleep?" Johnny said.

"Well, 'ere's plentya room in the barn loft," Jake said.

"But we ain't got no pillors, no covers, no nothin'," Sarah said.

From the river, a high-pitched squeal shot into the room, and Houdini barked.

"What was that?" Sarah said.

"We just caught supper," Jake said. "I set out some rabbit snares a while ago."

"Dang! That was spooky!" Mark said.

"Yeah, a little bit," Jake said. "But we'll have a good supper if'n I can get him 'fore he gets loose."

As Jake headed to the backdoor, Mark ran after him. "I wonna go, too."

"No, young feller, you stay here. Animal killin' and cleanin's ugly work."

Sarah grabbed Mark's arm. "Yeah, Marky, Mr. Jake's right. You don't need to see that. It'll give ya bad dreams."

Jake walked back into the yard a half-hour later, and the kids ran to meet him. Besides the rabbit, he carried one straight stick and two forked sticks. Houdini had stayed behind to feast on the discarded rabbit parts.

Jake laid the carcass on the grass beside the well and rinsed it.

"Is that really a rabbit?" Mark said as he stared at the animal's body.

"Yep, it shore-nuff is," Jake said.

"Ain't very big, is it?"

"Well, I bet it's big enough to fill all of our bellies. How much of it do ya thank ya can eat?"

"All of it," Mark said.

Jake laughed and carried the meat to the fire pit. The way Mark ate that might be true.

"What can we do to help ya?" Sarah said.

"I need farewood," Jake said.

The kids fanned out across the yard and carried dead limbs to the pit. While they broke them into short pieces, Jake drove one of the forked sticks into the ground on each side of the pit and started the fire. When the wood had burned into coals, Jake buried four potatoes in them. Then he stuck the straight stick lengthwise through the rabbit and hung it over the fire on the forks.

While the meat roasted, Sarah turned it and sprinkled it with salt. As it sizzled and browned, its aroma drifted across the yard.

"Umm! That smells good," Mark said as he and Johnny laid more limbs beside the fire.

"Yep, it won't be long now," Jake said.

He pulled the potatoes from the coals with a stick and laid them on the back porch to cool. Then he took the rabbit off the fire. "Missy, I need somethin' clean to lay this on."

"I got just the thang," Sarah said. She ran inside, returned with the lunch bag, tore it open, and spread it on the porch.

Jake pushed the rabbit off the stick onto the paper, then quartered it and the potatoes with his knife.

"Okay, it's suppertime," he said, and they gathered at the porch to eat.

As usual, Mark swallowed his portion and asked for more, so Sarah shared hers with him.

"Who wonts dessert?" she said as she got up to pick a cantaloupe.

"Just a minute, Missy. I got somethin' special," Jake said, and he set out four peaches. "I found 'ese when we's comin' home today."

"I wont some candy," Mark said.

"Well, okay, Marky, since it's your birthday, you can have a piece or two," Sarah said.

While she fetched the sweets, Mark ate a peach. Sarah returned, handed the candy to Mark, and he popped a piece into his mouth. "This ain't as good as it was at noon," he whined.

"That's 'cause ya just et that peach," Jake said. "It was sweeter'n the candy, so now, ya cain't taste it as much."

They finished supper, threw the rabbit bones over the fence, and Jake doused the fire.

While everyone else strolled to the front porch, Johnny stopped at the outhouse. The instant his heinie touched the toilet seat, a sharp sting shot through it, and the story of his mother's Uncle Clyde "Snake Bite" Hood flashed through his mind. Johnny leaped from his perch, ran bare-bottomed into the backyard, and shouted, "Snakebit!"

Everyone–including Houdini–jumped off the porch and ran to him.

"I been snakebit!" Johnny shouted.

"Whur?" Sarah said.

Johnny turned his bottom to the group and pointed to a single red bump. "Here!"

"What kinda snake was it?" Jake said.

"Copperhead!" Johnny said as he held his bottom and bounced up and down on his toes.

The group eased to the outhouse, cracked open the door, and peeked inside. There, on the toilet seat, lay a squashed red wasp, and Sarah bellowed out laughing.

"What you laughin' at?" Johnny yelled and frowned.

"You silly boy! You ain't snakebit! You're just wasper stung!"

Johnny peered down at the wasp. Then he burst out laughing, too.

Chapter 7

FOUND OUT

FOR THE REST of the week, Jake fed the kids and himself by any honest means he could find. He caught fish, snared rabbits, and worked at Mr. Zimmerman's store, where he took most of his pay in merchandise. In fact, as they all settled into barn life together, Jake brought home so many things that the loft took on the appearance of a house. And despite the rough lifestyle, the atmosphere changed into one of a home and family.

During the same time, a clean and tidy side of Jake emerged that he didn't even know he had, and he bathed every day while the kids were at school.

One day, Jake got so carried away with his cleanliness that he even bathed Houdini, which caused the dog to moan and shiver like he was being punished for something. And from then on, he stayed away from Jake when they were at the river.

All that bathing soon wore Jake's soap bar down to a nub. So the next time he worked at the store, he bought four soap bars, four toothbrushes, two tubes of toothpaste, and a can of dog food that Houdini flatly refused to eat.

Then, life threw them a curve.

On Friday evening, as usual, Miss Gibson walked the short distance from her house to Mr. Zimmerman's store to do her weekly shopping. While she gathered items and set them on the counter, their conversation meandered through a maze of subjects. Then Mr. Zimmerman asked, "Do you know anything about a man named Jake Dooley, who's supporting three children in our community?"

"You must mean Mrs. Pinscher's brother, Jake," Miss Gibson said. "He's here visiting."

"Ah! So that's who he is!" Mr. Zimmerman said.

But that answer only led to more questions. Why hadn't Mrs. Pinscher been in lately to buy groceries? Why were the kids being supported by their uncle? Had something happened to their parents?

Miss Gibson decided to pay the Pinscher family a visit. So Saturday morning, she stuck a small bag of fudge into her purse and headed to their house.

As she crossed the empty schoolyard, the familiar sound of steel on steel screeched behind her. Expecting to see someone, she peered over her shoulder but only saw a swing pushed by the wind and still swaying as if a ghost child had just leapt from its seat. She smiled and continued her journey.

When Miss Gibson arrived at the Pinschers', she stopped in front of the house, stared at the derelict old place, and a tingle ran down her spine. Mr. Pinscher's junky old car was gone, the front door stood half open, and not a soul stirred. She walked through the gate, crossed the yard, and stopped at the porch steps. "Mrs. Pinscher?" she called.

When no one answered, she stepped onto the porch and knocked on the door. "Oh, Mrs. Pinscher? It's me, Elsie Gibson, from Austin School."

Still, no one answered, so she eased inside–to an empty house, and her heart sank.

A few yards away, the kids lay asleep in the barn loft. In her dream, Sarah heard Miss Gibson call her mother. When she heard the voice again, her eyes popped open. She crawled to the wall and peeked at the house through a crack.

Mark sat up and rubbed his eyes. "Is breakfast ready?"

Johnny woke and peered at Sarah. "What's hap'nin?"

"It's Miss Gibson! What's she doin' here?"

Sarah scrambled down the ladder and tiptoed to Jake, who was kneeling just inside the barn door and holding Houdini. "Ya know that woman?"

"Yeah, she's our school teacher," Sarah said as the boys joined them.

"Looks like we been found out," Jake said. "Best not to tell 'er 'bout me. Somebody might get the idy somethin' bad's been goin' on here. If'n ya hafta leave, then go to the back porch and wave to me. And remember, ya gotta do what's best for y'all. If'n I don't see ya no more, it's been good knowin' ya."

Sarah threw her arms around Jake and pecked his cheek. "Ah, don't worry. I'll fix it."

The kids dashed to the house and ran into the front yard just as their teacher walked back outside onto the front porch.

"Miss Gibson! What're you doin' here?" Sarah said.

"Oh, there you are!" Miss Gibson said. She stepped down from the porch and ambled to the kids. "I've come to see your mother."

"Well, she ain't here right now," Sarah said. "Her and Hank took Uncle Jake to Piggott to catch his train back to St. Louie. I expect they'll be gone all day. Mama's aimed to do some shoppin' while she's there."

"Oh, I see."

Since Miss Gibson had a clear view of the barn from where she stood, Sarah crossed in front of her and drew her attention to the other side. "Whatcha wonna see her 'bout?"

"I just wanted to check and see. . ." Miss Gibson paused and peered into Sarah's eyes. "Are you sure that's where your mother is?"

"Yes'm," Sarah said and glanced at her brothers. "Ain't that right, boys?"

"Yes'm, that's right," Johnny said.

Feeling uneasy, Sarah turned away from Miss Gibson's penetrating gaze. "Would ya like a drank of water, ma'am?—Johnny, go fetch the bucket—"

Miss Gibson raised her hand. "No, Johnny, that's not necessary."

For a moment, the group stood there in awkward silence. Sarah's mind raced as she tried to think of something to say. But there wasn't anything left to say.

Miss Gibson took hold of Sarah's hand. "You know, I've been a school teacher long enough to tell when someone's lying to me, so tell me the truth, Sarah. Where's your mother?"

"Like I said, Miss Gibson, she's gone to town to take Uncle Jake to the train de—"

"Sa-rah!" Miss Gibson said as her gaze deepened. "The house is empty. There's no furniture, no dishes in the cupboard, and no food in the cabinets. So tell me. What's going on here? I know you're in trouble, and I want to help you."

Sarah struggled to invent an explanation for why everything was gone. *Hank was buying them new furniture—no, Miss Gibson would never believe that. They had to sell the furniture to pay the rent—no, she wouldn't believe that either.* Too tired to pretend anymore, Sarah closed her eyes, slumped her shoulders, and her throat tightened. Suddenly, her emotions gushed forth like a breaking dam, and she threw her arms around her teacher. "Oh, Miss Gibson, our Mama's gone! Hank took her away with him to St. Louie. She said they'd come back to get us, but they shoulda been here by now."

Miss Gibson wrapped her arms around Sarah. "There, there! Let it all out!" She pulled out her handkerchief and wiped Sarah's tears. "Bless your hearts. Why didn't you tell me?"

"We's afraid we'd get split up," Sarah said.

"So what's gonna happen to us now?" Johnny said.

"Well, the first thing we're going to do is go to my house and have a good breakfast."

Mark looked at Miss Gibson through his tears and giggled. "Breakfast? Oh, boy!"

"Oh, that reminds me," Miss Gibson said. She pulled the fudge from her purse, handed pieces to the kids, and took one herself. Mark swallowed his morsel and asked for another one. Miss Gibson gave him another piece and then stuffed the bag back into her purse. "That's all you can have before breakfast. Now, let's go home."

"Just a minute," Sarah said. "I gotta get somethin'." She ran to the bedroom, pulled off the wallboard, and took out her gold locket. She opened it and gazed at the picture of her mother and father. They were both young, and her mother was pretty. She closed it, kissed it, and slipped it into her dress pocket.

Then she ran to the back porch and peered at the barn. Jake was sitting just inside the doorway. She smiled and waved to him. She wanted to go thank him for everything he had done, but was afraid Miss Gibson would see him.

Jake waved back to her, and Sarah threw him a kiss. As she turned to leave, she saw Hank's church key hanging on the porch post. She grabbed it, dropped it into her pocket with the locket, and ran back to the front yard.

"Okay, I'm ready to go now," Sarah said, and Miss Gibson led them out the front gate. As they marched down the lane for the last time, Mark peered back at the place, and tears trickled down his face. That old farm was the only home he had ever known, so it must have saddened him to leave it. But, for Sarah and Johnny, it was just a temporary stop. Hank moved them there when their mother married him after their real father was killed. It had *never* felt like home to Sarah.

Chapter 8

AT MISS GIBSON'S HOUSE

THE FIRST THING the kids noticed about Miss Gibson's house was that it had electricity. Sarah had seen the men setting the poles and stringing the wire on them, but the only place she knew of that already had electric power was Mr. Zimmerman's store. It had those long white tube lights on the ceiling and those pretty colored tube signs in the windows advertising ice cream, soda pop, and cigarettes.

As Miss Gibson opened the refrigerator, the kids watched. All they had ever had was an icebox that seldom contained ice. She removed a water pitcher, filled four glasses, and handed them out. A fresh bucket of cool well water was as cold as the kids' water ever got in the hot summertime. But this water was so cold it hurt Sarah's teeth.

Mark set his glass on the table, tiptoed to the refrigerator, and jerked open its door. "Who's turnin' on the light?" he said as he peered inside.

"They say Yehudi does it," Miss Gibson said. "But it's really done by a door switch."

The kids finished their drinks. Then the boys ran outside to play, and Sarah stayed in the kitchen. "Is there anythang I can help ya do, Miss Gibson?"

"Have you ever made biscuits?"

"No, ma'am, but I watched Mama do it."

"Well then, scrub your hands, and I'll teach you how."

While Sarah washed, Miss Gibson set a big wooden mixing bowl, a rolling pin, and the biscuit-making ingredients on the table.

When Sarah returned, Miss Gibson handed her an apron. "You'd better put this on. Biscuit making is a dusty job."

Sarah unfolded the flower-print, frilly-edged pinafore and slipped it over her head. "Wow! This is perty!" she said as she tied its sashes behind her. "Mama has one kinda like it that her Mother made for her."

Under Miss Gibson's guidance, Sarah soon had the biscuits in the oven.

As the delicious aroma wafted out the doors and drifted across the yard, it lured the boys to the back porch.

Sarah carried a washbasin, a soap bar, and a towel outside and set them on the porch banister.

"Is it time to eat yet?" Mark said.

"Almost," Sarah said.

Then the boys laughed.

"You look like a ghost," Mark said.

Sarah looked at her reflection in the washbasin. "Oh, that's flour. I been makin' biscuits." She rinsed her face and dried it. "Y'all get warshed, then come inside and help me set the table."

In the dining room, Sarah and Johnny set the plates and cups on the table, and Mark distributed the silverware. Then Sarah placed cloth napkins beside the plates while Miss Gibson stocked the table with biscuits, gravy, eggs, and bacon. When she poured cocoa into their cups, the kids giggled. Sarah couldn't remember the last time she had cocoa.

"Okay, let's eat," Miss Gibson said. "Sarah, you sit by the window. Johnny, you sit at the other end of the table. And Mark, you sit across from your sister."

"Give me some of ever'thang," Mark said as Miss Gibson took her seat at the end of the table nearest the kitchen.

"Okay, Mark, but first, we've got to say grace," Miss Gibson said.

"What's grace?" Mark said.

"Our prayer to thank God for the food," Miss Gibson said. "Didn't you say grace at your house?"

"No," Mark said.

"Oh, yes, we did, Marky," Sarah said. She didn't want Miss Gibson to think they were total heathens. "We did it all the time, remember?"

Mark gawked at his sister and shook his head. "No!"

Sarah grimaced and kicked him.

"Ouch!" Mark said as he frowned and rubbed his shin. "What'd ya do that for?"

Miss Gibson clamped her lips together and fought back a grin.

Sarah glared at Mark. "Well, we *did*!" she hissed through clenched teeth. "Didn't we, Johnny?"

"Uh-huh," Johnny grunted.

"Well then, Sarah, perhaps you'd like to say grace for us this morning?" Miss Gibson said.

"Oh, well, ah, ma'am, I thank you'd better do it this time. I'll do it next time."

"Okay, let's all join hands and bow our heads," Miss Gibson said.

Mark didn't know what "bow our heads" meant, so he watched his sister. He lowered his chin, but his eyes stayed focused on Sarah while Miss Gibson spoke the sacred words. Then he heard a new word that would become very important to him at mealtimes.

"Amen!" Miss Gibson said.

They released hands, and Mark grabbed his fork.

Miss Gibson picked up the platter and walked to Sarah. She laid two strips of bacon and an egg on her plate, then did the same for Johnny.

When she laid the bacon on Mark's plate, he picked up a strip and stuck it in his mouth.

"Put that down, Marky!" Sarah scolded.

"Why?" Mark said and laid the bacon back on his plate.

"'Cause we cain't eat till ever'body's ready."

Mark shifted his eyes from side to side. "Ain't ever'body ready?"

"No, silly. Miss Gibson hadn't set down yet."

Mark rested his elbows on the table, cupped his puffed cheeks in his hands, and stared at his food. *Hungry! Hungry! Hungry!* He had been hungry ever since his mother left.

Miss Gibson walked to Mark, broke up a biscuit in his plate, and poured a ladle of gravy over it. Then she sat down. "Okay, let's eat."

Mark stuck his fork into a big piece of biscuit and raised it to his mouth. It smelled so–

"Hold it, Mark," Miss Gibson said. "I forgot something."

Mark froze–fork in mid-air–and his eyes watered.

Miss Gibson returned to him and tucked his napkin into his shirt collar like a bib. Why was she fussing over such a silly little thang?

By the time she finished, Mark could no longer hold back. He stuffed the biscuit into his mouth, closed his eyes, and let the taste make his mouth happy as tears streamed down his face. "Ummm! This is soooo good!" he mumbled.

When they finished eating, Miss Gibson poured more cocoa into their cups.

Mark took a drink, set his cup down, and Sarah giggled. "Marky, you got a mustache."

He looked back at her and grinned. "So do you."

"Well, you can wash them off when you take your baths this afternoon," Miss Gibson said.

"Baths?" Mark grimaced and shook his head. "I don't need no bath! I'll just warsh my face."

"No, you'll take a full bath," Miss Gibson said. "Tomorrow's Sunday, and we've all got to be clean for church."

"Ya mean, 'sides takin' a bath, we gotta go to church, too?" Mark said.

"Yes, I always go to church on Sunday, and tomorrow you all will go with me."

As much as Mark enjoyed the food, he wasn't sure it was worth having to take a bath and go to church. He felt he could get along just fine for the rest of his life without taking another bath. And as far as church was concerned, he had never been, so he *knew* he could do without *that*.

While the women washed and put away the dishes, the boys lounged on the living room couch and listened to the radio. It was Johnny and Mark's first time to hear a complete program.

When the kitchen was clean, Miss Gibson set the tea kettle and three large pans of water on the stove to heat. Then she and Sarah carried the long galvanized bathtub inside to the back bedroom. While Miss Gibson made final bath preparations, Sarah joined her brothers on the sofa beside the radio.

"Okay, Sarah, your bath's ready," Miss Gibson said as she stepped into the living room. "You boys go outside and stay there."

"Why?" Mark said. "We wonna listen to the radio."

"Because your sister's going to take a bath, and you shouldn't see her naked."

Mark laughed. "Sarah's seen me nekkid lotsa times."

"Well, not anymore. You're too old for that now, so run along. You can help me get things ready to do the laundry. Go to the backyard and fill the buckets by the pump. I'll be out in a minute to help." Miss Gibson turned off the radio and shooed the boys out the backdoor.

At the well, Mark and Johnny wrestled the long handle of the big iron pump and filled the two five-gallon buckets. When Miss Gibson came out, she emptied the water into the two large black kettles, built a fire under the wash kettle, and left the rinse kettle cold.

A few minutes later, Sarah stepped out onto the back porch dressed in a robe with her wet hair wrapped in a towel.

"Okay, boys, who's next?" Miss Gibson said.

Mark crossed his arms, puffed out his jaws, and stood his ground.

"I guess I am," Johnny said and followed Miss Gibson into the house. After getting him squared away, she returned to the yard and the kettles.

A short time later, Johnny came back outside dressed in a long nightshirt.

"Okay, Mark," Miss Gibson said. "It's your turn."

Mark frowned and shook his head. "Nope! Don't wont one!"

"Well, whether you want one or not, you're taking one. You've got to be clean for church in the morning."

"I don't wonna go to church, neither."

"But, you'll like church. Some of your school friends will be there."

Mark shook his head. "I ain't got no friends."

Sarah laughed. "Oh, Marky! Yes, you do. You got lotsa friends!"

"Baths hurt," Mark said.

Miss Gibson glared at him. "How do they hurt?"

"The soap burns, and the warshrag scratches."

"Well, I'll help you, and I promise not to scrub you raw, okay?"

"Nope!"

"Oh, go on, Marky," Sarah said and pushed him toward the house. "The sooner ya get done, the sooner ya can come back out and play."

Miss Gibson took him by the hand and pulled him inside to the tub. "Okay, Mark, this is a stickup," she said as she formed her hand into the shape of a pistol and pointed it at him. "Get those arms up in the air."

"Why?" Mark said.

"Because we're going to skin a monkey."

Mark glared at Miss Gibson. "Skin a monkey? What monkey?"

"The Mark monkey."

Mark raised his arms and held his pout, but as Miss Gibson stripped him, a crooked grin sneaked onto his face. Her touch wasn't rough like Sarah's. She soon coaxed him into the water and gave him a thorough but gentle scrubbing.

When finished, Miss Gibson dried Mark, dressed him in a long shirt, and sent him back outside. Then she and Sarah emptied the bathwater in the backyard and carried the tub back to the bedroom.

After putting three fresh pans of water on the stove to heat, the women gathered the dirty clothes, carried them outside, and laid them beside the kettles. As Miss Gibson poured soap powder into the boiling water, suds bubbled over the kettle's sides and hissed as they dripped onto the fire. She picked up the garments a few at a time, dropped them into the hot, soapy water, and stirred them with a long wooden pole. When they were clean, she moved them to the cold rinse water. Then the kids wrung them out, and Miss Gibson hung them on the clothesline.

When the job was done, Miss Gibson and Johnny dumped the water onto the fire and turned the big black pots upside-down to drain.

"Okay, now it's my turn to bathe," Miss Gibson said and went into the house.

A short time later, she called the kids inside, and while they listened to more radio, she made telephone calls.

Just before sunset, the kids brought in the dry laundry and put on their clean clothes, while Miss Gibson cooked a supper of white beans, stewed potatoes, turnip greens, and cornbread.

"Okay, let's eat," Miss Gibson said as she set the last bowl of food on the table.

The boys charged into the dining room, and Sarah frowned. "Y'all quit bein' so rowdy! We don't wont Miss Gibson to thank she's brung a bunch of white trash home with her."

"What's white trash?" Mark said.

"Somethin' we don't ever wonna be," Sarah said.

Miss Gibson walked to the living room and turned down the radio. On her way back, she stopped and fixed Mark's bib.

Sarah smiled. This felt like home. They were clean and had plenty of food. Even Mark was getting enough to eat.

"Would you like to say grace this time, Sarah?" Miss Gibson said as she sat down.

"Yes'm," Sarah said. She paused a moment, then began. "Dear God. Thank You for this wonderful food and for ever'thang You and Miss Gibson are doin' for us. Please take care of Mama, and help us get back with her real soon. Amen."

"That was very nice," Miss Gibson said. Then she walked back to the living room and turned up the radio.

"This is clear channel 650, WSM, Nashville, Tennessee," the announcer said. Then he paused a moment and continued. "Live from Ryman Auditorium in downtown Nashville, Tennessee, this is the *Grand Ole Opry* starring George Morgan."

As a fiddle played, Miss Gibson passed out the cornbread, and Sarah spooned potatoes onto their plates.

"Whur's the meat?" Mark said.

"There isn't any," Miss Gibson said. "This is a vegetable and cornbread meal."

Mark frowned. "Well, I like meat."

"Sorry, Mark, but there's not any tonight. We'll have meat tomorrow for lunch."

Mark puffed out his jaws, then took a bite of cornbread.

When they finished eating, Miss Gibson cleared the dishes from the table. "Who wants more cocoa?" she said as she carried the pot of hot chocolate into the room.

"I do," the boys' voices rang out in unison.

"Yes'm, please," Sarah said.

As Mark finished his cocoa, his eyelids drooped. "I'm tard," he murmured.

"Well, it's almost bedtime," Miss Gibson said and wiped off his chocolate mustache. "While you boys go to the outhouse, I'll fix you a pallet on the living room floor."

When the boys returned, they crawled into bed, and the women visited the privy. Then Miss Gibson turned off the porch light and locked the backdoor.

"G'night, Johnny. G'night, Marky," Sarah said as she headed to her bedroom.

"G'night, Sissy," Mark said.

"G'night," Johnny mumbled.

"Knock on my door if you need anything," Miss Gibson said as she checked on the boys one last time. "Oh, and stay covered. It gets chilly before morning, and we don't want anyone getting sick."

"Yes'm," Johnny muttered. Then Miss Gibson went into her bedroom and closed the door.

Sarah turned off the light in her room and slid onto the feather bed. It reminded her of home before her daddy died, and tears filled her eyes. In the background, soft orchestra music played on the radio. Miss Gibson had forgotten to turn it off. And it played all night.

Chapter 9

CHURCH AND
REVEREND RICHTER

ON SUNDAY MORNING, Miss Gibson woke the kids and had them wash and dress while she made breakfast.

"Why we gotta warsh so much?" Mark said as they ate.

"Because the Bible says, 'Cleanliness is next to Godliness,'" Miss Gibson said. "And we all need to be as close to God as possible."

Mark didn't understand her answer but accepted it since he didn't know what else to do. He knew the Bible was a book, and books had important things written in them, but that was all he knew about it. Besides, the washing didn't hurt as much when Miss Gibson helped him. It was almost fun the way she did it. For a moment, he thought he might even get used to it. Then he frowned. *No, warshin's still warshin', and that's never fun.*

At nine o'clock, while Miss Gibson and Sarah put away the last clean breakfast dishes, a shiny, new green Plymouth sedan drove up in front of the house.

"Okay, children, our ride's here," Miss Gibson said. As they gathered in the living room, a nice-looking, middle-aged man in a gray suit stepped out of the car and walked to the front porch.

"Come in, Al. We're ready," Miss Gibson said.

The man took off his hat and stepped inside.

70

"Al, these are the Skaggs children I told you about yesterday on the phone. Children, this is my friend, Mr. Al Peterson."

Sarah held out her hand. Other than him being Miss Gibson's friend, she wasn't sure who he was, but right now, she felt she needed to be friendly to all grown-ups who might help them. "G'mornin', Mr. Peterson. I'm Sarah, and these are my brothers, Johnny and Mark."

Al shook her hand. "Nice to meet you, Sarah." Then he nodded to the boys. "Johnny, Mark."

"Well, we'd better go," Miss Gibson said. "We don't want to be late."

Mr. Peterson walked to the porch and held the screen door open while everyone filed out. Then Miss Gibson locked the door, and they hurried to the car.

The kids knew where they were going since the church house sat near the schoolhouse. It was a white, rectangular, concrete block building with pointy-topped windows whose panes had been painted various colors to look like stained glass. Sarah had been there once before with her mother and the lady who had invited them to services, but Johnny and Mark had never attended.

Mr. Peterson parked the car beside the building, and they walked inside. In the small room just past the front door stood a tall, slender, stern-faced man dressed all in black.

"Good morning, Brother Peterson and Sister Gibson. Are these the unfortunate children we've all been hearing so much about?" the man said without losing his stern scowl.

"Yes, Reverend. Perhaps you should preach a sermon on the disrespectful practice of party line eavesdropping," Miss Gibson said. "These are the Skaggs children. This is Sarah, this is Johnny, and this is Mark," she said as she tapped each child on the shoulder.

"I'm pleased to hear they've all been named from the Holy Scripture," the Reverend said.

"Children, say hello to Reverend Richter," Miss Gibson said.

"Hello, Reverend Richter," Sarah said, but the boys said nothing. Sarah looked at them and frowned. She would have to talk to them about that. They needed to start being polite to people.

Then the Reverend turned his gaze on Sarah, and the hair bristled on her neck. So that was why they hadn't answered. He scared them. Sarah smoothed her neck hair and peered at the Reverend. She usually liked everybody, but this man had a black heart and an evil soul.

Miss Gibson nudged the kids down the aisle and guided them into a pew. As they took their seats, the congregation eased into a spontaneous hymn. After two more songs and a prayer, the Reverend strutted to the pulpit.

When the sermon began, Johnny fell asleep with his head propped against the back of the hard wooden bench. Sarah peered at him. So long as he didn't snore, he would probably go unnoticed. Then she looked at Mark, who was scratching his britches legs and squirming.

Suddenly, the woman sitting behind them rapped Mark on his head with her bony knuckles.

"Ouch!" he said out loud as he rubbed his head and frowned at the pickle-pussed old woman.

Miss Gibson glanced over her shoulder and was greeted with a self-righteous smirk as though the woman expected a "thank you" for her actions. Instead, Miss Gibson grimaced. "Keep your hands to yourself, Belladonna Hemlock," she whispered. "If there's any disciplining to be done here, I'll do it."

Miss Gibson had Mark move to the seat between her and Sarah, where she put a protective arm around him. And in the comfort of that arm, he fell asleep.

Although Sarah yawned several times, she stayed awake during the entire sermon. But, by the time the congregation stood to sing what she found out later was called the "invitation song," she was exhausted.

While the song dragged on, the Reverend stood beside the pulpit with outstretched arms gazing over his flock as if he were beaming some holy message into their hearts and minds. But even at that distance, Sarah could still see the evil in his eyes.

"Repent, brothers and sisters, before God rains down his wrath upon your wicked souls!" he shouted during the song's final verse.

Near the back of the room, a young woman with tears streaming down her face stepped from a pew and ran down the aisle.

Sarah's brain snapped wide awake. How often did this kind of thing happen?

The Reverend bolted from the platform, threw his arms around the woman, and guided her to a front-row seat. Then he marched back to the podium and stretched his arms out over the congregation again.

"Be seated," he said as the song's last note faded.

He stepped off the podium, sat down beside the woman, and they whispered to each other. Except for a crying baby, the room was dead silent.

A moment later, the Reverend returned to the pulpit. "Brothers and sisters, the angels are rejoicing this morning because one of our own children, Angela Billings, has come forward to accept our Lord Jesus Christ as her savior and be buried with him in baptism. Most of you already know Angela, but for those who don't, she is one of my and Sister Richter's foster daughters.

"For reasons known only to her and God, she left our midst over a year ago but, to our great joy, has now returned.

"She will now make her confession of faith."

The Reverend walked back to Angela, took hold of her hand, and she stood. "Angela, do you believe, with all of your heart, that Jesus Christ is the son of the living God?"

"Yes, Daddy, I do!"

"May God bless you, my daughter, for having the courage and conviction to confess His Son's name. And may you remain faithful to Him all the days of your life so that when your earthly journey is done, you shall hear Him say, 'Well done, my faithful servant. Enter ye into *the kingdom of heaven*.'"

As they left for the changing rooms, the song leader stepped onto the podium and started another hymn. This song was fast, and the congregation knew it by heart. Sarah smiled and swayed to its rhythm. She wanted to clap her hands, but since no one else did, neither did she.

The song ended, and the song leader opened a curtain that covered a window behind the pulpit. There stood the Reverend and Angela. In the background, water sloshed and echoed like they were in a big rain barrel.

Angela stood sideways to the audience, and the Reverend faced them. He raised his right hand and tilted his eyes heavenward. "Angela Billings, having made your confession that Jesus Christ is the Son of God, I now baptize you in the name of the Father, the Son, and the Holy Ghost. Amen!"

While Angela held on to the Reverend's forearm, he placed a handkerchief over her nose and mouth and supported her back with his other hand.

Sarah's eyes bulged as the Reverend laid Angela backward into the water and plunged her completely under its surface. Her school friends had told her about the baptism ceremony, but this was the first time she had seen it.

As Angela rose from the water, the congregation leaped to its feet and began singing, "Oh, How I Love Jesus."

Johnny popped awake and bounced to his feet. "What's hap'nin'?" he whispered.

"A woman was just baptized," Sarah said. "Ya shoulda seen it."

"What's baptized?"

"I'll tell ya later."

The service ended, and Miss Gibson and Mr. Peterson ushered the kids to the exit where the still-damp Reverend stood and shook hands with each person who filed past him. At his side stood Angela with a baby in her arms as several people fussed over them. For a moment, Sarah and Angela's eyes locked, and they smiled at each other.

As the kids shook the Reverend's hand, he glared down at them. "Sister Gibson, next Sunday, we'll expect you and these children here for Bible school. We'll also expect you here for service tonight. These youngsters need the Lord in their lives. I sense their spiritual guidance has been severely neglected."

"Well, we'll see," Miss Gibson said. But by the tone of her voice, Sarah could tell she had no intention of ever attending anything more than Sunday morning worship, which suited her just fine. The less she saw of the Reverend, the safer she would feel.

Mr. Peterson drove them back to Miss Gibson's house, and she sent the kids outside to play. Sarah volunteered to help prepare lunch, but Miss Gibson insisted that she and Al could handle the job alone.

When lunch was ready, they called the kids back inside. As they filed past the table on the way to wash their hands, they gawked at the biscuits, chicken, green beans, gravy, mashed potatoes, and pitchers of sweet tea, milk, and water.

"Oh, boy! Let's hurry up and sit down," Mark said.

While Mr. Peterson said grace, Mark eyed the fried chicken.

'Amen,' Mr. Peterson said, and Mark shouted, "I wonna drumstick!"

"Okay, Mark," Miss Gibson said. She stood up, fixed his bib, and filled his plate.

At the end of the meal, Miss Gibson carried in an apple pie.

"Wow! Whur'd that come from?" Mark said.

"Al brought it." Miss Gibson said as she served the dessert.

"I'm 'bout to pop!" Mark said when he finished his pie, and Sarah and Johnny laughed.

"Don't tell me you're full, Marky?" Sarah said.

"Yeah, I am. Why?"

"'Cause we ain't never heard ya say that 'fore," Johnny said. "Ya usually ask for more, no matter what."

"Maybe this is the beginnin' of somethin' new," Sarah said.

After lunch, Miss Gibson sent the kids back outside. As they played in the yard, several cars came and went from the house. Each one stayed only a few minutes, and each lady carried a bag inside. The boys paid no attention, but Sarah recognized the women from the church.

At five o'clock, they ate a supper of leftovers. Then, while Miss Gibson and Mr. Peterson washed the dishes, the kids played in the living room and listened to the radio.

Just past sunset, Sarah tiptoed to the window and watched Miss Gibson and Mr. Peterson stroll hand in hand to his car. When they kissed, she giggled. As Mr. Peterson drove away, Miss Gibson headed back inside, and Sarah returned to the couch.

"I've got surprises for you," Miss Gibson said as she entered the living room. She hurried to her bedroom, returned with three new coats, and handed them to the kids. "Aren't these nice?"

"Wow! They sure are!" Sarah said as she slipped hers on. It was green and knee-length, with a black felt collar and cuffs. "Are these really ours?"

"Yes, they really are," Miss Gibson said.

This must be what her mother meant about the church people taking care of them. Sarah hugged her teacher and giggled. "Thank you, Miss Gibson!"

Maybe they should have come to her at the very beginning. They wouldn't have been so scared and wouldn't have had to steal food. Then Sarah frowned. But if they had done that, they wouldn't have met Mr. Jake, and he had been so kind to them when they needed help the most. A tear trickled down Sarah's cheek. She loved and missed him, but not being scared anymore and not having to find food was like being in heaven.

Sarah cleared her head and watched her brothers try on their coats. Johnny's was dark brown, Mark's was dark blue, and each had a hood that zipped up into its collar. The boys also got caps with earmuffs that folded up on the outside, and Sarah got a pretty hat, some gloves, and regular earmuffs. Then Miss Gibson brought in shirts and pants for the boys, blouses and dresses for Sarah, and new shoes for all three. It was like Christmas, only better, because they only got one thing each at Christmas.

Sarah could hardly wait to wear her new things to school and show them to her friends. She spent the rest of the night dressing up and looking at herself in the mirror while the boys laughed at her. They couldn't figure out why she was so excited about a bunch of clothes. But *she* knew why. It was simple. They were beautiful.

Chapter 10

THE ESCAPE

ON THE KIDS' first day of school after their transformation, all the girls gathered around Sarah and fussed over her new look, but Johnny and Mark weren't so lucky. Two boys cornered them during morning recess and called them "sissies." Johnny knocked the boys to the ground, but they gave him a bloody nose before the teacher could stop the fight.

Miss Gibson had expected the kids to encounter some teasing, but she hadn't expected violence. She gave Johnny and the other two boys four licks with her paddle and made them apologize to each other in front of the class. However, that just humiliated them, and the fight broke out again at noon. This time, Johnny dished out the bloody noses with black eyes to boot. He wasn't going to take any name-calling or bullying.

Again, Miss Gibson broke up the fight and paddled the boys. Although she knew Johnny hadn't caused the trouble, she punished him anyway, so the other boys wouldn't blame him for their paddling and continue the feud.

By the next day, the kids' schoolmates had accepted their new look. Sarah's circle of friends grew from two girls to a half dozen. And one boy even befriended her. She giggled every time she thought about it because he acted like he wanted her to be his girlfriend.

Then, on Thursday, a strange woman and man came to school. When they asked to speak to Miss Gibson alone, she gave the pupils an early lunch break.

As Sarah walked past the visitors, she glared at them. There was something eerie about them.

A few minutes later, Miss Gibson called Sarah and her brothers back inside.

"Whatsamatter, Miss Gibson?" Sarah said as her eyes shot back and forth between her teacher and the visitors. The man looked all right, but the woman had lying eyes.

"Sarah, Johnny, Mark, this is Miss Galloway, and her associate, Mr. Bradford from the Child Welfare Off–"

"Whatcha wont?" Sarah snapped.

Miss Gibson frowned. "Sarah! Behave yourself!"

Miss Galloway smiled a fake smile and walked over to Sarah. "Yesterday, we were informed of your situation and have decided to place you in a foster home."

Sarah crossed her arms and backed away from the woman. "No! We ain't goin' to no 'foster home,' whatever that is. We're stayin' with Miss Gibson."

"Sa-rah!" Miss Gibson said. "These folks are here to help you and your brothers."

"We don't need their help," Sarah said. "We're fine just the way we are."

Miss Gibson eased to Sarah and put her arm around her. "But they'll place you and your brothers in a nice home with a nice family who'll take proper care of you. I can't give you the help you need, but they can."

"But we like it at your house, Miss Gibson."

"Yes, I know you do, but my house is small, and I don't have time to give you the attention you need. Your brothers are even sleeping on the floor."

"What's wrong with that? We been sleepin' on floors all our lives. And I can help ya take care of us."

"Yes, I know you can. I'm not saying you're any trouble. You're not. I'm just saying you deserve better, and I can't give it to you."

"Ya give us new clothes, didn't ya?"

"Yes, with help from the ladies at church, but that was only one of the many things you need. My teacher's salary won't support all four of us, and I need time to grade papers and prepare for classes. I didn't mean for you to think you'd be staying at my house permanently."

Sarah pulled away from Miss Gibson and glared at her. "So you're just gonna hand us over to 'em and let 'em take us away?"

"No, Sarah! That's not how it is! This is simply the best thing for you, so you've got to go with them."

"Will we still getta go to school here?"

"Yes, at least for now," Miss Galloway said. "We've arranged for you to stay with the Richters. They live in this school district."

A chill shot down Sarah's spine. "You mean the preacher at Miss Gibson's church?"

"Yes, they're good people and will take good care–"

"No, they're not!" Sarah said. "He's a wicked, evil–"

"Stop that, Sarah!" Miss Gibson said.

"–old devil!"

As Sarah spoke, Johnny and Mark squirmed.

Miss Galloway cocked her head and peered at Sarah. "I hope you're not going to be trouble."

"Oh no, she's not," Miss Gibson said. "She's just high-spirited."

"When we gotta go?" Sarah said.

"Right now," Miss Galloway said. "But you'll be back here at school tomorrow."

Sarah squinted at Miss Gibson. "Will we getta keep our new clothes?"

"Of course–They're yours."

Mr. Bradford glanced at his wristwatch. "We've got to go, Gloria, if we're going to get these children processed and delivered to the parsonage by the end of the day."

"Yeah, we do," Miss Galloway said. "Come on, children."

As they headed to the door, Miss Gibson gazed at Sarah. "Don't worry. It'll be all right. Al and I'll bring your clothes to you this evening."

"Don't forget my locket," Sarah said, "–and my church key."

"Your locket and your what?" Miss Gibson said and squinted.

"My can opener. I hung it on the dresser with my locket."

"Oh, okay. I'll hand-deliver them to you."

Miss Galloway herded the kids outside, and they slid into the back seat of Mr. Bradford's black sedan. As the door slammed, it echoed like the prison door in a radio show Sarah had heard. They should have stayed with Mr. Jake. Her worst nightmare was coming true.

At the Welfare Office, the kids ate lunch. Then they answered dozens of questions while a woman at a typewriter filled out forms. Later, a doctor examined them at the hospital, did blood tests, and gave them each three shots.

Sarah and Johnny took their shots in the arm, but when Mark fought the nurses, the doctor gave him his shots in the hip.

At four-thirty, Mr. Bradford drove Miss Galloway and the kids to the Richters' house. It was a white, two-story frame structure with three dormers. Two large oak trees with limbs, just right to hang swings, stood in the front yard. But there were no swings, which Sarah took as a bad sign.

Miss Galloway led the kids and Mr. Bradford onto the front porch, knocked on the door, and the Reverend opened it. "Ah, Miss Galloway. How pleasant to see you again. Please come in."

"Good afternoon, Reverend," she said and pushed the kids inside. Then she gestured toward her coworker. "This is my colleague, Mr. Gene Bradford."

As the men shook hands and made small talk, a chubby, plain-faced woman wearing an apron entered the room from the kitchen. Sarah peered into her eyes but read nothing. They were as blank as the eyes of a porcelain figurine.

"And this is my wife, Edna," the Reverend said. She shook hands with the caseworkers and then hurried back to the kitchen.

"Reverend, these are the Skaggs children," Miss Galloway said.

"Yes, I had the pleasure of meeting these wonderful children at worship last Sunday morning. Welcome to our humble–"

"Whur's Angela?" Sarah blurted out, and the Reverend glared at her.

"Angela has gone home. She was only here visiting. Now, as I was saying before I was interrupted. Welcome to our humble home. It isn't much, but the Lord has blessed us with sufficient comforts. I'm sure it will meet your needs."

When the kids didn't reply, Miss Galloway nervously giggled. "Yes, I'm sure it will."

"Please, come in and have a seat," the Reverend said and led everyone to the center of the living room.

Sarah pulled her brothers to the sofa, where they sat down and huddled together.

"Oh well, thank you, Reverend," Miss Galloway said, "but Mr. Bradford and I need to get back to the office. We still have a few things to do before the end of the day."

"Well then, you'll just have to come back when you can stay longer."

"Yes, we will," Miss Galloway said. Then she walked over to the kids. "We're leaving now, but we'll be back occasionally to check on you. Enjoy your new home and behave yourselves."

While the Reverend escorted Miss Galloway and Mr. Bradford outside, the kids ran to the window and watched them. "We gotta get outta here," Sarah whispered.

"Why?" Johnny said.

"'Cause my heart's tellin' me this is a evil place."

"How we gonna do it?"

"I don't know," Sarah said while they watched Miss Galloway and Mr. Bradford drive away. "But I'll fig're out somethin.'"

As the Reverend headed back inside, Miss Gibson and Mr. Peterson pulled into the driveway, and he glared at them.

"We've brought the children's clothes," Miss Gibson said when they got out of the car.

"Just set them here on the porch, and Sister Richter will take care of them," the Reverend said. "She'll want to wash and press them before putting them in the closet."

"Well, they're already clean, Reverend, but I suppose they do have a few wrinkles," Miss Gibson said. "They're really nice garments."

"I'm sure they are," the Reverend said, "but Sister Richter will still want to check them."

"May I speak to Sarah for a moment?" Miss Gibson said.

"Yes!" Sarah whispered as she made a fist and punched the air. She wanted to grab her brothers, run outside, and jump into Mr. Peterson's car, but she couldn't.

"Well, they're just getting settled," the Reverend said. "Can't you talk to her at school tomorrow?"

"No, sir, I need to speak with her now," Miss Gibson said.

"Oh, well, all right," the Reverend said and frowned. "Sister Richter, fetch the girl and bring her out here."

As Sarah stood up to head for the door, Mark jumped up to go with her. "No, Marky! You and Johnny stay here. I'll be right back."

Sister Richter stepped in behind Sarah, put her hands on her shoulders, and guided her through the door.

"Hey, Sarah, we've brought your clothes. Come here, I want to talk to you," Miss Gibson said, and Sarah ran to her.

"Did ya brang my locket and church key?"

Miss Gibson took Sarah's hand and folded the items into her palm.

"This locket means the world to me. It's all I got left of Mama and Daddy."

"Yes, I can see you cherish it, but what's the significance of the can opener?"

"Oh, it's just a trinket I'm keepin'. I thought it might come in handy sometime." Sarah dropped the things into her pocket and hugged Miss Gibson. "I'll see ya tomorra," she said, then hurried back inside and rejoined the boys at the window.

As Mr. Peterson and Miss Gibson drove away, the kids scampered back to the couch. The Reverend walked inside, locked the door, and then scowled at the kids. "Well, welcome to your new home!

"Now, let's talk about rules. Rules are necessary for order, and there *will* be order here because all rules *will* be obeyed.

"Rule number one: You will call me 'Reverend Richter' and my wife 'Sister Richter.' Failure to address us properly will earn you a night locked in your room without supper."

The kids gawked at the Reverend.

"Rule number two: You will only speak when spoken to. Children never interrupt adults, and females never interrupt adult males. Speaking out of turn will earn you a night locked in your room without supper.

"Rule number three: You will not back sass. Doing so will get your mouth washed out with soap and will earn you the rest of the day locked in your room without meals.

"Rule number four: All meals will be eaten in the dining room. Food is *never* allowed anywhere else in the house unless you are sick and bedridden. Breakfast is at seven, lunch is at noon, and dinner is at six. You *will* be present and on time for all meals. If you're late, you will be locked in your room and go without the meal.

"Rule number five: Grace will be said before every meal, and you *will* bow your heads in reverence to God while the prayer is offered. We will also read from the Holy Scripture three times a day, mornings after breakfast, evenings after supper, and nights before retiring to bed. And everyone will read." He glared at Johnny and Mark. "Those who fail to read well will be required to read the scripture aloud for an hour every day until they can read fluently. God abhors terrible readers.

"Rule number six: All schoolwork will be completed between scripture reading after dinner and scripture reading before bed. God expects us to be educated as well as obedient. Grades of less than 'A' *will not* be tolerated. For every subject without the grade of 'A,' you will receive three sharp lashes from my strap."

Johnny squirmed.

"Rule number seven: Because your presence here will create additional work, you will perform daily chores. There will be no idle hands. The Holy Scripture says, 'He who does not work, neither shall he eat,' and that 'idle hands and idle minds are the devil's workshop.' Neither idleness nor the devil will be tolerated here. We will all work from Monday through Saturday, but on Sunday, the Lord's Day, we will rest. If you are assigned a chore and do not complete it to *my* satisfaction, you will receive three sharp lashes from my strap.

"Rule number eight: You can go to the outhouse without permission during the day and until bedtime. After that, you will use the slop jar in your room. First thing every morning, you will empty and wash the slop jar. Those who fail to do so will receive three sharp lashes from my strap. Anyone who wets or soils his bed will be made to clean up the mess and wash the sheets. Sister Richter will not deal with such filth. The offender will also receive three sharp lashes from my strap."

Mark squirmed.

"Rule number nine: Each of you will bathe on Saturday, and that bath will last you the entire week. Anyone needing an additional bath during the week will make his own preparations and clean up afterward. He will also be required to bathe using lye soap.

"Rule number ten: You will obey all rules.

"Are there any questions?"

All the cruelty and evil Sarah had seen in the Reverend's eyes the first time she met him was now right there in the open. And she would tell Miss Gibson about it the first chance she got. But until then, she had to find somehow to deal with this old devil. Hank was bad, but he was nothing like this man.

The Reverend glared at the kids and turned red. "You've just been spoken to, and I demand an answer! Do You Have Any Questions?"

"No, sir!" Sarah said, while the boys only shook their heads.

"Don't you shake your empty heads at me, or you'll feel the sting of my strap! Answer me with your tongues!"

Mark covered his ears, closed his eyes, and curled up into a ball. The Reverend grabbed him by the hair, jerked him to his feet, and Mark screamed.

Sarah leaped to her feet, with Johnny right behind her. She punched the Reverend's face with her fists and kicked his bony shins. Johnny jumped on his back, pulled his hair, and gouged his eyes.

"Leave him alone, ya dirty old devil!" Sarah screamed. "He's just a little boy! He don't know what you're talkin' 'bout!"

Johnny slid off the Reverend's back, grabbed an umbrella from the stand beside the desk, and pounded him with it until he dropped Mark.

Sister Richter bounced into the room carrying a big wooden spoon and whacked Johnny on the head. He whirled around and landed three hard knocks on her head and shoulders with the umbrella.

The Reverend fought to break away and shield his wife, but Sarah held on to him.

Sister Richter raised the spoon to hit Johnny again, but Mark grabbed her hand and bit it until she dropped the weapon.

As the Reverend and Sister Richter backed away, the kids huddled together on the other side of the room.

"Animals!" the Reverend bellowed. "They've brought us a pack of wild animals! Well, I know how to handle animals!"

"If you ever touch us again, we'll knock your brains out!" Sarah yelled.

"We'll see about that!" the Reverend shouted. "You're all going without supper!"

Sarah laughed. "That ain't gonna hurt us! We done without supper before!"

The Reverend picked up a black book from his desk and scribbled something in it. "This incident has now been officially logged in my journal and will be reported to the proper authorities!" He strode to his wife and examined her bloody hand. "This is an outrage! You may be an undisciplined rabble now, but you *will* learn obedience here! God as my witness, you will learn obedience!"

The Reverend marched from the room and returned with a razor strap in his hand. "'Spare the rod and spoil the child!'" He swung the strap back and forth and charged the kids. Sister Richter fell in behind him with a raised broom handle.

The strap caught Mark in the back, and he screamed. Sarah jumped in front of him and took a hard slap across her shoulders. The kids withdrew to the staircase, and the preacher herded them up the steps into the narrow hallway between two bedrooms.

Cornered, Sarah faced the Reverend and shielded her brothers with her body.

The preacher pointed to the bedroom on his right. "You boys, get in there!"

"We ain't gonna let ya separate us!" Sarah yelled.

"Oh, is that so?" the Reverend said. He swung his strap, struck Sarah across the waist, and she fell against her brothers. "You're going to do whatever I tell you to do! Now, you boys, get in that room! I'm not telling you again!"

Johnny glanced at Sarah, and she nodded. She wasn't going to risk them getting a real beating–she had seen what Hank did to her mother–it was awful. And this man was a *lot* meaner than Hank.

The boys eased into the room, and the Reverend locked the door. Then he turned to Sarah and headed toward her with the razor strap in one hand and the room key in the other.

"And *you*!" His lips quivered as he backed her toward the other bedroom. "You wicked little tramp! Get in there!"

Sarah stepped over the threshold and tried to slam the door, but the Reverend shoved his way in and locked the door behind him.

"You filthy little harlot. Behold the wrath of God. Your time of reckoning is at hand. Stand before thy Lord and receive His punishment."

Sarah peered into the Reverend's eyes. This man was crazy. He just liked to hurt people for the fun of it. Hank may have been mean, but at least he wasn't crazy.

Sarah jumped onto the bed and tried to escape to the other side of the room, but the Reverend caught her foot. He subdued her and covered her mouth and nose with his hand until she passed out. She came to, lying on her stomach, with her hands and ankles tied to the bed. Her heart pounded. What was he going to do?

Across the hallway, Johnny pressed his ear to the door while Mark lay curled up on the bed with a pillow over his head and his thumb in his mouth like he had always done when Hank was on a tear. Sarah screamed, and Johnny beat on the door. "Leave her alone, ya dirty old buzzard! If ya hurt her, I'll kill ya!"

But there was nothing he could do.

"Untie me, ya nasty old devil!" Sarah screamed.

The Reverend pulled out his handkerchief, stuffed it in her mouth, and she bit him. He slapped her and poked the cloth down her throat until she choked and almost passed out again. Sarah coughed and puffed at the rag but couldn't dislodge it. She stopped fighting just to breathe.

"You can't escape the wrath of God!" the Reverend said as he ran his fingers over her pale skin.

This wasn't punishment for anything she had done. This was just plain wrong–more than wrong–this was evil! Sarah twisted and turned to avoid his touch, but nothing worked, and she burst into tears.

The Reverend picked up the razor strap and ran his fingers down its slick surface. "The Lord demands obedience, and you have disobeyed Him. Therefore, you must be punished." He glared down at Sarah and raised the strap over his head. "Behold the wrath of God!" he shouted and struck a hard blow on Sarah's thighs. Fire shot through her legs and she screamed.

"You *will* learn obedience!" He swung the strap again and landed a slap on Sarah's back. "You *will* learn respect!" Again, again, and again, the lash tore into her back, thighs, and legs. The more Sarah twisted and screamed, the faster and harder the Reverend swung the strap. She passed out again and came to sobbing. The exhausted Reverend sat crumpled on the floor at the foot of the bed.

He pulled himself up, and Sarah arched away as he caressed her body a final time. "You must learn to respect and obey men," he said. "It's God's law." Then he shuffled out of the room and closed the door.

Sarah bit the gag. This wasn't *her* God's law! This was a bunch of hooey! Someday, her God would send this old devil to hell. Then *he* would learn *real* right from wrong.

A few minutes later, Sister Richter entered the room carrying a wash pan and set it on the nightstand. She pulled the handkerchief from Sarah's mouth but left the ropes tied. "My dear, dear child," she said and shook her head. "If you disobey, you will be punished, but if you cooperate, you will get along just fine. By divine right, men have dominion over women. That's God's law, and we must accept it."

Sarah winced and stared straight ahead as Sister Richter washed her. She didn't know what "dominion" meant, but she knew enough to know it was more hooey.

"Oh, you may hate us now, and I understand that, but soon you'll see what we're trying to do for you, and then you'll love us. It always happens that way. Over the years, we've had dozens of children pass through our home, and they've all left filled with love and respect for us. Some of the girls have even had their first babies here."

Sister Richter rinsed the washcloth and wrung it out. "Okay, there you are, all clean again. Now, I'll put some salve on you."

Sarah flinched and moaned as the cold gel touched her wounds.

Sister Richter finished the treatment and dropped the ointment tube back into her pocket. "Okay, I'll untie you now, but if you fight me, you'll get more strap. Understand?"

"Yes'm," Sarah mumbled.

Sister Richter untied Sarah's hands, then stood. "You can do the rest yourself. Get some sleep now, and I'll check on you again in the morning." She picked up the wash pan, walked out the door, and locked it.

Tears flowed down Sarah's face, and her wounds burned as she tried to untie her feet. She pushed the pain out of her mind and concentrated on ways to escape this hell hole. She didn't know how they would do it, but if she thought about it long enough, a way would come to her.

Sarah untied the last knot, rolled off the bed, and picked up the ropes. She would probably get another whipping for this, but the Reverend wouldn't tie her with these things again. She opened the window, threw the ropes onto the shingles, and as she did, the tree limbs touching the roof caught her eye. She closed the window, lay down on the bed, and thought about what she had just seen. *It might work.*

"Sarah? Can ya hear me?" Johnny called from across the hallway.

She crawled to the door and sat down. "Yeah, I hear ya."

"You okay?"

She hurt all over and was scared, but she wasn't going to let her brothers know that. "Yeah, I'm okay. That old devil whupped me with his strap."

"Yeah, we heard. What we gonna do 'bout it?"

"I don't know, but I'll fig're out somethin'. How's Marky?"

"Ah, he's okay–just sceared."

"Well, tell him ever'thang's all right. Y'all go to sleep now, and I'll see ya in the mornin'."

"Okay, g'night."

Sarah crawled back onto the bed and laid down on her stomach. All night, she wrestled with her conscience. She had never hated anybody, not even Hank, the way she hated Reverend Richter, and it gnawed at her. Because of her hate and pain, she lay awake most of the night. But by morning, she had worked out a plan.

Just past sunrise, footsteps squeaked on the staircase. Sarah sat up, drew her knees against her chest, and pulled the sheet up around her neck. The lock clicked, and the Reverend walked inside. "I trust you're feeling well this morning?"

"Yes, Reverend Richter, I'm okay."

He stepped in front of the dresser and straightened his tie. Sarah clenched her teeth and stared at him in the mirror. Then he turned and gazed at her. "Sister Richter is preparing us a wholesome breakfast. Perhaps you'll feel better when you've eaten something. She'll be up shortly to check on you." He left the door open and ambled back downstairs.

Sarah crept to the door and peeked down the staircase. Then she tiptoed across the hallway and tapped on her brothers' door. "Hey, Johnny, it's me."

"Sarah? What's hap'nin'?"

"Sister Richter is fixin' breakfast. Get Marky up, and be ready to go downstairs when they call us."

"Okay, I will."

"Johnny, I got a plan to get us outta here."

"Yeah? What is it?"

"I'll tell ya later. You and Marky stay outta trouble today, or it might not work."

"Okay, we will."

"I gotta go now. I'll see ya at breakfast."

"Okay, see ya at breakfast."

Sarah eased back to her room and sat down on the bed. A moment later, the stairs squeaked again, and Sister Richter waddled into the room. Besides the washbasin, she carried something draped over her arm. "Good morning, sweetheart," she said as though nothing had happened the night before.

"G'mornin', Sister Richter," Sarah groaned.

"I've-brought-you-some-thing," the woman said in a sing-song voice. She set the washbasin on the dresser and held up a green and white checked dress accented with white lace and green ribbons. "I think you'll look really pretty in this, don't you?"

Sarah stared at Sister Richter. She still couldn't read anything from those figurine eyes, which puzzled her. Until now, Sarah had thought she could read anyone's heart by their eyes. But that didn't work with this woman. There was something wrong with *her*.

"When you've washed, put this on and come down to breakfast," Sister Richter said.

"Yes'm," Sarah said.

"Hur-ry-up-now. We'll-be-wait-ing-for-you."

Five minutes later, Sarah eased into the dining room. Reverend and Sister Richter were seated at the table–just them–without the boys.

"Ooohhh! Don't-you-look-love-ly!" Sister Richter said.

The Reverend patted the chair seat next to him. "Come here and sit by me."

A chill ran through Sarah as she sat down. "Whur's Johnny and Mark?" she said in her most humble voice.

"They'll eat later," the Reverend said. "We have some things to tell you that they don't need to hear right now."

Sarah peered at him. "What thangs?"

"Nothing to be alarmed about. We're just making a few changes. We'll talk after breakfast. Now, let's thank the Lord for our food."

While the Reverend prayed, Sarah's mind raced. What changes? Why couldn't the boys hear about them? Something terrible was about to happen.

Although the food looked tasty, and Sarah needed it to stay strong, the knot in her stomach wouldn't let her eat.

"Is something wrong, dear?" Sister Richter said. "Would you like something different to eat?"

"No, thank you, Sister Richter. I'm just not hungry."

The Reverend finished his meal, walked to the living room, and sat down behind his desk. A moment later, Sister Richter led Sarah into the room and sat her in the chair facing him.

"Well, it's like this," the Reverend said. "We believe it would be best if your brothers were put in a different foster home."

Sarah's heart missed a beat. "What 'different foster home?'"

"We don't know yet. That hasn't been decided."

"Why do they need to be put somewhur else?"

"Because we want to avoid any repeats of yesterday's events."

"If I promise not to cause no more trouble, can they stay?"

"Well, of course, you would say that, but we must take precautions for our own protection."

Sarah stared into the Reverend's eyes. "Please, Reverend Richter, I promise we'll never do anythang like that again."

"I'm sorry, but the decision has been made."

Tears filled Sarah's eyes. "Will I ever get to see 'em again?"

"Of course, you will. They won't be far away."

"How often?"

"I don't know, but often enough, you'll not miss them."

"When are they leavin'?"

"Miss Galloway's coming to get them tomorrow."

Sarah stared straight ahead with a blank expression on her face. She hadn't expected to have to use her plan so soon, but she wasn't about to lose contact with her brothers. And she certainly wasn't going to believe anything the Reverend told her. Since they would have to escape that night, she needed to go over the plan one more time. "May I be excused now?"

"Yes, you may."

Sarah hurried back to her room and left the door open. A couple of minutes later, the Reverend came to get the boys, and the kids caught sight of one another.

"Hey, Sarah. You okay?" Johnny said as he paused in the hallway.

"No talking," the Reverend said.

Sarah nodded and pressed her finger to her lips.

The Reverend nudged the boys forward. Then he closed Sarah's bedroom door and locked it.

While the boys ate breakfast, Sarah lay on her bed and reviewed the plan. She couldn't see anything wrong with it. It should work.

From the living room, the drone of the Reverend's voice drifted upstairs as he told the boys about their upcoming move.

A few minutes later, Sister Richter came and took Sarah downstairs. Because it was their last day together, the Reverend let the kids skip school.

Mark cried until Sarah got the chance to tell the boys about her plan. Then his tears stopped.

When the Reverend locked the kids in their rooms that night, Sarah took off the pretty dress and put on her regular clothes. Then she lay down on the bed and listened until the Richters' bedroom door closed.

From experience, Sarah knew she could read ten Bible pages an hour. She picked up the book, let it fall open, and looked at the passage. It was Psalms 71. "In thee, O Lord, do I put my trust.... Deliver me in thy righteousness and cause me to escape...."

Sarah's heart pounded. "*Escape!*" It was a sign from God. They were going to make it.

Ten pages later, she read the end of Psalms 94. "... the Lord is my defense; and my God is the rock of my refuge ... he shall ... cut them off in their own wickedness; *yea*, the Lord our God shall cut them off."

Sarah closed the Bible, laid it down, and raised the bedroom window. She peered back at the green and white checked dress accented with white lace and green ribbons and wondered if she would ever have anything that pretty again. Then she stepped out onto the pitched roof, edged to the boys' window, and tapped on it. Johnny opened it, and she slid inside.

"Are y'all ready?"

"Yeah, let's get outta here," Johnny said.

"Okay, be careful. It's steep and slippery out there. Marky, stay between Johnny and me, and you'll be all right."

Sarah eased back onto the roof and helped Mark crawl out. Then Johnny followed.

"I'm scared," Mark whimpered.

"Yeah, I know," Sarah said. "Me too, but we gotta do this. It won't take long."

The kids scooted to the limb, straddled it like a horse, and eased down it to within six feet of the ground. Sarah slid off, dangled as low as she could, and dropped. She scrunched up her face and looked up at the boys. "Nut'in' to it," she whispered as she rubbed the scrapes and scratches on her legs and arms. "Okay, Marky. Now you do it."

"No, it's too high!" he whined.

"Here, lemme go first," Johnny said. Then he slid off the limb. "See, it's easy."

Mark still hesitated, but Sarah and Johnny kept talking and coaxed him into their arms.

As the kids ran to the highway, Johnny glanced at the house and did a double-take. "Look! The box!"

Sarah squinted at the porch through the darkness. "The Reverend forgot to take it in."

They carried the container to the driveway, pulled out their coats, and put them on.

"What we gonna do with the rest of this stuff?" Johnny said.

"Nothin'," Sarah said. "Gotta leave it."

"Well, dang! I wonted 'em shirts," Johnny said.

Sarah laughed. "I ain't never seen ya fuss over clothes 'fore."

"That's 'cause we ain't never had none to fuss over."

"Yeah, you're right," Sarah said. "Okay, come on–Let's go! We got a train to catch!"

Chapter 11

HOBOING WITH BO JESUS

WHILE THE KIDS marched along the highway, a starry canopy sparkled above them. When sweat trickled down Sarah's back, she removed her coat and had the boys do the same.

Mark tucked his under his arm, but it fell to the ground. He tried again, and the same thing happened. "This ole thang's too hard to carry!" he whined.

"It ain't if ya do it right," Sarah said. "Hook your fanger in the collar and slang it over your shoulder."

Mark did as told, but it still fell. He stopped, slouched, and burst into tears.

Johnny picked up the coat, pulled out its hood, slipped it over Mark's cap, and let the rest dangle down his brother's back. "'Ere, try that."

Mark took a few steps, the coat stayed in place, and he giggled. "Gee! Thanks, Johnny!"

Sarah smiled. Maybe she wouldn't have to do everything herself after all.

As the kids passed the Piggott city limit sign, a dog approached them. It laid back its ears, lowered its head, and slunk around them. Sarah slung her coat at it, and it snapped at her. "Get outta here, ya mangy ole mutt!"

Mark knelt and held out his hand to the dog. "Aw, let him come with us."

Sarah grabbed her little brother's arm and pulled him back to his feet. "Leave him alone! Ya don't wonna get bit. He might have hydrophobia."

"Ah, he ain't got no hydrophobi."

As the dog trotted away, a police car turned onto Main Street, a block in front of the kids.

"Quick! Hide behind that hedge!" Sarah whispered, and they darted into the bushes.

As the car passed, the policeman glanced in their direction but didn't stop.

"Good, he didn't see us," Sarah said. "That was ole Poodle Payne, the night marshal."

"How do you know thangs like that?" Johnny said.

"'Cause Daddy told me."

At the railroad tracks in front of the depot, the kids stopped. Sarah peered up the tracks one way and then down them the other. "Mr. Jake said St. Louie's north of here."

"Which way's north?" Johnny said.

Sarah looked up and down the tracks again. "I ain't sure." Then she peered up at the Milky Way. "The North Star! Mr. Jake showed it to me! That'll show us!"

"What's the North Star?" Johnny said.

"It's the last star in the handle of the Little Dipper, and it never moves."

"Whur's the Little Dipper?"

"Just above the Big Dipper."

"Well, 'ere's the Big Dipper," Johnny said. "See that buncha stars yonder that looks like a big water dipper?" He stepped behind Sarah, laid his arm over her shoulder, and traced the outline with his finger.

"Yeah, that's it! Mr. Jake said a straight line through the two stars on the front of the Big Dipper points to the North Star." Sarah followed the line to a tiny bright dot. "There it is! And that's the last star in the Little Dipper's handle." She pointed up the tracks to the right. "That's north. We gotta go thataway."

While they walked along in the darkness, Sarah and Johnny played a game to see who could walk the rail the longest. When Mark tried it, he fell and bit his tongue. As he cried, Sarah wiped the blood off his lips with her dress tail.

"Dang it, Johnny! We gotta remember that Marky cain't do ever'thang we can!"

From the south, a train whistle echoed. "Oooh, that sounds spooky!" Mark said, and his tears stopped.

As the kids dashed into the bushes and hid, the train rumbled up the rails toward them. Its light beacon whipped a long, narrow beam through the darkness like the eye of the Cyclops searching for runaways in the story Miss Gibson had read to them.

While the big black engine rolled past the kids, the train's brakes squealed, then it skidded to a stop. A man carrying a lantern jumped to the ground, hurried up the tracks a few yards, and threw a lever. As he raised and lowered the light, the locomotive's wheels spun, and sparks flew. When they caught hold, the train jerked. Then it eased onto the side track, and the man with the lantern hopped back on board.

"What's hap'nin'?" Mark said.

"I thank there's another train comin' from the other direction," Sarah said.

Mark's eyes bulged. "Is it gonna run over this'n?"

Sarah laughed. "No, silly. That's why this'n's pullin' over on the other track. It's a lucky break for us. Now, all we gotta do is hop on when this'n stops."

In the distance, the second train's whistle blew.

"Okay! Come on!" Sarah said, and they ran alongside the stopped train to an open boxcar. Sarah threw her coat inside, laid her hands flat on the floorboards, and jumped as hard as she could. The train jerked, bounced her out onto the rocks and crossties, and a sharp sting shot through her knees and palms. For a moment, she just sat there and rubbed them. Then she pushed the pain out of her thoughts and jumped back to her feet.

"Hurry! Throw your coats in! We gotta get on this thang 'fore it starts movin'!"

As the passing train's engine shot past, Sarah and Johnny lifted Mark into the boxcar. Then Sarah held out a hand stirrup to Johnny, and they heaved him aboard. Again, Sarah laid her hands flat on the floorboard and jumped as hard as she could, and again, the train bounced her out.

"Dang it!" Sarah said as she stood back up. "I'm beginnin' to thank this train don't wont me to ride it!"

Sarah took position one more time, and while Johnny and Mark's tugged on her, she jumped up and rolled aboard. As she stood up, the passing train's red caboose light streaked past the open door on the other side of the car, and their train eased forward.

"Darn, that was close!" Sarah said. "If catchin' all trains is this hard, I ain't sure how many times I can do it."

The kids picked up their coats, walked to a corner, and sat down. As the passing train's sound faded, the roar and clickety-clack of their train replaced it.

Sarah gazed at her brothers and grinned. "We're doin' it! We're really, really doin' it! We're on our way to St. Louie!" Then she thought about what lay ahead and shivered. How long would it take to get there, and then, how would they find their mother? Although it was scary, she would make it happen. But for now, everything was good except for the uncomfortable ride.

"This ole floor's hard," Mark said.

"Yeah, it is," Sarah said. "We could sit on our coats if it wudn't so dirty in here. I'll go see if I can find somethin' soft." She crawled into the darkness, and a moment later, she screamed.

"What is it?" Johnny said.

"Somethin's got me!"

Johnny jumped up and charged headlong into the darkness. Mark backed up against the wall, stuck his thumb in his mouth, and pulled his coat over his head.

As Sarah and Johnny fought whatever had hold of them, two big arms swept them up into the air. While they kicked and hollered, the beast carried them into the starlight and tossed them onto the floor.

Johnny crabbed backward and flopped down beside Mark. "It's a big ole nigger!" he shouted.

"Who are ya, and whatcha wont?" Sarah said.

"Seems to me, I ought to be the one askin' the questions. I's here first," the man's voice boomed. "There I was, sleepin' like a baby when y'all came bustin' in. I ought to throw ya back out that door."

Johnny jumped to his feet, doubled up his fists and took a fighting stance. "Just try it!"

Sarah stepped in front of Johnny. "Look, Mister. We got real trouble back whur we come from. We're tryin' to get to St. Louie to find our folks. I promise we'll be real quiet if ya just leave us alone. You can have one end of this thang, and we'll take the other'n."

"Well, okay" the man said as he peered down at the kids. "But if I hear the slightest peep out of ya, I swear I'll throw the lot of ya off this train."

"Yes, sir," Sarah said.

The kids hurried back to their corner and huddled together as the man disappeared into the darkness. A few seconds later, he stepped back into the light and tossed a piece of cardboard at their feet. "There, that'll make sittin' a little easier."

Sarah pulled the mat to them and smiled. "Thanks, Mister!" she said as he disappeared into the darkness again.

She laid the mat flat on the floor and spread their coats on it. Then they crawled on top of them and laid down. "Is that better, Marky?"

"Yeah, lots better!"

"Good! Now, let's get some sleep."

"I cain't sleep with that ole nigger in here," Johnny whispered. "He might try'n throw us off the train."

"Ahh, he's just bluffin'," Sarah said. "He ain't gonna do that. He just wonts to be left alone. And stop callin' him a 'nigger,' Johnny. That ain't nice."

"Well, if he tries somethin', I'm gonna hurt him," Johnny said.

Sarah laughed. "Yeah, sure ya are. There ain't no way you're gonna hurt him. Besides, he's prob'ly asleep again by now, and that's what we oughta be doin'. Here, Marky. I'll be your pillor," she said and leaned back against the wall.

Mark laid his head in her lap and fell asleep. Then Sarah and Johnny dozed.

A short time later, the kids woke to the squeal of brakes. As the train rolled to a stop, a harsh shaft of light streamed in through the open door.

Mark sat up and rubbed his eyes. "What's hap'nin'?"

"And whur's that ole nigger?" Johnny said.

"I don't know what's hap'nin', Marky. And I don't know whur the man is, Johnny," Sarah said as she glanced toward the other end of the boxcar. "I told you to stop callin' him that, and I mean it!"

She eased to the door and peered out onto a railroad yard. The light was coming from a locomotive parked a few yards away. At the edge of the yard set a water tower with a word painted on it. "M-A-L-D-E-N," Sarah said and then looked at her brothers. "We're in Malden, Missouri."

"How far's that from St. Louie?" Johnny said.

"I don't know, but I thank it's still a long way off."

In the distance, someone yelled, and Sarah peeked back outside. Two men with clubs in their hands were walking alongside the train, banging on the boxcars and shining flashlights inside them.

Suddenly, three hoboes leapt from one of the cars. The last one out tripped and fell, and the men with the clubs beat him unconscious.

"Come on! We gotta get outta here!" Sarah said. "Grab your coats and follor me!" She led the boys to the other side of the boxcar and peeked out. Two men with clubs were also walking down that side of the train. Three cars away from the kids, they stopped.

"Well, looka here! Lovebirds!" one of the men said. "Okay, you two, come outta there."

A young man and woman eased to the door. The man jumped to the ground, and the men with the clubs knocked him out. While the woman fought and screamed, the men pulled her out and touched her the same way the Reverend had touched Sarah.

"Ahh, whatsamatter, baby?" one of the men said. "Didn't ya save no lovin' for us?"

"Take your filthy hands off of her," the same voice the kids had heard boomed out of the darkness. The big black man stepped from between two boxcars into the light, and the bulls attacked him. Sarah watched wide-eyed as the big man wrenched the clubs from the bulls and knocked them both cold. Then he lifted the young man to his feet and led the couple away.

"Let's go!" Sarah said.

She and Johnny jumped to the ground and lifted Mark out. Hand in hand, with their little brother in the middle, they ran to the edge of the rail yard and hid behind a building. Then they crept onto the street and ran until they could no longer see trains. At the city limit sign, they plopped down on an old truck seat and rested. Then they strolled back to the tracks.

As they crossed a trestle that spanned a creek, the kids saw the glow of a fire through the trees on the other side.

"What's that?" Johnny said.

"Looks like some kinda camp," Sarah said.

"Ummm! I smell cookin'!" Mark said.

The kids inched forward until they could see the whole area. A half dozen hoboes sat on logs that encircled the fire, and several more lay asleep on the ground behind them. When Mark sneezed, a 'bo stood up, pulled the matchstick from his mouth, and stared at the kids. "Hey, y'all! Come outta there!"

He didn't sound mad, so Sarah stepped into the firelight, and the boys followed.

"Who are ye? What ye wont? And why're ye carryin' 'em coats in the summertime?"

"Whatsamatter, Bulldog?" one of the other 'boes said. "Don't ye recognize bandits when ye see 'em? 'Ey're here to take ye money. And by golly, 'ey're willin' to whup ye to get it." The camp roared with laughter.

"Shut your trap, Mop Head!" Bulldog said as he glared at the 'bo.

"We're just passin' and don't wont nothin'," Sarah said.

"Then, why'd ye stop? Why didn't ye just keep on goin'?"

"We seen your fire and wondered what this was," Sarah said.

"This here's a hobo jungle. It ain't no place for kids, so get on home whur ye belong."

"We ain't got no home," Sarah said. "We're hoboes, just like y'all."

Bulldog chuckled. "Shore ye are." He glanced at the other 'boes. "We believe that, don't we, boys?"

The laughter woke the sleeping 'boes, and they joined the circle around the kids.

Bulldog stuck the matchstick back into his mouth, walked around the kids, and looked them over. Then he pulled the toothpick out again. "If ye're hoboes, then whur are ye bindles, and whur are ye headed?"

Sarah didn't know what bindles were, but she wasn't going to let him know it. "We ain't got bindles, and we're headed to St. Louie. Our Maw died, and we're goin' 'ere to find our paw."

Mark's eyes shot to his sister, and she winked at him.

"He's workin' up 'ere and don't know she died."

Bulldog glared at her. "So ye'all are travelin' by yeselves?"

"Nah, Bulldog. 'Ey got their nanny with 'em, and she's gonna treat you real nice," Mop Head said, and the other 'boes bellowed.

Bulldog spat on the fire. "How'd you like to kiss 'ese flames, Mop Head?"

The laughter stopped.

"Is 'ere somethin' to eat in that pot over yonder?" Mark said.

Bulldog glanced at Mark, then looked back at Sarah. "Whur'd ye'all come from?"

"Texas," Sarah said.

"Humph, that's a loada horseshit," Bulldog said. "'Ere ain't no way you kids rode the rails all the way up here from Texas by yes-elves—Whur at in Texas?"

"Hurdy-Gurdy Falls," Sarah said. She didn't know what "hurdy-gurdy" meant. She just liked the sound of it, so she used it.

Bulldog smirked, scratched his ear, and shook his head. "Ain't never heard of it. And I been all over Texas . . . and then some."

"I don't care if ya ever heard of it or not. That's whur we're from," Sarah said.

"And another thang," Bulldog said. "Texans don't need no coats this timea year."

"Oh yeah?" Sarah said. "Well, we're headed up north whur it gets cold, so we brung 'em with us. And why're you so dumb ya don't thank kids can hobo?"

Bulldog leaned over into Sarah's face. "Ye got a smart mouth on ye, Maeve. You ain't nothin' but jailbait. Somebody oughta teach ye some manners." He grabbed Sarah, bent her over his knees, and all the 'boes whooped.

Johnny jumped up to help his sister, but before he could do anything, the same thunderous voice they had heard on the boxcar and in the rail yard boomed in from the darkness.

"I wouldn't do that if I's you," the big black man said and stepped into the light.

Bulldog jumped up and dumped Sarah on the ground. "Who in hell are you?"

"They call me, 'Bo Jesus.'"

Bulldog laughed. "'Bo Jesus?' What kinda damn moniker's that?"

"A righteous one," Bo Jesus said. He backhanded Bulldog and sprawled him in the dirt.

Bulldog jumped up, jerked a flaming stick from the fire, and swung it at the big man.

Bo Jesus caught Bulldog's hand in midair and crushed it.

"You sonuvabitch!" Bulldog screamed. "I'll have your head for this!" He staggered to the other 'boes, and they huddled around him.

Bo Jesus pulled a tin cup from his bindle, dipped it into the steaming stew, and sat down on a log. As he ate, the kids strolled over and sat down beside him.

"What is that?" Mark said.

"Mulligan stew," Bo Jesus said.

"What's Mulligan stew?"

"Anything ya can find to throw in the pot. Why? Are ya hungry?"

"Starved!" Mark said.

"Oh, Marky," Sarah said as she glanced at her little brother. Then she looked at Bo Jesus. "We ain't starved, but yeah, we are hungry."

Bo Jesus peered at the cook. "Well, hasher? You gonna feed these kids or not?"

The cook peered back at him. "Yeah, I'm gonna feed 'em–and by the way, you know me–my name's Wink. We met on the West Coast. I'd be obliged if ye'd call me that. Now, you young'uns, go over yonder, get ye some tin cans outta that trash pile, and I'll dip ye some stew."

The kids dashed to the fly-covered trash heap, where Sarah picked out two fairly clean cans for Mark and herself while Johnny chose his own. Then Wink wrapped the cans with newspaper and filled them with stew.

"What's the paper for," Mark said.

"To protect your fangers," Wink said. "This stuff's hot.

Sarah took hers, sat back down beside Bo Jesus, and the boys sat down on the log next to them. Mark sucked in a mouthful of the stew, his eyes watered, and he spat it on the ground.

"Hey! Don't waste food!" Wink shouted. "If ye don't wont it, dump it back in the pot!"

"Oh, he wonts it," Sarah said. "It just burnt his mouth."

"Well, I told ye it was hot!"

"Blow on it, Marky," Sarah said. "That'll cool it down."

Johnny looked at Wink. "What kinda stew'd ya say this is?"

"Vegetable," Sarah said.

"How ya know?" Johnny said.

"'Cause it's got beans and corn in it."

"Well, it does have a little bitta meat in it," Wink said, "but most of it's already been et."

Johnny took a big gulp and swallowed it. "What kinda meat?"

"Dog," Wink said. "Frosty seen it get kilt by a truck yesterd'y mornin', so he brung it in for me to cook."

Sarah and Johnny stopped eating and stared at Wink.

"This stew's got dog in it?" Sarah said.

"Yeah!" Wink said. "Perty tasty, ain't it?"

Sarah grabbed her throat and gagged. "Eww, yuck! I thank I'm gonna be sick!"

"Sick? From eatin' good dog stew?" Wink said. "Well, that beats all I ever seen!"

"He's right, ya know," Bo Jesus said. "It's good food and the last you'll get till St. Louis."

But Sarah just couldn't stomach dog. As she tipped her can to dump what was left onto the ground, Wink snatched it from her. "Whatsamatter with you? Are ye stupid? Put it back in the pot! Somebody else'll be glad to get it! Food's hard to come by out here!" He dumped what was left back into the pot, and Johnny did the same with his.

When Mark raised his can and took another big swallow, Sarah bounced off the log, pulled it from his fingers, and emptied it back into the pot. "Marky, we don't eat dog!"

Mark puffed out his jaws and frowned. "But it's good."

Suddenly, a train whistle echoed from the south, and several 'boes picked up their bindles.

Sarah looked at Bo Jesus. "What's hap'nin'?"

"Our train's comin'."

"Our train?"

"Yeah, it's a hotshot cannonball to St. Louis."

"What's that mean?"

"It's a fast train that only makes a few stops. I thought I'd help ya catch it since I'm headed that way, too."

Sarah was glad they would have his company and protection for a while longer. She smiled and kissed his cheek.

Bo Jesus peered at her and chuckled. "I'm surprised you'd do that after me threatenin' to throw ya off that train like I did."

"Well, I knowed ya was bluffin'."

Bo Jesus cocked his head and glared at her. "Are you sayin' my 'tough guy' image is slippin'?"

"No, I'm just sayin' I know a good guy when I see one."

Johnny strolled over to Bo Jesus and looked him in the eye. "I'm sorry I called ya that bad name back yonder."

Bo Jesus peered at Johnny and nodded. "Well, you're not the first to do that, and ya won't be the last. But you are the first to ever say you're sorry. And I appreciate it."

Johnny blushed and sat back down.

Again, the train whistle echoed from the south.

"Okay, if you've gotta use the toilet, jump behind them weeds over yonder and do your business," Bo Jesus said. "This'll be your last chance till St. Louis, and it's gonna take ya a while to get there."

Sarah dashed into the bushes one way, and the boys and Bo Jesus dashed into them the other. When they met back at the logs, they each took a drink from the water dipper.

"All right," Bo Jesus said as he picked up his bindle. "Let's get to the tracks."

The kids picked up their coats and lined up behind him.

"Stick with me, now," Bo Jesus said, "'cause when the time comes to board, we'll have to move and move fast."

While the train approached, the group crouched in the bushes beside the tracks. Right after the locomotive passed, two 'boes jumped into a boxcar.

"Fools!" Bo Jesus said. "They'll be the first ones caught when the train stops. That's okay, though. They'll cover your escape. Never ride the cars close to the engine or caboose. They're the first ones the bulls check."

Near the middle of the train, they spotted an open boxcar and ran to it.

Bo Jesus threw his bindle inside, picked up the kids one at a time, and tossed them on board like sacks of potatoes. Then he boarded, searched both ends of the car, and kicked a pile of straw to Sarah. While she spread the coats on the padding, he closed one of the doors.

"To railroad bulls, an open boxcar door means somebody's probably in it," Bo Jesus said. "But since we're on a cannonball, we'll leave one door open for fresh air."

They all laid down, and by the time the train roared to full speed, they had fallen asleep.

As the sun rose, golden light flickered into the car through the trees along the tracks and woke Bo Jesus. He got up, walked to the open door, and peered outside. A moment later, Sarah joined him.

"Looks like a nice day," Bo Jesus said.

Sarah tilted her face to the sun. "Yes, it's beautiful."

For a moment, Bo Jesus gazed at her. "Ya know, you're pretty spunky and savvy for bein' so young."

"Well, I gotta be," Sarah said. "I'm the oldest, so that makes me the boss. It's up to me to take care of us."

"Yeah, you're right," Bo Jesus said. Then they peered back outside at the morning's beauty.

Back in Austin, Reverend Richter climbed the stairs, unlocked Sarah's door, and stepped inside a vacant room.

He poked his head out the open window and looked on the roof. Nobody there! He ran to the boys' room and unlocked the door. Nobody was there, either!

"God damn them to hell!" he shouted.

Sister Richter rushed to the bottom of the staircase. "What's wrong?"

"They're gone!" he said as he ran back downstairs. "They crawled out the windows."

He hurried outside and searched the yard. Nothing there either but a box of clothes in the driveway. He marched back inside, cranked the telephone, and picked up the receiver. "Genevieve, this is Reverend Richter. Get me the sheriff."

Midmorning, the train slowed and pulled onto the sidetrack at Gorham, Illinois.

"Well, this is where I get off," Bo Jesus said as he peered out at the countryside.

"Whatcha mean?" Sarah said. "Ain't ya goin' to St. Louie with us?"

"No, I'm headin' east from here."

Sarah closed her eyes, slumped her shoulders, and hung her head. First, it was her daddy. Then it was her mother. Then it was Mr. Jake, and Miss Gibson. And now, it was Bo Jesus. She was losing all the important people in her life. "I sure wish you's goin' on with us."

Bo Jesus lifted her head with his finger and looked into her eyes. "Ah, don't worry. You'll make it okay now. You're only a couple of hours from the city. You'll know you're there when ya cross the Mississippi River. Be sure to close the doors before ya get to the rail yard. Then, after the train stops, crack it open just enough to look out. When ya see 'boes jumpin' off and runnin', wait till the bulls go after 'em. Then you all run for it. You should be all right while the bulls are chasin' the other 'boes."

Sarah looked at Bo Jesus and then hugged him. "Thanks for all your help. I don't thank we'da made it without ya."

"Sure ya would've. Nothin' nor nobody's gonna stop *you*. You're too set on makin' it for that to happen."

Then Bo Jesus rubbed Mark's red hair and knelt. "It's been good knowin' ya, Mark. You take good care of your sister and brother for me, okay?"

Tears filled Mark's eyes. "Okay, I will," he said. Then he threw his arms around the big man's neck and squeezed him. "I'm sure gonna miss you, Bo Jesus."

"Yeah, I'm gonna miss you too. But if we're lucky, we'll meet again someday."

As Bo Jesus stood back up, he and Johnny shook hands.

"I hope ya ain't mad at me for callin' ya that bad name back yonder," Johnny said. "I take it back."

"Well, I'm glad you know it was a bad thing to say. As kids, we learn a lot of bad things. But when we grow up, we're supposed to understand that and change. You're a good kid, Johnny, and if you'll hang in there, you'll make a good man."

Then Bo Jesus turned back to Sarah. "I hope you find your daddy and everything turns out okay."

"Well, I lied back yonder at the jungle. Sometimes I do that when I ain't sure I can trust people. It's really our Mama we're lookin' for." Sarah pulled out her locket and opened it. "This is her and our Daddy, who got killed. Our stepdaddy took her away with him, and now we're tryin' to find her."

"Well, I hope you do," Bo Jesus said. "I'm headed to see my Mother, too. She's been sick, and I'm going home to see her one more time before she dies."

"Ahh, that's sad!" Sarah said.

"Yeah, it is. She was forty-five when I's born, and now I'm forty-five. Except for me wanderin' around all over the place and seldom bein' home, she hasn't had many regrets. My two brothers and sisters live close to her, and they've always been there for her."

"But mothers want all their kids around 'em all the time," Sarah said.

"Yeah, I reckon so, but I's always too curious about the world to stay home for very long. I visit her five or six times a year and never miss her birthday, so it's not like I'm *never* there."

In the distance, the passing train whistled, and their train eased forward. "Well, I reckon I'd better be goin'," Bo Jesus said.

"Wait, I wonna give ya somethin' to remember us by," Sarah said and handed him the church key. "I wish I had somethin' better to give ya, but I don't."

Bo Jesus looked at the can opener and then winked at the kids. "It's perfect. It'll be handy, and I'll always keep it with me," he said and stuck it into his pocket.

Then Sarah threw her arms around him and pecked him on the cheek, Mark hugged him around the waist, and Johnny gave him a manly handshake.

As the train eased away, Bo Jesus jumped to the ground and headed down a dirt road. For a moment, he looked back and waved. Then he disappeared, and the kids returned to their corner.

"I'm hungry," Mark said as they settled back onto their coats.

"So's Johnny and me," Sarah said. "But whinin' ain't gonna help. There ain't nothin' we can do 'bout it till we get to St. Louie."

"I coulda et that good dog stew if you'd let me," Mark said.

"No, ya couldn'ta," Sarah said. "People ain't supposed to eat dogs."

Mark puffed out his jaws and glared at his sister. "How much longer is it to St. Louie?"

"Long enough for ya to take a nap, and that'll make time pass faster."

Mark laid his head on Sarah's lap and fell asleep. Johnny had already conked out. Sarah leaned back against the wall, and soon she dozed.

By the time the bloodhounds tracked the kids to where their trail ended on the railroad, they were already three-quarters of the way to St. Louis. It took another hour for authorities to notify railroad officials that the runaways had probably hopped on one of their trains and another hour to inform the bulls to watch for them.

While the kids slept, the train chugged through several more towns. Then, just before noon, it slowed.

Johnny got up, walked to the door, and peered outside. "Hey! 'Ere's a big river out here with a great big town on the other side of it!"

Sarah and Mark ran to the door and looked out. "It's St. Louie!" Sarah said, and a smile flashed onto her face. "We're here! We're really, really here!"

The kids joined hands, danced in a circle, and sang: "We're-in-Saint-Lou-ie! We're-in-Saint-Lou-ie!"

Sarah rushed back to the door, gazed across the river at the city's tall buildings with their backdrop of fluffy white clouds, and her heart pounded. She had expected St. Louie to be big, but she didn't know towns came big enough to fill the whole sky. How would they ever find their mother in this place? At least they were there, and that was a start.

When the train pulled onto the Mississippi River bridge, Sarah tried to close the door as Bo Jesus had instructed, but her foot slipped, and she fell outside the car.

"Help!" she screamed as she dangled from the door handle and kicked at the floorboard.

Johnny dashed to her, grabbed her legs, and pulled her back inside.

"O-o-h-h-h!" she said in a shaky voice. "I didn't like that!"

After Sarah caught her breath, she and the boys closed the door. Then they sat down and waited until the train stopped.

"Put your coats on," Sarah said as they stood up to leave.

"Why?" Johnny said.

"'Cause they'll be easier to carry that way, and we won't lose 'em. When we jump outta here, we're gonna hafta run like crazy to get away from the bulls."

Sarah cracked open the door and peeked outside. Like Bo Jesus said, some 'boes had already jumped out, and the bulls were chasing them.

"Okay, let's go!" Sarah said. They jumped to the ground and crossed under several long strings of freight cars. At the edge of the rail yard, they came to a high chain-link fence with barbed wire across its top and followed it to a locked gate. Sarah kicked at the dirt underneath it, and it was soft. "Come on, boys!" she said. "We got some diggin' to do!"

They took off their coats, dropped to their knees, and scratched at the dirt. As Johnny dug, he slung rubble in all directions.

"Easy, Johnny!" Sarah said. "You don't hafta get us dirty!"

"Hey, you kids!" someone hollered in the distance. "What in the hell do you think you're doin'?"

It was a bull, and he was headed straight for them.

"Faster!" Sarah screamed, and they all slung dirt as fast as they could. She jumped to her feet and pulled up on the gate. "Quick, Johnny! Slide under!"

He jumped under the gate and crawled to freedom.

"Here! Take these!" Sarah shoved their coats under, and Johnny pulled them through.

She tugged on the gate again, and it lifted a couple of more inches. "Go, Marky!"

Mark wriggled under, and Johnny pulled him free. Then Sarah dove under.

Halfway to freedom, the bull grabbed her legs. "Oh no, ya don't, ya little bitch!"

While Johnny pulled on Sarah's arms, Mark threw a handful of dirt into the bull's face. The man shut his eyes but didn't let go. "Shit, ya little bastard! You'll go to jail for that!"

"Turn loosa my sister!" Mark yelled and flung another handful of dirt into the bull's face.

Sarah pushed against the gate with all her strength while Johnny pulled on her arms, but she didn't budge. Mark picked up a stick and poked it through the fence into the bull's eyes. When the man grabbed it, Johnny pulled Sarah free.

As the bull stood up, he reached into his pocket.

"He's got a key!" Sarah shouted. "Grab your coats and run!" But the bull didn't have a key.

"Dammit! I'll get your asses for this!" he yelled as he pounded on the gate, and the kids bolted to the street.

Chapter 12

THE STREETS OF ST. LOUIE

THE KIDS RAN until they could no longer see the bull. Then they flopped down on a bus stop bench and giggled. Although they would have been in big trouble if they had gotten caught, Sarah still enjoyed the game of the chase. She stood up and pointed to the city's skyline. "That's whur we're goin'. There's food over there."

"Well, come on then! Let's go!" Mark said and ran in that direction.

At first, crossing streets wasn't much harder than it was in Piggott. But the closer they got to downtown, the thicker and more dangerous the traffic became.

"Hold on tight and stay with me," Sarah said as she led the boys off the sidewalk in the middle of a block. "When I say, 'Go!' we'll run across."

She glanced up and down the street until a gap opened between cars. "Go!" she shouted, and as they dashed into the traffic, drivers honked and yelled at them. One car skidded to a stop just inches from them, and the driver flipped them a hand gesture they didn't know. Safe on the other side, they glared back at the cars.

"These folks ain't nice like the ones in Austin," Sarah said.

As the kids stepped off the curb to cross another street, a man stopped on the sidewalk behind them. "Hey, you kids! Hold on, there!" he shouted. "Jaywalkin' will get you arrested in this town if it doesn't get you killed first."

Sarah led her brothers back onto the sidewalk. "Sorry, Mister. We ain't from here. We don't know how this street crossin' works."

The Clark Gable look-a-like reared back and grinned. "Yeah, I figured you were newcomers from your coats." He propped his fists on his waist and walked around the kids. "So, where are you from?"

"Arkansas," Sarah said.

"Arkansas?" the man said and squinted. "Then what's up with the coats?"

"Our school teacher give 'em to us," Mark said.

Sarah stepped between her brothers and the man. "We ain't ever seen this many cars 'fore."

"Well, you'll stay out of jail and live longer if you go to the corner and cross at the stoplight like you're supposed to."

"Yes, sir," Sarah said. "Thanks, Mister."

The kids ran to the corner and stopped beside the people standing there.

"What they starin' at?" Johnny said.

"I don't know," Sarah said.

"How we gonna know when to cross?" Johnny said.

Sarah shrugged. "We'll just cross when ever'body else does."

"You cross when the sign tells you to," a lady standing beside them said. "See that sign that says, 'DON'T WALK?'"

"Yes'm," Sarah said.

"Well, in a minute, it'll say, 'WALK.' Then we'll go."

"Oh, okay! Thanks, ma'am," Sarah said. Too bad everybody in St. Louie wasn't that nice.

The sign changed, and the group crossed the street.

"Dang! That was easy," Johnny said.

While the kids wandered the sidewalks, they window-shopped. Mark stopped in front of a toy store, but the crowd didn't and knocked him down. Someone stepped on his fingers, and he screamed.

Sarah felt like whacking people but instead helped Mark to his feet and pulled him aside. "Ya gotta watch out for these people,

Marky. They're as bad as the cars. They'll run over ya if ya get in their way."

"No wonder he stopped," Johnny said. "Look at all 'em toys."

"Yeah," Mark said as he wiped his tears. "I wont that tractor, that gravel truck, that dragline, and that–"

"Oh, what the heck? We'll just take 'em all," Sarah said, and they laughed.

Farther down the street, the kids ran into a gang of dirty, greasy-haired adolescent boys who surrounded Sarah.

"Hey, baby. How 'bout givin' me some nookie," the leader said. He puckered his lips like he meant to kiss Sarah while the other boys danced around them and threw punches at Johnny and Mark.

"What's nookie?" Mark said.

"What's nookie? Hey guys, getta loada this clodhopper. He don't even know what nookie is," the leader said, and the gang laughed.

"Why're you hicks carryin' them coats?" the gang leader said as Sarah pushed hers into Mark's arms.

"None of your beeswax!" she said. Then she landed a solid right hook on the gang leader's nose and knocked him to the ground.

"Get 'em!" the leader shouted and jumped back to his feet.

Sarah and Johnny backed up to each other with Mark sandwiched between them and dished out a whole lot better than they took.

Half a block away, a policeman blew his whistle. As he ran toward the fight, the gang scurried away. Sarah pulled her brothers into an alley, and they hid behind some trash bins. The officer paused, looked down the passage, then continued after the gang.

The kids stepped back into the open and examined each other's wounds. Johnny had minor cuts and bruises, and his left eye was turning purple, but Mark and Sarah didn't have a new scratch on them.

As they continued down the sidewalk, they came to a hamburger stand with outside tables. For a moment, the kids froze and watched people eat.

"When we gonna eat?" Mark said, and his voice broke Sarah's trance.

"Huh? . . . Oh, I don't know, Marky. Maybe it won't be too much longer," she said, but she really didn't have a clue how to make that happen.

As darkness set in, the air cooled, and they put on their coats.

"I gotta pee," Mark said.

"Me too," Johnny said.

Sarah peered down the dim alley beside them and led the boys into the passage. "Maybe we can find a place down here."

Mark walked a few feet into the darkness and stopped. "This is spooky."

"Yeah," Johnny said, and he stopped too.

"Ah, come on, you fraidy cats," Sarah said and continued walking. "I smell food."

''Food?" Mark's feet unlocked. "Well, let's go!" He ran to Sarah, and Johnny followed.

A moment later, Sarah stumbled over something and almost fell.

"Hey! Watch where you're goin'! I'm sleepin' here!"

Sarah peered down at a scruffy man with a wine bottle clutched to his chest. "Sorry, Mister!" she said and then frowned. She hadn't thought about where they would sleep.

"I cain't wait no longer," Johnny said. "I'm goin' over yonder in that corner and pee."

"Me too," Mark said.

"Okay, I'll wait here and stand guard," Sarah said.

The boys disappeared into the darkness and returned a couple of minutes later. Then Sarah took her turn, and they continued down the alley.

At every open door, the kids peeked inside. Outside the last one, delicious smells filled the air. As they peered in, the cook scooped a hamburger patty from the grill, put it on a bun, and laid it on a plate of French fries. "Order up," he said and set the dish on the shelf in front of him.

"It's a cafe!" Sarah said.

The trio hurried to the garbage cans and looked inside them. "Empty," Johnny said.

Suddenly, the screen door opened, and the kids dashed for cover. A young man dragged a full garbage can outside and pushed it to the others. Then he gazed up at the sky, pulled a cigarette off his ear, and lit it. As he exhaled the smoke, it vanished into the air. He finished his smoke, hocked and spat on the garbage, then strolled back inside.

"Eww, yuck!" Sarah whispered. "That was nasty!"

The kids eased to the garbage can and peered inside it. Several nice pieces of bread and meat lay on top of the other garbage.

"Too bad he spit on it," Sarah said.

"Hey, look yonder," Johnny said. On the ground lay a water hose with a small stream trickling from it. "I'm gettin' me a drank."

"Me too," Mark said, and they ran to it.

Johnny picked up the hose, turned on the faucet, let it run a moment, and then drank. "Umm! That's good," he said and wiped his mouth on his coat sleeve. He lowered the hose, and Mark drank. Then he passed it to Sarah.

"I didn't know I was so thirsty," she said as she turned off the faucet. "Now, if we can just find somethin' to eat."

"Hot Stuff!" someone yelled in the kitchen, and a man set a tray of fresh-baked rolls on the counter next to the back door.

"Lookee at that!" Mark whispered.

"Yeah!" Sarah said as the aroma wafted into the alley.

"Dang! I'm gettin' us some of 'em!" Johnny said.

Sarah still didn't hold with stealing, but they were hungry. "Well, you be careful."

They crept to the door, peeked through the screen, and Sarah eased it open just wide enough for Johnny to get his hand to the tray. He pulled off two rolls and handed them to Mark, who stuffed one, almost whole, into his mouth.

Johnny reached back in, pulled off two more, and handed them to Sarah. When he reached in the third time, the man who had dragged out the garbage can grabbed Johnny's arm. He pulled to break free, but the man's grip on him was as tight as his grip on the rolls.

"Whatcha think you're doin', boy?" the man said as he raised a knife in his other hand. "How'd you like to lose that hand?"

"I wouldn't!" Johnny whined.

"We's just tryin' to get somethin' to eat, Mister," Sarah said. "We ain't et in two days, and we're starvin.'"

The man glanced at Mark, who was stuffing the last of his rolls into his mouth. Then he looked back at Johnny and Sarah. "Ya know, I oughta call the cops, don't ya?"

"Yes, sir, we know," Sarah said. "But we'd be obliged if ya wouldn't."

"Well, since you're just kids, I'll let it go this time. But if ya do it again, I'll turn ya in."

"Yes, sir. I promise we won't do it no more, Mister," Sarah said.

With the rolls in their hands, the kids turned to leave.

"Ah, what the heck? Hang on a minute," the man muttered, and the kids looked back at him. "Don't go away. I'll be right back," he said and returned to the kitchen.

"Let's go!" Johnny whispered. "He's callin' the cops!"

"No, he ain't," Sarah said. "But he is up to somethin.'"

The man marched back outside and handed Sarah a paper bag. "There's three pieces of fried chicken and some more rolls in that. But don't open it till ya get someplace safe. There's lotsa bums in this town who'll steal it from ya if they get a chance. So watch out for 'em."

"Yes, sir! We sure do thank ya, Mister!" Sarah said and smiled. Then she tucked the bag inside her coat and led the boys back to the sidewalk. St. Louie was getting better all the time.

A couple of blocks from the cafe, the kids found an open area in a small park where they could be alone. They sat down beside a water fountain, and Sarah opened the bag. She broke a chicken breast into three parts, handed each brother a piece with a roll, and then took one of each for herself.

Mark devoured his portion and asked for more.

As Sarah opened the bag again, a man jumped out from behind a tree and tried to grab it. Johnny slugged him in the face, and Sarah kicked him until he ran away. When they turned around, Mark had the bag tucked inside his coat, his knees drawn up against his chest, and his arms wrapped around his legs. "Ain't nobody gettin' this bag!" he said as Sarah and Johnny laughed. Then they finished their meal.

With their bellies full, the kids fell asleep in the cool evening air. Sarah dreamed she was back at the Richters', and the Reverend was poking her with a broom handle. When a voice woke her, she opened her eyes. There stood two policemen—one chubby–the other thin. They looked like Laurel and Hardy. When the chubby one nudged Sarah again with his nightstick, she flinched, and it woke the boys.

"What are you kids doing here, all alone, sleeping on this park bench?" the thin man said.

Sarah faked a cough to stall and gather her wits. "Well, we was playin', got tard, and just fell asleep. How long's it been dark?"

"Since eight-thirty," the officer said. "You mean you've been here since before dark?"

"Yes, sir," Sarah said. "What time is it now?"

"Almost nine-thirty. Where are your parents?"

"At Uncle Gus's," Sarah said and stood up. "Come on, boys. We gotta go. We're in a heapa trouble. They're prob'ly wonderin' whur we are."

"Just a minute. We'll go with you," the officer said.

Sarah turned and faced the men. "Nah, that's okay. We can find it by ourselves."

"Yes, I'm sure you know the way," the officer said, "but that's not the issue. We want to know why your parents aren't looking after you better. These streets are dangerous at night. You shouldn't be out here by yourselves like this."

Sarah glanced up the street one way, then down the other, and smirked. "Looks safe enough to me. Ain't nobody bothered us."

"Maybe not," the officer said, "but believe me, there *are* people out here who'll do you harm if they get a chance, so we need to talk to your folks."

"Well, okay. It's this way."

Sarah put Mark in-between Johnny and herself. "Grab Marky's hand, Johnny. We gotta run for it," she whispered. Then she shouted, "Go!" And they pulled Mark into a hard run.

As the policemen blew their whistles and gave chase, the kids ducked into an alley and hid behind a discarded couch. When the chubby policeman's flashlight beam found them, they took off again, and the out-of-breath officer fell into a half-hearted run behind them. In the middle of the park, the kids dashed behind a clump of evergreen bushes and hid until the officers gave up pursuit. Then they came back out and sat down under a big maple tree, where Sarah kept watch for the rest of the night and only dozed while her brothers slept.

Chapter 13

Garbage Can Delicacies

Early Sunday morning, Sarah opened her eyes and looked across the park. A few yards away, a policeman strolled down the sidewalk twirling his nightstick. She shook her sleeping brothers, and they sat up. "We gotta get outta here. There's a cop headed this way."

They picked up their coats and hurried away. At the edge of the park, they each took a bathroom break behind some bushes. Then they headed downtown. Along the way, Sarah noticed that the policemen were stationed two or three blocks apart. As they passed one officer, he eyed them. Sarah covered her face, looked the other way, and tugged her brothers past him. "There's too many cops on these sidewalks," she said. "So we're stickin' to the alleys. And besides, that's whur the food is, anyhow."

At the entrance to the next alley, the kids stopped. The whole area smelled of pastries. They walked to the garbage can behind the shop, and Sarah opened it. "Donuts!"

Johnny reached into the can and pulled out one with a single bite taken out of it. "This'n don't look too bad," he said and handed it to Mark. Then reached back into the can.

"Give me that, Marky," Sarah said and snatched the pastry from his fingers as he was about to shove the whole thing into his mouth.

"Hey, Sissy, that's mine!" Mark said and grabbed for it, but Sarah shoved his hand away.

"Hold your horses, Marky. I'll give it back in a second. We don't wonna get other people's germs." She tore off the part where the bite had been taken, handed the rest back to Mark, and he wolfed it down.

"That was great, Johnny. Give me another'n."

"I sure never thought we'd be eatin' outta garbage cans," Sarah said as she also picked through the pieces.

In the distance, a bell clanged.

"Why's that bell rangin'?" Mark said.

"'Cause it's Sunday," Sarah said. "And ya know what that means?"

"No, what?" Mark said.

"Sunday dinners—fried chicken and ever'thang that goes with it. People eat in cafes on Sunday."

Mark grinned. "I wont me some of that fried chicken."

All day, the kids wandered alleys and dug through garbage cans. By evening, they had eaten their fill of fried chicken and other delicious things. They had even enjoyed some apple pie that looked like it hadn't been touched.

At twilight, they hiked back to the park.

"Look, 'ere's a water fountain," Johnny said as they approached a small concrete block building. They ran to it and drank all they could hold.

"Hey, this is a bathroom," Sarah said as she glanced up at the "Men's" and "Women's" signs. "We won't hafta go in the bushes no more."

Mark grabbed his bottom and bounced up and down on his toes. "I gotta go right now!"

"Okay," Sarah said. "Johnny, go with him. Somebody might be in there. I'll check out the women's side."

"Hey, Sissy," Mark said as they all met back outside. "'Ey got real toilet paper in 'ere. It ain't rough and scratchy like the leaves we been usin' and the corn cobs and catalog pages we use back home. 'Ey even got a place to warsh your hands with soap and hot water, and paper towels to dry 'em on."

Sarah squinted. "Then why're you dryin' yours on your pants?"

Mark tucked his hands behind his back and grinned. "I don't know."

"Ya know, Marky, sometimes, you're just plain goofy."

A few yards past the restroom, the kids passed a small pavilion where a man, covered with newspapers, lay asleep on a picnic table.

"Sissy, let's sleep here tonight, like him," Mark begged. "I don't wonna sleep on the ground no more with 'em ole bugs."

"I wish we could, Marky," Sarah said, "but the police could see us. I know sleepin' on the ground is icky, but we gotta do it for now. Maybe tomorra we can fig're out somethin' better."

The kids walked behind the shrubs under the big maple tree and spread their coats on the ground. As her brothers drifted off to sleep, Sarah took her guardian position and scanned the hundreds of lit windows around the park. Was their mother behind one of them, and if she was, would they ever find her?

Although Sarah fought to stay awake and on guard, exhaustion finally overtook her.

Chapter 14

CAUGHT

HANK AND ELIZABETH got up at dawn on Monday, and while he shaved and dressed for work, she made breakfast.

Hank had gotten a job with decent pay at a truck assembly plant in the city, and they had rented a small but comfortable, four-room apartment just two miles from the factory.

After breakfast, Elizabeth packed Hank's lunchbox and set it on the counter beside the back door while he drank a second cup of coffee.

"I wont pork chops for supper," he said. "Pork chops, mashed taters, biscuits, and gravy. And I wont it on the table when I walk through that door. Ya hear me?"

"Yeah, I hear ya," Elizabeth said as she peered at him and dried her hands on the dishtowel. "I'll need grocery money."

Hank reached into his pocket and tossed a five-dollar bill on the table. "'Ere, that oughta be aplenty, and dontcha go wastin' none of it. I wont change back."

Elizabeth stuffed the money into her pocket. "I never waste nothin'," she said. Then she frowned. "'Cept myself bein' your slave."

"What'd you say?" Hank muttered.

"Nothin'," Elizabeth said and turned back to the dishes.

"If you know what's good for ya, you'll shut your mouth and do like you're told."

Hank jerked his lunch bucket off the counter, tromped out the door, and slammed it.

Elizabeth tiptoed to the window, peeked out the curtain, and watched him drive away. Then she sashayed to the bathroom, gazed into the mirror, and ran her fingers over the bags under her eyes. She wasn't a pretty woman, but she wasn't ugly, either. She could have found herself another good man who loved her if she had had time. She did it before, when she found Ralph, and she could have done it again.

While she combed her hair and tucked it behind her ears, the mailbox rattled. She laid down the comb and hurried outside.

"Well, good morning, Elizabeth," her next-door neighbor said as they met on the porch. "Sure is a pretty day, isn't it?"

"Yeah, it sure is," Elizabeth said. "Listen, Kate, I gotta go grocery shoppin' this mornin', and I'm still sceared of this big ole town. Can you go with me?"

"Sure. I'm always ready to get out of the house for a while. I'll even treat us to a soda pop at the drugstore. What time are you going?"

"About ten."

"Okey-doke. Just come and get me whenever you're ready."

Elizabeth picked up her mail and looked at the three letters, all marked "Return to Sender." A lump rose in her throat, and tears filled her eyes as she walked back inside. Why hadn't her kids gotten them?

While she pondered that question, she finished the dishes and got ready to go shopping.

Downtown, the kids ate another garbage can breakfast, then wandered more alleys.

"Whur we goin'?" Johnny said as Sarah led them onto the sidewalks.

"I don't know. Mama's here somewhur," Sarah said, "but I don't know how to find her."

"Well, let's ask somebody," Johnny said.

Sarah peered at him. "Ask who?"

"Anybody–ever'body."

"Ask 'em what?"

"Ask 'em if 'ey know Hank and Elizabeth Pinscher."

"Well . . . Yeah . . . . I reckon that's one way of doin' it," Sarah said.

The kids began approaching random passersby and asking their question. Most people just ignored them and pushed on by. But then, a woman with caked-on makeup and smeared lipstick stopped and took a genuine interest in them. "Whatsamatter, children? Are ya lost?"

"Well, sorta, ma'am," Sarah said. "We're lookin' for our Mama. She moved here with our stepdaddy, Hank Pinscher, but we don't know whur they live or how to find 'em."

"Oh, what a shame!" the woman said. "Follow me. I think I can help you."

The kids fell in behind her, and she led them to–a policeman.

"Well, hello there, Beulah," the officer said as they stopped in front of him. Then he and Sarah gawked at each other. He was the same chubby officer who had confronted the kids in the park on Saturday night.

"Run!" Sarah shouted, and they took off with the policeman right behind them.

By nine o'clock, a police squad had surrounded and captured the kids. They hauled them to headquarters, put them in a holding room with two armed guards outside the door, and Sarah laughed. Because they had been so hard to catch, they were being treated like "real" criminals. But she was glad their running was over. She was too exhausted to do it anymore.

A few minutes later, a man in a business suit dismissed the armed guards and entered the room. "I'm Detective Berry Hill," he said and sat down across the table from the kids. "Who are you all, and what're you up to?"

Sarah gazed into Detective Hill's eyes. They were tough but honest and sincere. Maybe he really could help them.

"I'm Sarah Jane Skaggs, and these boys are my brothers, Johnny and Mark. We're lookin' for our Mama. She moved here with our stepdaddy, Hank Pinscher, and we're tryin' to find her."

"Why didn't you move here with them?" Detective Hill said.

"'Cause our stepdaddy don't wont us around no more," Sarah said.

Hill cocked his head and raised his eyebrows. "So they just moved away and left you?"

"Yes, sir," Sarah said. "Mama didn't wonna leave us, but Hank made her."

"So, where are you from?"

"Austin Community in Arkansas."

"Ah!" Hill sighed. "Hey, Murph, come here!"

An officer pranced across the hall and into the room. "Yaw'sur, what'z up, Boss?" he said, and the kids laughed.

"It looks like we just picked up those Arkansas kids from Saturday's APB. Call child welfare and have them send a caseworker over here."

"Sho'-nuff, Boss!" Murphy blew a kiss to Hill, shuffled backward on tiptoes out of the door, and the kids giggled.

Then Sarah cringed. "Dang it! Here we go again–Another caseworker! I wish we hadn't stopped that Beulah woman this mornin'."

"Beulah woman?" Detective Hill said. "What, Beulah woman?"

"That funny-lookin' Beulah woman who tried to help us this mornin' just 'fore we got caught."

Hill chuckled. "So you met 'Downtown Beulah Brown,' did you? Yeah, she's funny, all right. That's because she's not a woman–She's a man."

"A man?" Sarah said. "Then why's he dress like a woman?"

Detective Hill smirked, shook his head, and shrugged. "Who knows? I guess every place has its share of strange people. Speaking of strange–" He looked across the hall. "Hey, Murph, get Antsy Yancey to come and stay with these kids. I have work to do–oh, and ah, rustle up some hamburgers and sodas." He glanced at Mark and winked. "These kids look hungry to me."

"Yaw'sur, Boss. Sho'-nuff, 10-4," Murphy said with an Amos 'n' Andy accent. He made a funny face and saluted.

Hill leaned back in his chair, crossed his arms, and glared at Murphy. "You know, Murph, one of these days, I'm just gonna haul off and fire your silly ass."

Mark giggled and peered at Sarah. "'Ese guys are funny, Sissy, and 'ey're gonna feed us."

"Yeah, Mark," Detective Hill said. "Lunch and a show–Brought to you by the taxpayers of St. Louis."

A moment later, Officer Yancey wiggled into the room, and Detective Hill left.

"Is your name really 'Antsy?'" Sarah said.

The woman shook her head and smiled. "No, honey. These clowns around here just call me that because they think it's cute. My real name is Nancy."

While the kids ate their hamburgers and waited for the case-worker, Nancy gave them pencils and paper, and they each drew a picture of their mother. Mark drew her cooking supper, Johnny drew her hanging out the laundry, and Sarah drew a simple portrait of her. When Mark finished the picture of his mother, he drew a boxcar with Bo Jesus, himself, Sarah, and Johnny standing in its doorway.

mark
Skaggs

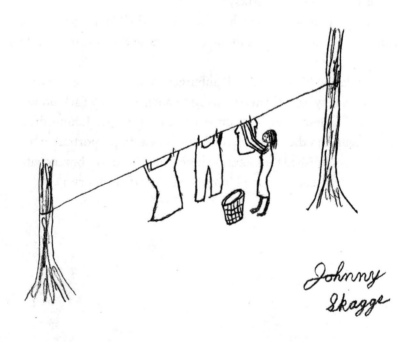

Johnny
Skaggs

132

Mary
Elizabeth
Skaggs by
Sarah Jane Skaggs

mark Skaggs

As the kids signed their finished pictures, Detective Hill brought in a pretty, kind-faced woman, who looked like a school teacher, and the kids straightened in their chairs. "This is child welfare caseworker Miss Alexis Jordan," Hill said. "She's going to help us sort things out."

"Hello, children," Miss Jordan said as she sat down. "What are your names?"

"I'm Sarah Skaggs, and these are my brothers, Johnny and Mark."

"So tell me, Johnny, how did you get that black eye?"

"I had a fight with some boys on the street. They tried to hurt Sarah, but me and the cops chased 'em away."

Sarah smirked. "You'd better be careful 'bout fibbin' like that, Johnny. Ya might get another black eye."

"So, you are from Arkansas. Is that correct?" Miss Jordan said.

"Yes'm," Sarah said.

"And how did you get from there to St. Louis?"

Sarah looked at Miss Jordan. She kind of reminded her of Miss Gibson. "We rode trains. We left Friday night and got here Saturday mornin."

"How did you get your tickets?"

Sarah squinted. "Tickets? We didn't need no tickets. We hoboed."

Miss Jordan's eyebrows shot up, and she snickered. "You hoboed?"

"Yes'm," Sarah said.

"And how did you do that?"

"We just hopped trains and rode 'em," Sarah said. "We caught a boxcar north of Piggott and rode it to Malden, whur the railroad bulls chased us off with clubs. Then we stopped at a hobo jungle and et some dog stew. That's whur we hooked up with Bo Jesus, and he helped us catch a hotshot cannonball to St. Louie."

"Hotshot cannonball?" Miss Jordan said.

"Yes'm, a fast train that only makes a few stops."

Miss Jordan grinned. "Well, Sarah, you certainly have a vivid imagination, don't you?"

Sarah cocked her head and glared at the woman. Was she making fun of them? Sarah gazed into Miss Jordan's eyes. No, she was okay, just dumb. "You ain't done much hard livin', have ya, ma'am?"

"No, I haven't. But I work with people who have and see its effects daily, so there is no need to be rude, Sarah."

"No, ma'am, there sure ain't."

"So you kids met the hobo, Bo Jesus?" Detective Hill said.

"Yeah!" Mark said and held up his boxcar picture for everyone to see.

"Yes, we did," Sarah said, "or at least that's what he said his moniker was."

"Where'd you learn the word 'moniker?'" Detective Hill said.

"At the hobo jungle," Sarah said.

"Do you have a moniker?"

"Yeah, two of 'em–'Maeve' and 'Jailbait.'"

Detective Hill chuckled. "Do you know what 'Jailbait' means?"

"No, but it sounds tough."

"Well, believe me, young lady," Miss Jordan said, "that is no name to admire."

Detective Hill covered his mouth like he was going to cough, but Sarah could see the grin in his eyes.

"Sarah, did anyone ever touch you while you were traveling?" Miss Jordan said.

"Well, yes'm. It's kinda hard to travel without touchin' people."

"No, that is not what I mean. Did anyone ever try to harm you?"

"Yeah, one ole 'bo grabbed me and tried to spank me, but Bo Jesus whacked him."

Johnny laughed. "Yeah, he sure did. Ole Bo Jesus knocked the fare out of him."

While Miss Jordan asked the kids more questions, Detective Hill called Murphy into the room and whispered something to him. A moment later, Murph returned with a document that had two photos on it. Hill held it up so only Mark could see it.

"Hey, that's Bo Jesus!" Mark said.

Then Hill showed the photos to everyone else. In one, Bo Jesus faced the camera. In the other, he faced to the side. His real name and some numbers, in a type too small to be read, were printed underneath the pictures.

"Yeah," Sarah said. "That's the man who helped us."

Detective Hill glanced at Miss Jordan. "Can I speak to you in private?"

They got up, walked into the office across the hall, and closed the door.

"Miss Jordan, these kids are telling the truth," Detective Hill said.

"Oh, how could they be? They're just children. They couldn't have ridden a freight train all the way here from Arkansas by themselves."

"Well, I believe they did," Hill said. "They know what they're talking about. I'm convinced they really did meet Bo Jesus. And their description of that hobo jungle?" He smirked and shook his head. "They couldn't have made that up?"

Miss Jordan stared at Detective Hill. Then she folded her arms and paced the floor for a moment. Perhaps she *had* misjudged both Sarah and the situation. After all, this was the third day since they were reported missing by Arkansas authorities. "That trip Sarah described. How long would it really have taken them to make it?"

"A day. Two at most," Hill said.

That meant the children had gone to great lengths to live secretly on the streets in a strange city for two full days. This was not just a case of abandoned children searching for their mother. This was a case of survival. They were on the run from something. But what? She needed the answer. "Detective Hill, I am taking these children with me."

They completed the paperwork and returned to the holding room.

"Get your things, children. We're going to the shelter," Miss Jordan said.

"What's a shelter?" Sarah said.

"Your new home," Miss Jordan said. "You will bathe and be given medical care."

"Huh-uh," Mark said. "I don't need no bath or no more shots."

"You will also get new clothes, hot meals, and nice clean beds."

Mark grabbed his coat. "'Hot meals and clean beds?' Oh boy! What we waitin' for? I'm tarda eatin' outta garbage cans and sleepin' with 'em ole bugs."

"Will there be other kids there?" Sarah said.

"No, not where we're going right now. You will have to be quarantined for a few days to ensure you do not have any contagious diseases. But then, you will be transferred to another shelter where there are many children, and you will remain there until your case is resolved."

As a policeman led Miss Jordan and the kids from the headquarters building to a police car, they passed a group of journalists awaiting the arrival of a local gangster who had been arrested.

"Hey, Joe, what's up with those kids?" one of the men yelled.

"They hoboed up here from Arkansas to find their missin' mother," the officer said, and the photographers rushed them.

While flashbulbs popped and movie cameras whirred, Miss Jordan nudged the kids into the car and slammed its door.

"What was that all about?" Sarah said as they rode away.

"Just St. Louis news reporters trying to get a story any way they can," Miss Jordan said.

As the officer strolled back to the building, the reporters surrounded him. "So what's the real scoop on those kids, Joe?"

"I'm not supposed to talk about it. Go inside and talk to PR," the officer said.

The reporters dashed inside and swarmed the public relations officer. She told them the kids' story and then announced that the gangster wouldn't be arriving. The FBI had moved him to a more secure, undisclosed location.

The reporters disbursed, and the TV crew returned to the studio. Since the gangster was a no-show, the TV news director aired the hobo children story instead.

At the shelter, Miss Jordan released the kids to the staff. Then, although she felt wary about it, she called the welfare administrator in Piggott and told him the children had been found. As she expected, he requested that they be returned as soon as possible, and she consented. If that happened and then their mother surfaced in St. Louis, she could still get them back together. However, the process would be easier if that happened before they left.

Chapter 15

ON TV NEWS

ON THEIR WAY home from the grocery store, Elizabeth and Kate stopped at the drugstore. As they drank their sodas and talked, neither woman paid attention to the news program on the television behind the counter until Elizabeth glanced up at the picture on the screen.

"In local news," the announcer said, "three children, ages six, nine, and twelve, who say they hopped a freight train in Arkansas and rode it to St. Louis in search of their missing mother, have been taken into custody by city police and turned over to child welfare authorities. They claim their stepfather forced their mother to abandon them two-and-a-half weeks ago and move with him to the city to find work. Since the children are minors, their names have not been released. So far, the police have no leads in finding the mother."

Elizabeth fainted and fell out of her chair.

Kate screamed, dropped to her knees, and laid Elizabeth's head in her lap. "Throw me a wet cloth!" she shouted to the man behind the counter. He tossed a damp towel to Kate, and she dabbed Elizabeth's face until she came to.

"What happened?" Kate said,

"My babies!" Elizabeth said. Now she knew why they hadn't gotten her letters. "Them kids on TV are my kids!"

"Your kids?" Kate said. "What do you mean?"

Elizabeth looked up at the crowd gathered around her and frowned. "Get me outta here, Kate," she whispered. "Take me home."

Kate helped Elizabeth to her feet, thanked the counterman, and picked up the groceries. At the Pinscher's apartment, Kate put Elizabeth to bed. Then she stowed the groceries and sat down beside her friend.

"Them kids on the news are my babies," Elizabeth said. "Hank made me leave 'em and move up here with him. Now, they've come lookin' for me. Bless their hearts."

"Well, I'll go call the police, and we'll have them brought here," Kate said.

"No!" Elizabeth said. "I'm sceared of what Hank'll do if he finds 'em here. They're safe whur they are for now. Just stay with me and let me rest a little bit while I fig're out what to do."

Elizabeth clutched Kate's hand and closed her eyes. Within minutes, they were both asleep.

A couple of hours later, the back door squeaked, and Elizabeth's eyes popped open.

"Damn it, 'Lizabeth! Whur's my pork chops?"

"Oh no! It's Hank! I gotta fix his supper!" She jumped up, staggered, and grabbed hold of Kate's chair.

Kate grasped Elizabeth's arm and eased her back down onto the bed. "I'll go help you."

Hank tromped into the room and glared at the women. "What's goin' on here?"

"Elizabeth's sick," Kate said.

"Sick? Whatcha mean, 'sick?' Who in the hell are you?"

"I'm Kate, your next-door neighbor."

"Well, Kate, you needta get outta here so 'Lizabeth can fix my supper."

"She can't fix it. She's sick."

"That's horseshit!" Hank jerked Elizabeth to her feet. "Get your sorry ass to the kitchen right now!" he said. Then he tramped back to the living room.

"Yeah, Kate, I gotta getta the kitchen. You go on home. I can do this myself."

"Are you sure?" Kate said.

"Yeah. You'd better go. He's awful mad."

"Well, if you need help, just holler or bang on the wall, and I'll come running."

"Okay, I will."

Kate and Elizabeth walked into the living room and stopped at the front door.

"Got yourself a girlfriend now, 'Lizabeth?" Hank said and smirked at them.

"Well, if I was her girlfriend," Kate said, "I'd take a lot better care of her than you do."

"I wudn't talkin' to you, bitch! Get the hell outta here 'fore I th'ow ya out!"

"You touch either one of us, and I'll have you arrested!" Kate said.

"That's a loada bullshit!" Hank grabbed Kate's arm, jerked open the front door, and shoved her outside. "This is *my* house, and no snoopy damn neighbor's gonna tell me what I can and cain't do in it!"

He slammed the door, locked it, and then glared at Elizabeth. "Didn't I tell you this mornin' to have my supper ready when I come through that door this evenin'?"

"Yes, ya did," Elizabeth said.

"Well, then, whur is it? You ain't even started it. Whatcha been doin' all day, layin' 'round holdin' your girlfriend's hand?"

Elizabeth hung her arms at her sides, slumped her shoulders, and stared at the floor. Her babies had hoboed all the way up here to find her, and here she was, still with this hateful ole bully instead of being with them. He would have beaten her, but she should have stood up to him and never left them.

"So, whatcha thank I oughta do 'bout it?" Hank said.

"I'll go fix it right now."

Elizabeth tried to push past Hank, but he blocked her. "Nah, too late. Ya had your chance and muffed it. You know what happens when ya cross me. You just never learn, do ya?" He doubled up his fist and punched her in the face.

"Stop it, Hank!" she screamed. "Please, stop it!"

But he didn't.

Kate hammered on the door and twisted the knob, but it wouldn't open. She could see and hear everything that was happening inside as clearly as if she was in there with them. "Hey, Randy!" she yelled and grabbed the broom from the teenage boy who was sweeping the porch. "Run and get the cops. This man's killing his wife!"

Randy bolted from the porch, and Kate smashed the window. She unlocked the door, dashed inside, and hammered Hank with the broom handle until he dropped Elizabeth. While she slid down the wall to the floor, Hank spun around and punched Kate in the face.

As Randy and the policeman raced into the apartment, Hank held Kate pinned to the wall with the broom handle against her throat. The officer whacked Hank on the head with his nightstick and crumpled him to the floor like a rag doll.

While the policeman telephoned for an ambulance, Kate held Elizabeth's head in her lap. Her left eye looked like a walnut, and her right cheekbone looked flat. Elizabeth came to and peered up at Kate's bruised face. "You look a mess," she murmured.

"Well, thanks a lot," Kate said as they smiled at each other. "You're no beauty queen right now, either."

As Hank lay unconscious, the police handcuffed him. By the time he revived, two more policemen and the ambulance had arrived.

"I'll get you bitches for this!" Hank yelled as the police led him away.

"No, you won't!" Kate shouted. "You're never going to touch either of us again."

"Can Kate come with us?" Elizabeth said as the attendants loaded her into the ambulance.

"No, ma'am. I'm sorry. It's against the rules," one of them said.

"That's okay, Elizabeth," Kate said. "I'll come straight to the hospital when I get things squared away here." Then she watched the ambulance speed away, its lights flashing and its siren blaring.

After Kate and Randy cleaned up the mess and locked the door, Kate freshened up and caught a bus to the hospital.

"I'm here to see Elizabeth Pinscher," she said to the emergency room receptionist.

"Are you family?"

From the question, Kate assumed they only allowed relatives to see critical patients, so she lied. "Yes, I'm her step-sister."

The nurse walked down the hall to the treatment rooms and returned a moment later. "It looks like they're still treating her. If you'll have a seat across the hall, I'll call you when they move her to a room."

"Okay, thanks," Kate said. She strolled to the waiting room and sat down.

Between the time the kids arrived at the shelter and supper time, they were deloused, bathed, and examined by a doctor. Except for their coats, which were sent to the dry cleaners, the rest of their clothes, including shoes, were thrown away, and they were given new ones. Before Sarah parted with her coat, she took her precious locket from its secret place in the lining and put it in the pocket of her new dress.

At five o'clock, the cook, a large black woman, served them a spaghetti supper.

"Are you Aunt Jemima?" Mark said as she set his plate on the table.

"Boy! What you mean callin' me, 'Aunt Jemima?' I'm not that fat. You watch your tongue, or I'll feed your supper to the dogs!"

Mark peered up at the woman, and tears filled his eyes.

"He didn't mean nothin' by it, ma'am," Sarah said. "You do kinda look like the woman on the pancake box, so he thought maybe ya really was her."

"Well, I'm not. My name's Rosella–Rosella Wilson." She smiled a broad smile and held out her hand to Mark. "What's yours?"

The little boy grinned and shook Rosella's hand. "Mark Skaggs."

"Well, Mark, from now on, don't you be callin' nobody, 'Aunt Jemima.'"

"Okay, I won't," Mark said, and he dug into his supper.

Sarah picked up some of the slippery spaghetti with her fork and tried to poke it into her mouth, but it didn't work. "How in the heck do ya eat this stuff? I cain't get hold of it."

"Like this," Rosella said. She took Sarah's fork and spoon and twisted the strands into a ball. Sarah and Johnny caught on right away, but Mark never did, so he just sucked the long strands into his mouth any way he could.

The kids finished supper, and while Johnny taught Mark how to play checkers, Sarah played with paper dolls, Jax, and pickup sticks.

At seven o'clock, night attendant Miss Judy Jackson walked into the lounge and turned on the TV. When its sound drifted into the playroom, the kids tiptoed to the lounge door and peeked inside.

"Come in and sit down," Miss Jackson said.

"Ya mean we getta watch television?" Mark said.

"Yes," Miss Jackson said. "Don't you usually watch TV?"

"No, ma'am," Sarah said. "We ain't never watched it, 'cept in store windors."

"You mean you've never watched a whole TV show before?"

"No, ma'am."

"Well then, you're in for a treat. There's lots of good shows on tonight."

The kids ran into the room, plopped down in its fluffy chairs, and sat spellbound for two hours by *The George Burns and Gracie Allen Show, I Love Lucy,* and *December Bride.*

At nine o'clock, the news came on, and Miss Jackson turned off the TV set. Then she and Miss Holly Harris, the other night attendant, led the kids to their bedrooms. At the end of the hallway, Sarah followed Miss Harris to the left, and the boys followed Miss Jackson to the right.

Sarah glanced back at her brothers. This sort of reminded her of their first night at the Richters' house when the Reverend separated them. She shook her head and cleared her mind. These were good people, and they were safe here.

In the bedroom, Sarah put on her new nightgown and crawled into the soft, clean bed. As Miss Harris turned out the light and closed the door, Sarah stared at the ceiling. Maybe now, with Miss Jordan's help, they would finally find their mother. And, with that happy thought, she drifted off to sleep.

At the hospital, the emergency room nurse walked over to Kate, who was dozing. "Miss, they've taken your sister to Room 334."

"Thank you," Kate said as she opened her eyes. Then she stood up and walked to the elevator.

At the room, Kate cracked open the door and peeked inside. Bandages covered Elizabeth's entire face except for her right eye, and bruises marked her arms. A nurse stood beside her taking her pulse.

When Elizabeth saw her friend, she burst into tears. Kate rushed to her side and hugged her.

"He's a mean, angry man," Elizabeth said.

"Yes, I know," Kate said, "but he's in jail now and can't hurt you anymore."

"You mean they really put him in jail?"

"Yes, they really did."

"Oh no! That'll make him even madder, and next time, he'll hurt me even more!"

"There won't be 'a next time,'" Kate said.

"Why do you say that?"

"Because I'm going to help you get what's called a restraining order against him. That way, he'll never be able to come anywhere near you again."

"No. I ain't gonna do that. Besides, he won't pay no attention to it, anyhow."

"Oh yes, he will, or they'll send him to prison like they did my ex-husband when he came back and tried to beat me up again."

"Ya mean your husband beat you too?"

"Yes, he sure did. He almost killed me. But he's in prison now, and I moved away. He doesn't know where I am."

"All I wont is to be with my kids and have a happy life."

"And you will," Kate said. "You absolutely will."

While Kate held her hand, Elizabeth drifted off to sleep, and when she woke the next morning, Kate was still holding it.

Chapter 16

THE ZOO

EARLY TUESDAY MORNING, the city was abuzz with newsboys waving a special edition newspaper in the air. A photo of a local gangster filled a quarter of the front page. When day attendants Miranda Martinez and Hazel Hastings exited the bus, they bought a copy and hurried into the shelter. While they drank their morning coffee, the ladies read about how the gangster had escaped from the FBI. The article also said that all city police resources had been reallocated to support an area-wide manhunt and that all non-critical investigations had been put on hold.

The small paragraph in the police report about a man named Pinscher who had almost beaten his wife to death and the human interest story about three children who had hoboed to the city in search of their missing mother went unnoticed.

Due to the police resource reallocation, Hank Pinscher was only held in jail overnight. Upon release, he was advised to seek counseling since domestic abuse was considered more of a family matter than an actual crime, but he ignored it.

After washing in a public restroom, he bought a bottle of whiskey and reported to work.

Blaming Elizabeth for his arrest, Hank's rage built all day as he drank from his hidden bottle. While working underneath a truck body that afternoon, his anger flared, and he kicked a jack. The chassis it was supporting fell and crushed him, and a few minutes later, he died.

Because Elizabeth was in the hospital, police efforts to notify her about Hank's death were unsuccessful, so they sent his body to the city morgue.

At noon on Wednesday, Miss Jordan joined the kids for lunch and returned their dry-cleaned coats.

"Have you found out anythang 'bout Mama?" Sarah said as she put her locket back into her garment's lining.

"No, not yet, but you must remember, there are almost a million people in St. Louis, so it will take time. And now that the police are involved in the manhunt, it will take even longer."

"Yes'm, I know," Sarah said. "But I was hopin' maybe you'd heard somethin.'"

"I have been in touch with the Piggott welfare office, though, and they want you brought back to them."

Sarah cringed. "Why? Mama's here."

"Well, we do not know that for sure, do we? We assume she is, but what if she has returned to Arkansas to get you, and you are not there?"

"No, Hank ain't gonna do that," Sarah said.

"What if she is no longer with Hank? What if she has left him?"

"No, she'd be too sceared to do that. She ain't got nowhur else to go."

"Well, if you do go back to Arkansas, and then she is found, I can still get you back together. It will just take longer."

They finished lunch, Miss Jordan left, and the kids returned to the playroom.

At five o'clock, they ate supper, then watched TV until bedtime.

Sarah tried to sleep but couldn't. If they got sent back to Austin, they would be returned to the Richters', and she couldn't let that happen. She wrestled with her thoughts until exhaustion pushed her into a restless sleep.

As the kids ate breakfast on Thursday, Miss Jordan unexpectedly joined them.

"What's wrong?" Sarah said. "You don't usually eat breakfast with us."

"Nothing is wrong," Miss Jordan said. "I just decided we would go to the zoo today."

Sarah breathed a cautious sigh of relief until she looked into Miss Jordan's eyes. There was something she wasn't telling them.

"What's a zoo?" Mark said.

"A place with animals," Johnny said.

"Like a farm?"

"Nah, not like a farm. It's got lions, elephants, and eagles. Not horses, cows, and chickens."

Mark's eyes bulged. "Dang, that's scary!"

"Nah, it ain't," Johnny said. "They're all in cages."

"We ain't never been to a zoo," Sarah said.

"Then you will really enjoy this one," Miss Jordan said. "It has all kinds of animals, and there are nice benches where we can sit and rest in the shade."

They finished eating, and while the kids used the bathroom, Miss Jordan called a taxi.

As they stepped from the cab at the zoo, a lion roared, and Mark ducked behind Sarah.

"Don't worry, Mark," Miss Jordan said as she led the group to the entrance. "It is safe here."

They walked through the gate and came to an exhibit of mountain goats.

"Johnny, I thought you said this wudn't gonna be like a farm," Mark said.

"It ain't," Johnny said.

"Then why're 'em goats here?"

"To feed the lions and tigers," Johnny said.

Mark froze in his tracks. "Dang, I wonna see that!"

"Ah, Marky, he's just kiddin' ya," Sarah said.

"Whatsamatter? Don't lions eat goats?"

"In Africa, but not here," Sarah said. "These are just for people to look at."

"But, 'ey're just goats," Mark said.

"Well, city folk ain't ever seen 'em before."

Just past the goats, they came to a pond, and Mark giggled. "Lookee at 'em sissy ducks!"

Sarah looked at him and scowled. "Them ain't ducks. Them's swans."

"Well, 'ey look like sissy ducks to me," Mark said. He puffed out his jaws, stuffed his hands into his pockets, and shuffled on down the sidewalk.

"Who wants a hotdog?" Miss Jordan said as they approached a snack bar.

"Me!" Mark shouted. Sarah and Johnny raised their hands.

"We would like four hotdogs and four orange drinks," Miss Jordan said and paid the man.

She distributed the food and drinks. Then they sat down at a picnic table under an oak tree.

When they finished their snack and headed back down the sidewalk, they came to a stone building with a long word engraved over its door.

"This is the herpetarium," Miss Jordan said as they stopped in front of it. "Is anyone afraid of snakes?"

Mark balked. "Snakes? What kinda snakes?"

Miss Jordan closed her eyes and shivered. "All kinds."

"Snakes don't bother me, none," Sarah said as a secret shiver slid down her spine.

"Me neither," Johnny said.

"Oh yeah? Since when? Mr. 'Snakebit' Skaggs!" Sarah said. She told Miss Jordan about Johnny's red wasp sting in the outhouse, and they all laughed.

"I still ain't sceared of 'em," Johnny said as he opened the door, and they stepped inside.

Behind the thick glass windows, they viewed all kinds of serpents, from king snakes to pythons and from rattlesnakes to boomslangs.

At the last window, Johnny marched up to it and peered inside. "Empty," he said. "Nut'in' 'ere." Suddenly, a long, thin snake reared up, flared the sides of its head, and Johnny fell backward onto the floor.

"What's that?" he shouted as everyone laughed.

"A cobra," Miss Jordan said. "It is very aggressive and very poisonous."

"I wouldn't wonna run into one of 'em in the woods," Johnny said as he stood back up.

"Don't worry," Miss Jordan said. "They are not native to this country."

"What's that mean?"

"It means you will never see one in the United States except in zoos."

"Thank goodness," Johnny said.

Over the next couple of hours, the group viewed prairie dogs, foxes, raccoons, owls, peacocks, monkeys, water buffalo, dromedary camels, and a silverback gorilla named Phil.

As they strolled away from the gorilla cage, they met a vendor with a cart.

"What'll ya have?" the man said as he approached them.

"Ice cream, anyone?" Miss Jordan said.

"Strawberry!" Mark shouted.

"Yeah, me too," Johnny said.

"I wont chocolate," Sarah said.

"And I will have vanilla," Miss Jordan said.

They carried their cones to a bright yellow round table and sat down under its red, yellow, and green umbrella.

Mark devoured his treat and licked his fingers clean. As they headed back down the sidewalk, Miss Jordan glanced at her watch. "Okay, it is time to start back to the gate."

"But we ain't seen the lions yet!" Mark said.

"That is because they are on our way out," Miss Jordan said. "We have saved the best for last."

At the big cat exhibit, they viewed the leopard, tiger, cougar, and black panther. As Mark ran up to the lion's cage, the cat roared, and he plugged his fingers into his ears. "Wow, he's big and loud!"

"Okay, let's get to the taxi," Miss Jordan said.

"Ahh, cain't we stay just a little bit longer?" Mark said.

"No, Mark, I am sorry, but we have to go," Miss Jordan said. "Rosella will have dinner ready, and she cannot go home until we have eaten."

"Dang, Marky!" Sarah said. "Have ya finally found somethin' ya like more'n eatin'?"

Mark puffed out his jaws and glared at his sister. He shoved his fists into his pants pockets and slogged to the taxi.

At the shelter, Rosella met them in the dining room. "I's beginnin' to think I's gonna hafta throw your supper out to the dogs," she said as she set the platter of pork chops and the bowl of mashed potatoes on the table.

"Sorry we are late, Rosella," Miss Jordan said. "We took extra time at the cat exhibit."

"Yeah! Ya shoulda seen 'em, Rosella!" Mark said. "'Ey's huge!"

"I have seen 'em, Mark. And I know what you mean–What can I get you to drink, Miss Jordan?"

"Just a glass of water."

When they finished eating, Rosella cleared the table and brought in four saucers of lemon meringue pie.

"Oh, no, thank you. None for me," Miss Jordan said as Rosella passed out the dessert, "but I will have a cup of coffee with cream."

While the kids ate their pie, Miss Jordan glanced at them several times, and her eyes turned sad. A lump filled Sarah's throat, and she laid down her fork. She knew it–bad news.

"Would you please ask Miss Jackson and Miss Harris to come here?" Miss Jordan said as Rosella picked up the empty dessert dishes.

"Yes'm, I'll have 'em come right in."

A moment later, the attendants walked to the table and sat down.

"I have something to tell the children that you ladies also need to hear," Miss Jordan said, and Sarah frowned.

"Okay, Miss Jordan, what is it?"

"Well, Sarah, despite our efforts to keep you and your brothers here, I am going to have to take you back to Piggott tomorrow."

Sarah clenched her teeth and glared at Miss Jordan. "What if we don't wonna go?"

"I am sorry, but you have to. It is a legal matter. You have no choice."

Sarah jumped up, ran to the lounge, and her brothers followed.

Miss Jordan looked at Miss Jackson and Miss Harris. "I was hoping she would take it better than this. I am afraid they may try to run away."

"Well, we'll be alert and lockdown especially tight tonight," Miss Jackson said.

"Yes, don't worry," Miss Harris said. "They'll still be here in the morning."

Miss Jordan eased into the lounge and gazed at Sarah, who was sitting in one of the big puffy chairs. "I understand how you feel."

"No, ya don't, or ya wouldn't send us back!"

Miss Jordan sat down beside Sarah and put her arm around her. "Yes, I do, but we have to obey the law."

"That's a buncha hooey! I don't give a hoot nor a holler for the law! It ain't done nothin' to help us find our Mama!"

"Oh yes, it has," Miss Jordan said. "The police have followed up on every lead they have received about your mother. I check with them daily, and they know I will dog them until this case is closed. The trouble is, they have been distracted by the manhunt, but I promise I will do everything I can to help you get back with your mother, so *please*, do not give up hope."

Sarah peered into Miss Jordan's eyes. They were honest and true. "I know you're really tryin' to help us, Miss Jordan, but it seems like somethin' goes wrong with ever'thang we do."

"Yes, it may seem that way to you now, but eventually, things will work out."

They all got up and walked back to the dining room.

"Don't worry, Sarah," Miss Jordan said as she picked up her belongings beside the door. "I promise I *will* get you through this."

Sarah tried to smile but couldn't. "Yes'm. G'night, Miss Jordan."

"Goodnight. I will see you in the morning," Miss Jordan said. She walked out the door, and Miss Jackson bolted it.

As everyone gathered in the lounge, Miss Harris turned on the TV. While the programs played, Sarah's mind raced. If only they hadn't gotten caught, maybe they could have found their mother.

Chapter 17

BACK TO AUSTIN

FRIDAY MORNING, ROSELLA served everyone a hearty breakfast. Then while Mrs. Hastings and Mrs. Martinez helped the kids gather and fold their clothes, Miss Jordan fetched a donated suitcase from the supply room.

"This will hold your regular clothes, but you will have to carry your coats," she said as she set the case on Sarah's bed and opened it.

"Well, we're used to that," Sarah said.

Miss Jordan packed the luggage and then handed it to Johnny. "Here, big boy, get this to Piggott, okay?"

"Okay," Johnny said as he shouldered his coat and took the suitcase.

"Are you ready?" Miss Jordan said and peered at the kids.

"Ready!" Mark said. He hung his coat's hood over his head and let the rest dangle down his back. "I'm Superman. I'm gonna flyin' to Piggott!" he said as he stretched out his arms and buzzed around the room.

The kids said goodbye to Mrs. Hastings and Mrs. Martinez and followed Miss Jordan to the dining room, where Rosella met them.

Sarah hugged the sweet woman and breathed in her pleasant fragrance of bath soap and cooked food. "G'bye, Miss Rosella. Thank ya for bein' so nice to us and for feedin' us so good."

"Goodbye, Sarah," Rosella said. "I've enjoyed you bein' here. Come back and see me some time."

"Yes'm, I'd like that."

"G'bye, Rosella," Mark said as tears filled his eyes. He threw his arms around the big woman and squeezed her. "You sure are a good cook. I wisht you's goin' with us."

"Goodbye, Mark. And remember, now. Don't you be callin' nobody 'Aunt Jemima!'"

Mark giggled. "Okay, I won't."

Johnny nodded to Rosella but didn't go to her. "Thank ya, ma'am."

Rosella squinted. "Whatsamatter, Johnny? Ain't ya gonna hug me?"

Johnny blushed and set down the suitcase but held on to his coat. He slogged to Rosella and put his empty arm around her.

"That's better," she said. "But ya coulda used both arms."

Johnny released her and hurried back to the suitcase.

Beside the door, Miss Jordan put on her hat, gloves, and sunglasses and glanced at herself in the mirror. Then she picked up her purse and briefcase and peered at the kids. "Are we ready?"

Mark stretched out his Superman arms. "Ready!"

"Okay then, here we go."

As Miss Jordan led the kids to the taxi, Rosella waved to them from the kitchen door.

On the ride to the station, Sarah peered out the window. "I'm gonna miss St. Louie. There's lots here I'd like to see. I wonder if I'll ever be back?"

"Sure you will," Miss Jordan said. "Your whole life is ahead of you. These troubles will end someday. And when you are grown, you will return. You are too curious not to."

As Mark and Sarah climbed out of the cab in front of Union Station, they peered up at the building.

"Wow! It's a rocket ship!" Mark said.

"No, silly boy! It's a castle!" Sarah said.

Johnny was too busy wrestling the suitcase to have an interpretation.

Inside the station, Sarah gazed up at the ceiling and gasped. "Wow! This is a palace!"

"Yes, it is beautiful, isn't it?" Miss Jordan said.

Sarah pulled her locket from her coat and fastened it around her neck. "Wearing this, I feel like a princess." She opened it and showed the picture to Miss Jordan. "This is our Mama and real Daddy. It's the only thang I got left they give to me."

Miss Jordan smiled. "Yes, it is lovely. Now I have something to show you." She positioned the boys under one end of the arch that curved above them. Then she and Sarah walked to the same position under its other end.

"Now, say something to your brothers in a normal tone of voice," Miss Jordan said.

"Hey, Johnny. Hey, Marky," Sarah said, and Mark giggled.

"Hey, Sissy, it sounds like you're right here next to us."

"It is called the 'Whispering Arch,'" Miss Jordan said. Then the boys rejoined them, and they headed to the train.

"Hold on to that suitcase, Johnny. It is crowded in here, and people will bump into you."

They walked through a set of doors to a series of long walkways beside strings of passenger cars, where people were scurrying on and off them.

"This is our coach," Miss Jordan said at its entrance, and a man in uniform held out his gloved hand to her. She took hold of it and climbed the steps into the car. Then the man offered his hand to Sarah. She put on a stern face, lifted her head high, and clasped the glove. *A princess must act like a princess.* But as she strutted up the steps, her pretty fantasy suddenly ended. She tripped on her coattail and stumbled inside. *Well, dang it, Sarah. You're still just a peasant.*

Superman Mark scuttled up the steps on all fours. Then the man helped Johnny aboard with the luggage.

Miss Jordan led the kids halfway down the aisle to two seats, one behind the other, and pushed her briefcase onto the overhead rack. "Sarah, you and I will sit here, and you boys will sit in front of us."

While Miss Jordan helped Johnny stow the suitcase, Sarah slid into the seat next to the window and peered out at the people rushing to and from their trains.

"No, I wonna set by the windor," Mark whined as Johnny sat down. So big brother scooted over, and little brother slid past him.

"I wish we'd found Mama. I know she's here," Sarah said as Miss Jordan sat down beside her.

"Yes, I wish we had, too," Miss Jordan said. "If she is here, the police *will* eventually locate her. It is simply a matter of time."

"All aboard!" the uniformed man outside the coach shouted. "All aboard for Pine Bluff, Shreveport, Dallas, and Waco!"

"He didn't say, 'Piggott,'" Johnny said.

"That's because the train goes through Piggott to get to them other places," Sarah said.

"Yes, that's correct," Miss Jordan said and smiled. "You're pretty smart, aren't you?"

A smug look spread across Sarah's face, then it faded. Smart though she was, she hadn't been smart enough to find her mother.

At nine o'clock sharp, by the big clock on the platform, the train eased away from the station. As it crossed the Mississippi River into Illinois, the conductor entered the car.

"What time will we get to Piggott?" Miss Jordan said as he stopped beside her.

The conductor pulled out his watch and glanced at it. "About two-thirty, ma'am, if we stay on schedule." He punched their tickets and continued down the aisle.

Mark rested his head against the window and gazed out at the stopped freight train on the track beside them. "Lookee, Sissy, box-cars. I wonder if Bo Jesus is in one of 'em?"

"No, he's at his mother's house," Sarah said. "He was goin' to visit her, remember?"

"Well, I sure hope we getta see him again someday."

Miss Jordan grinned, and Sarah glared at her. She obviously still didn't believe they had hoboed.

While Sarah and Miss Jordan talked, the boys slept. At noon, Miss Jordan woke them. "Are you hungry?"

"Starved!" Mark said.

"Okay, let's go eat."

In the dining car, they waited for a table to be bussed, then sat down.

"What do you want, Mark?" Miss Jordan said as the waiter handed her a menu.

"A hamburger, French fries, and strawberry sody pop."

"What about you, Johnny?"

"A hamburger, French fries, and a root beer."

"And, Sarah?"

"I wont a toasted cheese sandwich with a sweet pickle and sweet iced tea."

Miss Jordan closed the menu and handed it back to the waiter. "And I will have a salad with vinaigrette dressing and a cup of hot tea."

"Yes, ma'am, I'll be right back with your drinks."

When they finished eating, the waiter returned. "Who wants dessert?" he said as he picked up the empty plates.

Mark's eyes flashed. "Me!"

"Today's special is apple pie a la mode."

"What kinda apple pie's that?" Mark said.

"Apple pie with ice cream on it," Miss Jordan said.

"Yeah, that's what I wont."

"Marky, ya need to ask Miss Jordan if it's okay first," Sarah said. "There might not be enough money for dessert."

Mark's grin fell away to a frown. He puffed out his jaws and slumped his shoulders.

"Well, we are on a budget, but it will cover dessert," Miss Jordan said, and Mark's grin re-blossomed.

"Three apple pie a la modes," Miss Jordan said.

The waiter nodded and hurried away to the kitchen.

When the kids finished their dessert, they all strolled back to their seats in the coach.

A couple of hours later, the train rolled to a stop at the Piggott depot, and Miss Jordan glanced at her watch. "Two thirty-five. Right on time."

As the group stepped from the train, Miss Galloway and Sheriff Charlie Crane marched over to them.

Miss Jordan smiled and offered her hand to Miss Galloway, who sidestepped her, grabbed Sarah, and shoved her to the sheriff. "Here ya go, Charlie. Lock her in the car."

Sarah cocked her foot to kick Miss Galloway, but Miss Jordan stepped in-between them. "What is going on here?"

"Are you that snooty bitch we talked to on the phone?" Miss Galloway said.

"Well, I am Miss Alexis Jordan, if that is what you mean."

"Well, Miss Alexis Jordan, did you know these kids broke out of their foster parent's house in the middle of the night and ran away?"

"What do you mean, 'broke out?' Were they being kept under lock and key?"

"That's exactly what I mean."

"Why were they being treated like prisoners?"

"Because they're violent."

"I do not believe it. I have never had any trouble from these children."

"Well, then, you've just been lucky. These monsters should be sent to reform school for what they did to the poor Reverend and his wife."

"We didn't do nothin' to 'em they didn't deserve!" Sarah said. "That old devil pulled Marky's hair and slapped him!"

"That's a lie. He never did any such thing. It was you and your brothers who attacked them with umbrellas, broom handles, and anything else you could lay your hands on."

"All we done was defend ourselves!" Sarah said.

"Well, you're goin' to get what's comin' to you this time, young lady. We've dealt with troublemakers like you before."

"These children are not 'troublemakers,'" Miss Jordan said. "They just need help."

"Well, I beg to differ with you. Besides, they're in my custody now, and you don't have anything more to say about it. So get your prissy ass back to St. Louis, where you belong."

"I beg your pardon! I have not released these children to you yet. It is my duty to retain custody of them until I am satisfied they are in safe, competent hands."

The sheriff put his hands in his pockets and swaggered over to Miss Jordan. "Well, ma'am, Miss Galloway is authorized to take custody of these kids, and she's gonna do that."

Miss Jordan took out a piece of paper and held it in the air. "Not until we have both signed this custody release form."

Miss Galloway snatched the document, plucked the pen from the sheriff's shirt pocket, signed the form, and shoved it back in Miss Jordan's face. "Okay. There, I've signed it! Now you do the same, give me my copy, and get the hell outta here!"

"No, I am not signing it until I am sure these children will receive courteous and competent treatment. Maybe you do not follow proper procedures, but I do, and I will not be a party to any violation of those procedures."

"Well, ma'am," the sheriff said. "Miss Galloway is takin' custody of these kids whether you sign the form or not, so I suggest ya just sign it and be on your way."

"No, sir! And trying to coerce me is not helping your position!"

The sheriff jerked the form from Miss Jordan's hand, tore off the original, and handed the carbon copy back to her. "Well then, we'll just take the kids without your signature."

"Excuse me, but the original copy is mine," Miss Jordan said.

"So arrest me," the sheriff said and stuffed the form into his pocket.

Miss Galloway chuckled. "See there, Miss Smarty-pants, Alexis Jordan. We have law enforcement officers here who'll do the right thing regardless of so-called 'proper procedures.'"

"Well, I hope you are both prepared to lose your jobs and possibly go to jail because I *will* file a formal complaint against you, and there *will* be repercussions."

"Don't threaten us! You're in our jurisdiction, not yours." Miss Galloway said and pushed the kids to the sheriff. "Here, Charlie. Haul these scumbags away."

"I am warning you, Miss Galloway! I shall report this incident and give your names to the proper authorities!"

"You go right ahead," Miss Galloway said as the sheriff guided the kids to his car. "We have enough reliable witnesses here to refute anything you say."

Sarah looked at Miss Jordan. "Do we really hafta go with 'em?"

"I am sorry, Sarah. I cannot do anything to stop them. But I promise I will be working to correct this situation and will get back to you as soon as possible."

Miss Jordan glared at Miss Galloway and the sheriff as they drove away with the kids. She had never seen such disregard for children's welfare by a staff member. And especially for *these* children–intelligent, resourceful, interested only in finding their mother–to be manhandled into a police car like common criminals. It was insane. This called for a disciplinary hearing, and she was determined to see that Miss Galloway, at least, got one.

As the car drove out of sight, Miss Jordan marched into the depot where a man wearing a green visor on his head and garters on his shirtsleeves sat behind a desk and wrote as the telegraph clicked.

"How can I help you?" he said when the clicking stopped.

"I would like to send an urgent telegram to St. Louis."

"Yes, ma'am. Expedited telegrams are ten cents a word. Who's it going to?"

"Mr. Franklin Frazier, St. Louis Child Welfare Administrator."

Chapter 18

Unfinished Business

AT THE PIGGOTT welfare building, Miss Galloway and Sheriff Crane herded the kids into her office and closed the door. Then she sat down on her desk and picked up the telephone. "Hey, Jenny, this is Gloria Galloway. Ring Reverend Richter for me."

"We ain't goin' back to that old devil's house!" Sarah said.

"Hello, Reverend, this is Miss Galloway. How are you today?"

Sarah's heart pounded, and she jumped to her feet. "Grab your stuff, boys! We're gettin' outta here!" They ran for the door, but the sheriff blocked them.

"Oh, I can't complain," Miss Galloway said. "Especially now that we have these runaways back in custody. And that's why I'm callin'– to see when I can bring *her* back to you."

Sarah pushed the sheriff again but still couldn't budge him.

"Four-thirty? Yes, sir, that'll be fine. Okay, we'll see you then. Goodbye."

Miss Galloway hung up the phone and glared at Sarah. "You're goin' wherever I send ya. You don't have any say about it. And something else, we're not puttin' up with any more of your crap. You hear me?"

When Sarah didn't answer, Miss Galloway got face-to-face with her. "Do You Hear Me?"

Sarah broke loose, waved her hand in front of her nose, and coughed. "Your breath stinks."

"And that's another thing. You're gonna get that smart mouth of yours under control and start showin' us some respect whether ya want to or not. And from now on, violence will be answered with violence."

Then Sarah's mouth flew open. "Wait just a dang minute. You never said nothin' to the Reverend 'bout Johnny and Mark."

"Oh, so ya caught that, did ya?" Miss Galloway said.

"Whur they goin'?"

"I'm not tellin'. If ya don't know, ya can't get with 'em and run away again."

Sarah frowned. "You just wait. Miss Jordan'll fix you when she comes to help us."

"Oh, no, she won't. Miss Jordan's not gonna do anything. The sheriff's gonna see to that. Right, Charlie?"

He looked at Miss Galloway, then glanced at the wall clock. "We gotta go if we're gonna get to the Richters' by four-thirty."

"Yeah, we do. Go get Gene and bring him in here."

As the sheriff left the room, Miss Galloway blocked the door. A moment later, he returned with Mr. Bradford.

Miss Galloway pulled the bag from her trash can. "Here, Gene. Put the boys' clothes in this. Then take them to their new foster home while Charlie and me take Sarah back to the Richters'."

"We're goin' with Sarah," Johnny said.

"No, you're not," Miss Galloway said. "You're goin' somewhere else."

"We don't wonna go 'somewhur else.'"

"Well, tough. You don't get a vote. Get 'em outta here, Gene."

Mr. Bradford picked up the clothes bag. "Okay, boys, get your coats, and let's go."

"No!" Sarah shouted and grabbed her brothers. "Don't we getta say g'bye?"

"No, ya don't." Miss Galloway said. "Take 'em away, Gene."

"Hang on a second," the sheriff said as he raised his hand. "For goodness sake, Gloria, surely we got enough time to let these kids say g'bye to each other."

"Well, ain't you the Good Samaritan today?" Miss Galloway said.

"When will I get to see 'em again?" Sarah said.

"See 'em again?" Miss Galloway huffed. "I don't know, and I don't care. All I'm interested in right now is gettin' you back to the Richters.'"

"These boys are my brothers, and I ain't gonna let nobody stop me from seein' 'em."

"Oh yeah? And just how're ya gonna do that?"

"I don't know, but I'll fig're it out."

"Sure ya will," Miss Galloway said and laughed. "Maybe ya can get God to help ya. Maybe He'll work a miracle for ya."

The sheriff cringed and rubbed the back of his neck. "Damn it, Gloria! One of these days, you're gonna get lightnin' struck."

"Oh hell, Charlie, why don't you grow up? I hate to disillusion ya, but it's time ya stopped believin' in God and Santy Claus."

The sheriff bristled. "Go on out to the car, Gloria. I'll brang Sarah out in a minute."

"Good idea. I need a smoke." She grabbed her purse and tramped out the door.

Sarah stared at her brothers and burned their faces into her memory. "I don't know when we'll getta see each other again, but Miss Jordan's comin' back to help us, so don't give up.

"Johnny, take good care of Marky, and Marky, stay close to Johnny. Don't let nobody separate ya, and we'll get outta this mess. Remember, I love ya," she said and kissed them.

"I love you too, Sissy," Mark said as he clung to his sister, and tears streamed down his face.

For a moment, the kids just stood and looked at one another.

"Okay, boys, let's go," Mr. Bradford said.

Sarah's heart sank, and tears rolled down her cheeks as she watched her brothers walk out the door. This was even harder than watching her mother leave.

The sheriff picked up the suitcase, Sarah picked up her coat, and they joined Miss Galloway in the car. On the way to the parsonage, Sarah put her locket back inside her coat's lining.

As they pulled into the Richters' driveway, Sarah saw the big tree they had used in their escape lying on the ground, and tears filled her eyes. It had been cut down because of her.

Miss Galloway led Sarah and the sheriff onto the porch and knocked on the door. When the Reverend opened it, he glared at Sarah. "Well, look who's back!" he said, and a chill rolled down her spine. She could deal with dangerous people, like Hank, but not with evil people, like Reverend Richter. What scared her most was that he believed his evil had won.

"Yes, Reverend, here she is," Miss Galloway said and pushed Sarah into the living room. "But I'm afraid her attitude hasn't improved."

Sarah gritted her teeth and held back the hateful words that wanted to spew from her lips.

"Well, I'm sure we'll get along splendidly this time," the Reverend said.

"Well, if you don't," Miss Galloway said, "help is just a phone call away. Isn't it, Charlie?"

"Yes, Reverend," the sheriff said. "If ya need me, call me. We wanna stop any trouble before it gets started."

"Indeed, we do," the Reverend said.

Miss Galloway peered at Sarah. "So I suggest you behave yourself this time, girl."

Sarah wanted to spit in the woman's face but didn't.

"Well, I need to get back and close the office," the sheriff said and tugged Miss Galloway toward the door.

"Have a good evening, Reverend," Miss Galloway said.

"Thank you, and you do the same."

Reverend Richter watched them drive away. Then he locked the door, marched over to Sarah, and slapped her. "How dare you betray our hospitality and embarrass us by running away like that!"

Sarah rubbed her face and backed away. She tried to put furniture between them, but he blocked her moves.

"Sister Richter, is everything prepared for the Lord's work?"

"Yes, Husband. Everything is ready."

He grabbed Sarah's arms and pulled her to the staircase. "You're coming with me. We have unfinished business."

"Turn loose of me, ya old devil!" Sarah screamed as she fought him.

"'Old devil,' is it? Oh no, my dear. Quite the contrary. I'm the Lord's servant, and this time you'll feel His full wrath."

He dragged Sarah into the same bedroom she had before and shoved her face down onto the bed. While he held her down with his knee on her back, he tied her wrists and ankles to ropes he had already prepared. Then he tore off her dress, picked up his razor strap, and struck.

Sarah twisted and screamed as each blow ripped into her flesh. The more she squirmed, the faster and harder the Reverend swung the strap.

Downstairs, while four pans of water heated on the kitchen stove, Sister Richter carried a soap bar, a bath towel, and a clean set of the Reverend's clothes to the screened back porch and laid them on a chair beside the long, deep galvanized bathtub. For a moment, engulfed in memories of other girls who had passed through their home, she stood motionless and listened to Sarah's screams. All the previous girls had become "obedient, young women" and had never told anyone what happened to them there. And for Sarah's sake, she hoped the Reverend would subdue her the same way.

Suddenly, the lashes stopped, and only Sarah's whimpers floated downstairs. Sister Richter froze and held her breath. Then came the long, shrill screams. She covered her ears and scrunched up her face.

"Dear God, please let it pass quickly!" she prayed, then hummed a hymn to cover up the sound.

"Praise God!" The Reverend's loud voice echoed from upstairs. Then, except for Sarah's sobs, everything fell silent again.

Sister Richter carried the pans of hot water to the porch and filled the bathtub.

A few moments later, the Reverend staggered into the kitchen wrapped in a blood-streaked sheet. "A virgin!" he gasped. "The Lord hath sent me a virgin."

Sister Richter clasped her prayer hands and lifted her eyes heavenward. "Glory to thee, oh God!" she shouted in her church voice. Then it returned to monotone. "Now, let's get you into the bath."

She led her husband to the porch and helped him into the tub. Then she gathered what was needed to attend to Sarah and headed upstairs.

When Sarah heard footsteps on the staircase, she struggled against the ropes. As Sister Richter walked into the room, Sarah's fear turned to shame. She was lying naked on the bed, crying and trembling uncontrollably.

"Oh, there, there, child," Sister Richter said as she set the washbasin on the nightstand. "Don't you fret. I'll have you fixed up again, fit as a fiddle, in no time."

Sarah withdrew deep inside herself to where she could barely hear Sister Richter's voice.

Maybe none of this would have happened if she had cooperated with the Richters instead of running away. Maybe this was her own fault. But why had Miss Galloway and the sheriff brought her back here? Didn't they know what went on in this house? Hadn't Angela and those other girls ever told anyone what had happened to them here?

Then Sister Richter's voice became clear again. "You can't fight God, my dear! He will always bring you back into submission. Men must submit to God, and women must submit to men. Like I told you the first time you were here, that's how it is. But you'll soon get used to it."

Get used to it? She wasn't ever going to get used to being whipped and used. She had seen Hank beat her mother and had sworn never to let that happen to her, but now, here she was. And she would do whatever was necessary to get out of this awful mess, even if it meant killing someone.

Chapter 19
BACK TO SCHOOL

EARLY SATURDAY MORNING, Sister Richter woke Sarah and had her come downstairs to breakfast. Every time the Reverend looked at her, she trembled. When would he attack her again?

They finished the meal. Then for the rest of the day, Sarah and Sister Richter washed and ironed clothes while the Reverend wrote his Sunday sermon. Although the Richters had an electric washing machine and iron, the job still took most of the day.

Among the laundered clothes were several lovely dresses just Sarah's size. "Whose are these?" she said and held one up to herself.

"They're yours now," Sister Richter said.

"Mine?"

"Yes, they used to belong to a girl named Angela who lived here, but she grew up and moved away."

"Was that the Angela that got baptized?"

"Yes. I don't know why she didn't get baptized while living here. Reverend Richter studied with her in private every night. And he'll do the same with you."

Sarah shivered. She didn't want any private Bible lessons from him.

"After we finish the ironing," Sister Richter said, "we'll hang these in your closet, and you can wear them to church."

That evening, after bathing and eating supper, Sarah returned to her room and tried on her new dresses. They were all so beautiful she wished she had somewhere to wear them besides church.

Just before nine, Sarah put away the dresses and went downstairs for the bedtime devotional. While the Reverend read aloud from the Bible, Sarah stared at him and became nauseated. How could such an evil man even think he was Godly? She blinked and thought about other things–How much longer would she have to live here? Would Miss Jordan really come back to help them? What if Miss Galloway was right? What if Miss Jordan couldn't do anything to help them– What then? She needed a backup plan, but to make one, she had to know how to get to her brothers. That meant talking to other people, and Reverend Richter wasn't going to let that happen.

When the devotional ended, Sarah hurried back to her room and crawled into bed. As she pondered her problems, an uneasy sleep swept her away.

Just before seven on Sunday morning, Sister Richter entered Sarah's room. "Which dress are you wearing to church today, Sweetheart?" she said as Sarah got out of bed.

"This dark blue one with the white polka dots," Sarah said and pulled it from the closet.

"Oh, yes! Reverend Richter likes that one! Put it on and come downstairs to breakfast."

How could this woman just accept her husband's behavior?

After Sister Richter left, Sarah put away the pretty blue dress and put on a plain brown one. She wasn't going to wear anything that attracted that old devil's attention.

When Sarah entered the dining room, Sister Richter didn't even notice she wasn't wearing the pretty blue dress. Somehow that old woman's brain just didn't work like everyone else's.

All day Sunday, Sarah studied the problem of finding her brothers but found no solution.

On Monday, Sister Richter woke Sarah at dawn. "Get up and get dressed, sweetheart. You've got school today."

"School?" Sarah said.

"Yes, school. It's the law, you know. You must attend school."

Sarah's heart fluttered. Maybe her schoolmates had heard something about her brothers.

"Which dress are you going to wear?" Sister Richter said.

Sarah walked to the closet and pulled out a green one.

"Oh yes, that's very pretty," Sister Richter said and left the room.

As Sarah hummed and thought about returning to her school friends, heavy footsteps sounded on the stairs. She jumped into bed and pulled the covers up around her neck. A moment later, Reverend Richter entered the room and glared at her. "If you're thinking of telling anyone about what's happened here, I would advise against it. Who are people going to believe, a minister or God or a trouble-making runaway? And since you don't know where your brothers are, you can't afford to run away again for fear of never finding them. So if you know what's good for you, you will keep your mouth shut," he said and tramped back downstairs.

Sarah's mind whirled. He was right. Until she could find Johnny and Mark, he had her right where he wanted her.

At school, all the kids clustered around Sarah.

"Wow! Look at you!" Avis Potter said. "What a perty dress!"

"Yeah, Sister Richter give me six of 'em. The Reverend likes seein' me in 'em," Sarah said as she tugged at the sleeve and almost tore it.

"We heard that y'all ran away to St. Louie," Gracie Lamp said.

"Yeah, we did, but they caught us and brung us back."

"Whur's Johnny and Mark?" Brewster Holland said.

"I don't know. They took them somewhur else and won't tell me whur. Have any of y'all heard anythang 'bout 'em?"

All the kids shook their heads.

"'Ey say ya hoboed to St. Louie," Curlly Wayne Booth said.

"Yeah, we did."

Curlly laughed. "Well, that there dress shore-nuff makes ya look like a bum."

Without a word, Sarah marched to Curlly, landed a hard right hook on his nose, and knocked him to the ground. She wasn't sure why she did it. He had said a lot worse things to her before. But it sure felt good to whack him.

As Curlly staggered back to his feet, Miss Gibson stepped outside carrying the bell. "What's going on here?"

Gracie lit up like a sunburst. "Curlly insulted Sarah, and she punched him."

Sarah put on a stern face and stared at Miss Gibson, who was straining to hold back a laugh. "Well, Sarah! That's a fine way to return to school!"

"He had it comin'," Avis said. "He called Sarah a 'bum.'"

"Well, dust yourself off, Curlly, and everybody come inside. It's time to start classes," Miss Gibson said, and she clanged the bell.

At ten o'clock in St. Louis, the doctor released Elizabeth from the hospital. Since the landlord had already cleaned out her and Hank's apartment and sold their belongings to cover what he called "expenses," Kate took Elizabeth home with her.

As the women stepped off the bus in front of the drug store where they had seen the kids on TV, Elizabeth froze. "I gotta find my babies."

Seeing where they were, Kate grasped her friend's arm and tugged her past the shop. "And I'll help you. I'll make some phone calls, and by this afternoon, we'll know something."

At the apartment, Elizabeth sat down in the living room, and Kate got them both a glass of water. While they rested, Kate dug dimes out of her purse. "Okay, I'm going to make those phone calls, and when I get back, hopefully, I'll have good news."

Kate walked to the porch, picked up the phone receiver, and dialed "O." "Operator, get me the police administrative offices."

"I'm sorry, you'll have to dial that yourself," the operator said. "The number is Central 1212."

Kate got a new dial tone, deposited a dime, and dialed the number.

"Police Headquarters, Officer Cagill. How may I help you?"

"Hello, officer, my name is Kate Carson, and I'm calling on behalf of my friend, Elizabeth Pinscher, who is–"

"Excuse me–Did you say someone named 'Pinscher' is calling?" Cagill said as his voice raced.

"Yes, my friend, Mrs. Hank Pinscher, is trying to–"

"Just a moment, ma'am. I'll be right back." The sound muffled as the officer obviously covered the phone with his hand, but Kate could still hear what he was saying. "Hey, Lieutenant–This is that Pinscher woman we've been looking for."

The sound cleared, and another man spoke. "Hello, Mrs. Pinscher–Mrs. Hank Pinscher?"

"No, my name's Kate Carson, but I'm a friend of hers. She's staying with me right now."

"That's Colossal! Would you have her call Lieutenant Hickson at police headquarters? I've got an urgent message for her."

"If it's about her children, that's why I'm calling."

"Well, Ma'am, I'm not allowed to say what it's about. Just have her call me. I need to speak to her ASAP."

"Well, there's no need for that. Just hang on a minute, and I'll go get her for you."

Kate let the receiver dangle and ran back into her apartment. "This is really strange, Elizabeth, but there's a police Lieutenant Hickson on the phone who wants to talk to you."

"Talk to me? Why?"

"I don't know, but he says it's 'urgent.'"

Kate helped Elizabeth to the phone and handed her the receiver. "Hello, this is Mrs. Hank Pinscher," she said. Then she turned pale and crumpled to the floor.

"Elizabeth!" Kate shouted. She sat down, laid Elizabeth's head in her lap, and grabbed the phone. "What did you tell her? She just fainted."

"I told her that her husband was killed in an accident at the truck plant last Tuesday."

"Well, why didn't you just tell me? I could've broken the news to her a whole lot gentler than you did."

"Because we're not allowed to tell anyone but the next of kin when something like this happens. They have to be the first ones we notify."

"Well, you just told me, didn't you?"

"Yes, I did, but I had already told *her*, so the next of kin *had* already been notified."

"Why didn't you come over here and tell her in person?"

"Well, with everything else that's been happening lately, we'd lost track of her. We didn't know where she was till you called. We tried to contact her at the hospital, but she'd already been released."

"Yes, and now, thanks to your stupidity, she'll probably have to be readmitted," Kate said. She slammed the receiver against the wall and wrapped her arms around Elizabeth.

When Elizabeth revived, Kate took her back inside and helped her lay down on the couch. "I thought he said Hank had been killed."

"I'm sorry, Elizabeth, but that is what he said."

Elizabeth gasped and stared up at Kate. "So what am I gonna do now? I ain't got nowhur to go nor nobody to take care of me."

"Don't you worry!" Kate said. "We'll get you through this just fine! The first thing I'm doing is calling that police lieutenant's supervisor. They've got some explaining to do about why they notified you this way."

"What did you find out about my babies?"

"Nothing–I didn't get a chance–but I will. Right now, we're going to put you to bed so you can rest. Then I'll take care of everything else. And when you wake up, hopefully, I'll have some answers for you."

While Elizabeth slept, Kate called the Department of Child Welfare and the Police Headquarters. Both agencies agreed to send representatives to the apartment that afternoon to conduct interviews. Then Kate called the payroll manager at the factory where Hank had worked and arranged for his final paycheck to be sent to Elizabeth at her address.

At two o'clock, police internal affairs arrived, and Kate filed a formal complaint against Lieutenant Hickson. Nothing would probably ever come of it, but at least she got the satisfaction of filing it. And maybe, just maybe, it would end up in Hickson's permanent work record to remind him never to do anything that stupid again.

At three-fifteen, Kate answered another knock at her door.

"Hello, I'm Betty Turner from the Department of Child Welfare," the woman said. "I believe someone here called us?"

"Yes, come in," Kate said. "My friend, Elizabeth Pinscher, has some questions about her missing children. She's lying down in the bedroom."

"Oh, is she ill?"

They walked to the center of the room and stopped.

"I wish that's all it was," Kate said. "She just received word that her husband was killed last Tuesday in an industrial accident."

"Oh, my gracious! Should I wait and come back later?"

"No, she wants to talk to you now. But you need to know she looks pretty rough. She's been hospitalized all week because of a beating her husband gave last Monday."

"Well, I deal with abuse cases all the time, so I'm not easily shocked by such things," Miss Turner said, and they continued to the bedroom.

Kate knocked on the door, and they stepped inside. "Elizabeth? Are you awake?"

"Yeah, I'm just restin'."

"Well, we're finally going to find out something about your babies. This is Miss Turner from the child welfare office. She's here to get some information about them."

"That's wonderful!" Elizabeth said and shook Miss Turner's hand.

Kate brought in a kitchen chair, and Miss Turner sat down beside the bed. "If you ladies need anything, just call me," she said. Then she walked out of the room and closed the door.

"Well, Mrs. Pinscher, are you ready to begin?" Miss Turner said.

"Yes, but please, call me 'Elizabeth.'"

"Okay, Elizabeth, before we start, I want you to know I'll be asking some very personal questions. It's not that I'm trying to be snoopy. It's just that I'll need to know certain things for the investigation."

"Yes, I understand," Elizabeth said.

"So tell me your story, and I'll stop you when I need to ask a question."

Elizabeth told how Hank had forced her to leave her kids, how he had beaten her, and how he had been killed. Then she told about seeing her kids on the television news, and Miss Turner gasped.

"Oh! The Skaggs children!"

"Yes," Elizabeth said. "Sarah, Johnny, and Mark Skaggs. They're my babies."

Miss Turner bounced from her chair. "Oh, my goodness! Excuse me, Elizabeth! I've got to go make a phone call! I'll be right back!" she said and dashed from the room.

Thirty minutes later, a tall, elegant woman knocked on the front door, and Kate escorted her into the bedroom.

Miss Turner stood up and smiled. "Well, Alexis, it looks like we've cracked this one. This is Mrs. Elizabeth Pinscher, the mother of Sarah, Johnny, and Mark Skaggs."

"Well, hello, Mrs. Pinscher. I am Alexis Jordan," she said as they shook hands. "I enjoyed getting to know your children."

"You know my babies?"

"Yes, I do. They were with us at the shelter for almost a week while the police searched for you. When they failed to find you, we returned the children to Arkansas. I escorted them back to Piggott on the train just three days ago."

"Are they okay?"

Miss Jordan smiled. "Yes, they are just fine–healthy as horses and fit as fiddles, except that Mark is always hungry."

Elizabeth laughed. "Yeah, that's my little Marky. How can I get back to 'em? They need me."

"Well, we have connections with several philanthropic organizations that help us with cases like yours. When I return to my office, I will contact one of them and make the necessary arrangements. Are you well enough to travel?"

"Yes, ma'am! I'm well enough to do anythang to get back to my babies. When can we leave?"

"In a few days, I hope. We should have you back together within a week."

Elizabeth frowned. "A week? Why so long?"

"Because a lot has to be done to ensure everything goes smoothly. In the meantime, you can rest and get your strength back. I will come by and update you every couple of days."

The welfare ladies said goodbye. Then Kate escorted them outside and hurried back to the bedroom.

"I cain't believe I'm goin' back to my babies," Elizabeth said as tears trickled down her face.

Kate took hold of her hand and smiled. "See! I told you it would happen! Now, take a nap, and when you wake up, I'll fix us a nice supper."

With the detailed notes Miss Jordan made on her train ride back to St. Louis from Piggott, the St. Louis Welfare Administrator convinced the Clay County Welfare Administrator to investigate the conduct of caseworker Gloria Galloway and County Sheriff Charles Crane. And they scheduled a 3:00 p.m. hearing on Thursday, August 12th, at the Piggott Welfare Office.

Because Miss Jordan had to attend the hearing, she would also use the trip to escort Elizabeth to Piggott. So she booked them on the nine o'clock train Thursday morning.

On Tuesday, August 10th, Clay County Welfare Administrator Collier Collins notified Caseworker Gloria Galloway of the scheduled hearing, and she immediately called Sheriff Crane.

"Hey, Charlie, that bitch from St. Louis really did file a complaint against us, and there's gonna be a hearing Thursday afternoon."

"So? She cain't do nothin'. She don't have jurisdiction down here."

"No, *she* don't, but Mr. Collins does, and he's conducting the hearing. We'd better get a lawyer."

"Nah, that costs money."

"Maybe, and maybe not. What if I can work out an arrangement with him?"

Charlie's end of the phone fell silent. "'An arrangement?' What 'bout our 'arrangement?'"

"Well, this won't interfere with that. It just means you'll have to share me for a while."

"I don't like sharin'. Who ya thankin' 'bout gettin'?"

"Harry Hampton. He's always lookin' at me."

"I don't wonna hear that. How long of an arrangement?"

"Just long enough to get us past this."

"I still don't like it."

"Well, what else can we do?"

"How 'bout we just forget it and take our chances?"

"Take a chance on gettin' fired or goin' to jail? Oh no! Not me!"

"Oh hell, they cain't do that. Can they?"

"Yeah, I think they can."

"Well . . . all right then, call him," Charlie said and hung up.

 A few minutes later, Gloria called him back.

"Okay, it's all set. But besides the arrangement, he wants two hundred dollars."

"Two hundred dollars? That asshole!"

"Just pay him, Charlie. It might save us a whole lotta trouble."

"If you'd just kept your mouth shut at the depot, we wouldn't be goin' through this."

"Well, if that's how ya feel, then why don't I just cancel your arrangement and go full-time with Harry?"

"All right–All right–I'll pay it. But when this is over, I'm gettin' even with that little bastard. And since he's gettin' an arrangement, he'd better keep us outta trouble."

"Oh, get a grip, Charlie. It ain't like I'm your wife or nothin.'"

"Well, if ya was my wife, I prob'ly wouldn't care so much."

"You know, Charlie, sometimes you're a real horse's ass."

"Oh yeah? Well, sometimes you're a total slut whore."

"Yeah . . . and you love it. Don't tell me you don't. By the way, Harry wants us to come by his office in the mornin' for a consultation."

"Damn it! I ain't got time for that!"

"He's expectin' us to bring him his money, Charlie, in case you don't get what that's about. And he wants cash."

"Cash? That means I gotta go to the bank."

"Well then, do it! We can't afford any delays on this! And I hope you're in a better mood tomorrow."

"Don't count on it," Charlie said and hung up the phone.

Chapter 20

MAMA'S JOURNEY HOME

ALTHOUGH ELIZABETH STAYED busy every day until the trip, the hours still crawled by. On Wednesday night, she went to bed early, hoping to make the night pass faster. But, no matter what she did, sleep wouldn't come. Several times she got up, walked to the window, and gazed at the waxing moon with tears of joy in her eyes.

At first light on Thursday, she bathed and got dressed. Then she set her clothes bag beside the front door and sat down in one of the big living room chairs to wait.

Thirty minutes later, Kate shuffled into the room. "Good morning, Elizabeth. How'd you sleep?" she said as she propped open the front door.

"Hardly a wink," Elizabeth said.

"Oh well, tonight, you'll be back with your babies, and you'll all sleep cuddled up together."

Elizabeth smiled. "Yes, and I cain't hardly wait."

"Come on," Kate said and pulled Elizabeth to her feet. "I'll fix us a good breakfast. We don't want you heading to Arkansas on an empty stomach."

As they strolled to the kitchen, tears rose in Elizabeth's eyes. "I'm really gonna miss you, Kate. You been a wonderful friend to me. I don't know what I'd done without ya."

"Aww!" Kate said and hugged her. "You've been a wonderful friend to me too. But just because you're leaving doesn't mean we can't stay in touch. Stamps are only three cents. So when you get set-tled, send me your address, and we'll write to each other."

"I will, but that ain't the same as bein' able to do thangs together."

"No, but it's the next best thing, except for a phone call."

"Well, I ain't gonna have no money for phone calls. I don't know how I'm gonna make a livin'. I ain't ever worked no place but home since Ralph and me got married. I don't know how to do nothin' but clean house and cook."

"Well, lots of people hire housekeepers and cooks. Everybody wants a clean house, and everybody has to eat. You know people there, and they'll help you get started."

"Actually, I never got acquainted with many folks there since we lived way out in the country and always stayed home."

"Maybe not, but your kids will help you. With all of you working together, you'll do just fine. And besides, you don't have to stay there. You can move somewhere else if you want to."

Elizabeth shook her head. "I wouldn't know whur. All my folks are dead now, so I wouldn't wonna move back to Millcreek."

While they talked, Kate brewed coffee, fried sausage, scrambled eggs, and made toast.

When they sat down to eat, Elizabeth tugged on her dress. "I gained weight since I been here with you."

Kate chuckled. "Well, I always thought you were too thin. I'm glad to have fattened you up some."

As they finished eating, Miss Jordan knocked on the door.

"Come in," Kate said as she and Elizabeth entered the living room. "Would you like a cup of coffee?"

"No, thank you," Miss Jordan said. "I have already had my Java limit for the day." Then she smiled. "How are you this morning, Elizabeth?"

"Excited and nervous. I been awake all night and ready to go since six-thirty."

"Well, this will be a big day for you and your children. I have not told anyone in Piggott that we have found you, so they do not know you are coming. It will be a wonderful surprise for your children."

Then Miss Jordan glanced around the room. "Where are your bags? I will help you carry them to the taxi."

Elizabeth pointed to the paper sack beside the front door. "I only got one."

Miss Jordan frowned. "That is all?"

"Well, not exactly," Kate said. She scampered to her bedroom and returned with another large bag. "I gathered up a few things for you, Elizabeth. I meant to give them to you before Miss Jordan arrived. It's not much–just a couple of dresses, some underwear, and a little makeup–but it'll get you by for now."

Elizabeth smiled. "See what I mean, Kate? You saved me again."

Kate looked at Miss Jordan. "When Elizabeth was admitted to the hospital, and her husband was sent to jail, our landlord didn't think they were coming back, so he sold all their good belongings and threw away the rest."

"How did he get away with that?" Miss Jordan said.

Kate chuckled. "You've never lived in apartments like these, have you, Miss Jordan?"

"No, fortunately, I have not."

"Well, the landlords of these places know they can get away with almost anything, so they do."

Miss Jordan eased to Elizabeth and took hold of her hand. "I am sorry. I did not mean to embarrass you. Had I known you needed clothing, I would have brought you some. We have nice used garments at the shelter. I will call Miss Turner and have her bring some things to the train station before we leave."

"Ah, ya don't need to do that," Elizabeth said.

"Yes, I do!" Miss Jordan said. She dug a dime out of her purse and marched outside to the payphone.

"Oh, that reminds me," Kate said. She walked to the bureau, pulled out an envelope, and handed it to Elizabeth. "This is your husband's final pay from the factory. I called and had them send it here."

Elizabeth tore open the envelope, and her jaw dropped. "Fifty-four dollars and forty-seven cents!"

"See!" Kate said. "You're not broke after all!"

"I'd never thought to ask for this or even knowed how. Thanks, Kate! Now, whur am I gonna put it, so I don't lose it?"

"Stuff it in your bra. It'll be safe there," Kate said, and they laughed.

"Yeah, nobody but me'll be stickin' their hand in there."

Elizabeth stowed the envelope, then she and Kate picked up the bags and strolled to the front porch. While they hugged and said goodbye to each other, Miss Jordan finished her phone call. Then she took the bag from Kate, and she and Elizabeth hurried to the taxi.

At eight-thirty, the cab pulled up in front of Union Station, and the women walked inside.

"This place is beautiful!" Elizabeth said as they weaved through the crowd.

"Yes, it is. Your daughter called it 'a palace.'" Miss Jordan said.

Elizabeth smiled. "Yes, she's right. It is. Sarah's always liked perty thangs."

On their way to the platform, Miss Turner ran up to them carrying a suitcase. "I thought I was going to miss you. My cab driver was a slowpoke."

"What did you bring?" Miss Jordan said.

"Three dresses, some foundation garments, and some toiletries," Miss Turner said.

Elizabeth squinted. "What're 'foundation garments?'"

"You know–" Miss Jordan said and slid her hand up and down her thigh. "–underwear."

Elizabeth blushed and laughed. "Oh! I never heard it called that before."

Miss Turner set the luggage on a trashcan, packed everything from the bags into it, and handed it to Elizabeth. "Now you only have one thing to carry."

"Thank you, Miss Turner," Elizabeth said. "And thank you for helpin' me get back to my babies. I'll always be obliged to ya for that."

Miss Turner smiled. "It's my pleasure. Reunions like this one make our jobs rewarding. I'll have Miss Jordan tell me all about it when she returns."

"Well, we had better go," Miss Jordan said. "I will see you later, Betty. And thanks for bringing the clothes."

With the suitcase in hand, Elizabeth followed Miss Jordan to the train.

"Hello, gentlemen," Miss Jordan said as they approached two men standing beside the coach. "Elizabeth Pinscher, this is my boss, Mr. Franklin Frazier, and this other handsome fellow is Mr. William Diamond, a Missouri Department of Welfare lawyer. On our journey, they will brief you about the hearing."

"Hearin'?" Elizabeth said. "What hearin'?"

Miss Jordan explained the reason for the hearing, little of which Elizabeth understood. She also said that Franklin and Billy had contacted one of their Arkansas attorney friends who had agreed to represent Elizabeth and her children pro bono, whatever that meant, to prevent them from being bullied into any "unfavorable outcomes." And that confused Elizabeth even more. As she listened to their strange explanation, a knot formed in her stomach, and she burst into tears. "Are ya sayin' I might not get my babies back?"

Miss Jordan raised her hand and stopped the conversation. "Gentlemen, we are scaring her." She wrapped her arm around Elizabeth. "You are positively getting your babies back. There is absolutely no doubt about that. They will be at the hearing. However, you may not get to be with them until after the proceedings have ended. So you will need to be patient."

"I'll try," Elizabeth said as she smiled and wiped away her tears.

"All aboard!" shouted the porter standing beside the coach entrance.

"Okay, let's go," Miss Jordan said. "Billy, take Elizabeth's suitcase."

The porter helped the ladies up the steps. Then the men climbed aboard. Halfway down the aisle, Miss Jordan stopped at two seats facing each other. While she and the men stowed their cases in the overhead rack, Elizabeth slid into the first seat and scooted over next to the window. Then Miss Jordan sat down beside her, and the men settled in across from them.

"Elizabeth, have you ever ridden a train before?" Miss Jordan said.

"Yeah, when I's married to Jesse James," she said, and everyone laughed. "No, this is my first time."

"Well, it is pleasant in some ways and unpleasant in others. The scenery is nice, but the ride is bouncy and noisy."

Suddenly, the car jerked and eased away from the station. While the group made small talk, the train pulled onto the mainline and crossed the Mississippi River. As it picked up speed, the conductor entered the coach.

"What time will we get to Piggott?" Miss Jordan said as he punched their tickets.

He pulled out his watch and glanced at it. "About two-thirty, ma'am, if we stay on schedule."

"Thank you," Miss Jordan said. Then she chuckled.

"Whatsamatter?" Billy Diamond said.

"Oh, I just had a bit of déja vu. On my last trip to Piggott, I asked the conductor that same question and got the very same answer."

"Do you think that's some kind of omen?" Billy said.

"No, it just means the train is on schedule."

While Elizabeth stared out the window, she thought about her kids. In less than five hours, she would be back with them.

During the trip, Miss Jordan and the men discussed the hearing and reassured Elizabeth that she would get back with her children. But they also said hearings sometimes reveal information that can lead to unexpected twists, and if that happened, she shouldn't worry. They would bring things back into line when needed.

At nine-thirty in Piggott, Miss Galloway picked up the telephone.

"Good morning, Reverend. This is Gloria Galloway," she said when he answered. "I just wanted to tell you, I'll be picking up Sarah from school for a hearing at our office this afternoon."

"What kind of hearing?"

"Oh, that caseworker who escorted the kids back from St. Louis got snooty with the sheriff and me, so we laid down the law to her. Now, she's filed a complaint against us, but I'm sure it'll all blow over without much trouble."

"Well, Sarah will need to clean up before attending something that important, so I'll go get her, and you can pick her up here."

"All right. I'll be there at two."

"Okay, she'll be ready."

While Sarah and her friends played hopscotch during morning recess, the Reverend entered the schoolyard.

"Hey, look who's here," Gracie Lamp said.

Sarah turned just in time to glimpse the Revered as he disappeared into the schoolhouse. "What's he doin' here?" She handed the toss rock to Gracie and ran to the building just as the adults stepped outside.

"Hey, Sarah," Miss Gibson said. "Reverend Richter has come to take you home."

"Why? What's wrong?"

"Nothing's wrong," he said. "You're just needed at the welfare office."

Sarah cringed and then smiled. "Am I gonna get to see my brothers?"

"No, I don't think so," the Reverend said, and Sarah's smile faded.

"There's going to be a hearing this afternoon," the Reverend said as they walked along the highway. He grabbed Sarah by the shoulders and peered into her eyes. "While you're there, you'll behave yourself. You hear me?"

"Yeah, I hear ya," Sarah said and broke his grip. The silly old devil wanted her to love him like Angela did, but that wasn't going to happen.

At home, the Reverend watched Sister Richter bathe Sarah. Then he dried her and blotted her welts. "If you misbehave today, I'll have to give you more of these, but if you're good, I won't."

Sarah stared blankly across the room. "I'll be good."

While she was still naked, the Reverend led her upstairs. "Now show me what a good girl you can be," he said and pushed her onto the bed.

Once again, Sarah withdrew deep inside herself to her safest memory. Her mother was rocking her to sleep and singing.

"Je-sus loves-me this-I-know. For-the Bi-ble tells-me-so," spontaneously flowed from Sarah's lips.

At noon on the train, Miss Jordan led the group to the dining car. While everyone else ate, Elizabeth only drank a glass of sweet iced tea.

"Are you sure that is all you want?" Miss Jordan said. "It is a long time until dinner."

"Yes, I'm sure," Elizabeth said. "I just ain't hungry."

"Well, if you change your mind, let me know."

The group finished lunch and returned to the coach.

"What time is it?" Elizabeth said.

Mr. Diamond glanced at his watch. "Five minutes till one."

"Still a hour-and-a-half to go," Elizabeth murmured.

Miss Jordan took her by the hand. "Yes, only an hour-and-a-half more, and we can get off this bumpy old train. I have had just about all the bouncing I can take for one day, haven't you?"

Elizabeth grinned and nodded, but she hadn't even noticed the bouncing. Her thoughts were on her kids.

At two o'clock, while Sarah stood at the living room window and fastened her locket around her neck, a State Police car pulled into the Richters' driveway. Miss Galloway got out, walked to the porch, and knocked on the door.

"Remember what I told you," Reverend Richter said as he led Sarah to the door and opened it.

"Good afternoon, Reverend," Miss Galloway said and smiled her fake smile.

"And a good afternoon to you too, Miss Galloway. Well, here she is, all cleaned up and ready to go."

Sarah glared at the woman and gritted her teeth. Then she looked at the car. Behind the steering wheel sat Trooper Fred Johnson, who had once arrested Hank for drunk driving. But Trooper Johnson wasn't the only one in the car. Sarah squinted at the passengers in the back seat, and her mouth flew open. "Johnny! Marky!" she hollered and then dashed to the car.

"Come back here!" Miss Galloway shouted and ran after her.

Sarah yanked the car door open and hopped in beside her brothers.

As the kids hugged one another and giggled, Miss Galloway grabbed Sarah's legs and tried to pull her back outside. When that failed, she slapped Sarah's calves.

Trooper Johnson jumped out of the vehicle and pulled Miss Galloway away from Sarah. "Stop it, Gloria! You're out of control!" he shouted and shoved her into the front seat.

"Outta control, my ass!" Miss Galloway shouted back. "That girl's the one who's outta control!"

Sarah and her brothers clung to one another and gawked at the ruckus while the Richters watched from their front porch.

Trooper Johnson closed the passenger doors, waved to the Richters, and climbed back into the driver's seat.

As they drove away, Miss Galloway glared at Sarah. "You need your butt whipped, girl, and I'm just the one who can do it!"

Trooper Johnson scowled. "Gloria, if you say another word, I'll arrest you."

Miss Galloway faced forward, crossed her arms, and locked her jaws.

Then Sarah's mouth flew open, and she laughed. Miss Jordan must be back. What else could make Miss Galloway so mad?

When they arrived at the welfare building, Miss Galloway jumped out of the car and ran inside. Trooper Johnson took the kids to Mr. Bradford, then he went to the office and filed a report about what had just happened.

At two-thirty-seven, the train squealed to a stop at the Piggott depot. As the St. Louis group stepped from the train, two men in business suits approached them.

"Hello, I'm Collier Collins, Clay County welfare administrator," the man in front said.

"And I'm Franklin Frazier, St. Louis welfare administrator," Frank said, and they shook hands. Then Frank gestured to the group behind him. "And these folks are Missouri Department of Welfare Attorney William Diamond, Caseworker Miss Alexis Jordan, and Mrs. Elizabeth Pinscher, mother of the Skaggs children."

"Well, this is a surprise," Mr. Collins said as he reached out and took Elizabeth's hand. "Welcome, Mrs. Pinscher. It's a pleasure to meet you."

Then Mr. Collins gestured to the man standing beside him. "And I believe most of you already know Attorney Ustus Harlow."

"Yeah, we know the bum," Billy Diamond said as he and Ustus shook hands and hugged. "He used to steal my pocket change when we were roommates during law school."

Then Franklin and Ustus shook hands. "How've ya been, Harlow?"

"Obviously better than you guys from the looks of your clothes. Where'd y'all get them rags?"

Franklin straightened his tie, brushed his sleeves, and folded his arms. "I'll have you know, this is a genuine Scuzzy Duds outfit."

"Scuzzy's right," Ustus said. He reached up and felt Billy's lapel. "Just as I thought, straight off the thrift store rack."

"So, Ustus, what's that trash you're wearin'?" Billy said.

"Like it, do ya? This is gen-u-wine, Hong Kong, hand-tailored silk."

"Uh-huh! Well, it looks like a worn-out shoeshine rag," Franklin said.

"Haven't you guys made *any* money since we graduated law school?" Ustus said.

"Well, maybe we state attorneys don't get paid as much as you independent lawyers do," Billy said, "but at least we have a steady income."

Miss Jordan stepped in-between the men. "Okay, gentlemen, that's enough. Elizabeth is already nervous without you acting like a bunch of teenagers. Try being professionals for once."

The attorneys looked at Elizabeth and put on their humblest faces. Billy eased to her and put his arm around her shoulders. "She's right, Mrs. Pinscher. We may act like spoiled college boys when we're just goofin' off, but we're all top-notch professionals when we're expected to be. And I guarantee we'll have nothing but your interests in mind during this hearing."

Billy motioned to Ustus, and he walked over to them. "This is Ustus Harlow. He claims to be Jean Harlow's cousin, but he's never proved that to us–"

"My mother was one of the Kansas City Harlows. She's related to Jean's mother–"

"Yeah! Yeah! Yeah!" Billy said. "Anyway, he's here if you need him, and despite his bad manners, when it comes to lawyerin', he's darn good at it. In fact, he's never lost a case." Billy glared at Ustus. "That is still true, isn't it?"

"Yeah, it's still true."

"You probably won't need him, but we're holdin' him in reserve just in case. As they say, 'It's better to be safe than sorry.'"

"Well, that is good to hear," Miss Jordan said. "Now, one of you, pick up Elizabeth's suitcase, and let's get to the hearing."

Chapter 21

THE HEARING

AS MISS GALLOWAY and her group entered the conference room, she peered at Miss Jordan and her group. "Who's that skinny little woman in the hand-me-down dress?"

"I don't know," Harry Hampton said, "but I'll find out." He walked to the St. Louis group, introduced himself, and then returned. "She's the Skaggs children's mother."

"What? Where'd she come from?" Miss Galloway said. "I thought she was missing."

"She was until Monday when she contacted them," Harry said.

As they continued to discuss the matter, Mr. Collins led four new people into the room. "Let me have your attention," he said. "Before we begin, I'd like to introduce these folks. This is Arkansas Circuit Judge Preston Eiffel, Arkansas Child Welfare Attorney Virgil Stilly, Court Reporter Stella Langston, and Arkansas State Trooper Fred Johnson." Then Judge Eiffel and Miss Langston sat down at the head of the table, and Mr. Collins and Mr. Frazier sat down at its foot. The St. Louis and Piggott groups sat down at its sides, facing each other.

At three o'clock, Mr. Collins stood up and motioned for Trooper Johnson to close the door. "Mr. Frazier and I have asked Judge Eiffel to facilitate this hearing, and he has agreed. Although this is not a court of law, it will be conducted like one in many ways. However, this is simply a hearing to determine whether or not there has been any unethical, not criminal, behavior by a state employee and an

194

elected county official. Any disciplinary actions resulting from it shall be decided upon and carried out by the appropriate agencies. There will be *no* court-ordered sanctions.

"Are there any questions?" Mr. Collins said and scanned the faces around the table. "If not, then Judge Eiffel, I turn these proceedings over to you."

"Thank you, Mr. Collins." The judge said as he stood up. Then his demeanor shifted. "This hearing is now officially in session. It was requested by Clay County, Arkansas, Welfare Administrator Collier Collins after he received a complaint from St. Louis, Missouri, Welfare Administrator Franklin Frazier, alleging that improper procedures were followed by Arkansas Department of Child Welfare Caseworker Gloria Galloway and Clay County Sheriff Charles Crane, on the afternoon of Friday, August 6, 1954, when Missouri Department of Child Welfare Caseworker Alexis Jordan, accompanied Mrs. Elizabeth Pinscher's children, Sarah, Johnny, and Mark Skaggs, back to Piggott from St. Louis, where they were taken into protective custody after running away from their foster home in Austin Community on the night of July 30, 1954.

"Mr. Collins and Mr. Frazier, is that an accurate description of the filed complaint?"

"Yes, Your Honor," Mr. Frazier said.

Mr. Collins glanced at attorney Stilly and then answered, "Yes, Your Honor."

"Okay, then let's hear testimony," Judge Eiffel said. "Who will conduct questioning for the Missouri legal team?"

"I shall, Your Honor," Mr. Diamond said as he stood.

"Very well, Mr. Diamond. Call your first witness."

"Your Honor, I call Miss Alexis Jordan."

Miss Jordan rose, and Miss Langston administered the oath.

"Miss Jordan, on the afternoon of Friday, August 6th, did you escort Sarah, Johnny, and Mark Skaggs back to Piggott from St. Louis?" Mr. Diamond said.

"Yes, I did."

"Please tell us what happened when you and the children exited the train in Piggott?"

As Miss Jordan shared her version of the exchange, several times Elizabeth broke into tears. This was the first she had heard about her kids' hardships while searching for her.

When Mr. Diamond finished questioning Miss Jordan, Mr. Stilly cross-examined her.

"That was quite a tale, Miss Jordan. I'm curious how you can recall so many details from an event that occurred almost two weeks ago?"

"For several reasons, Mr. Stilly," Miss Jordan said. "First, I have an excellent memory. Second, because of the nature of my work, I have been trained to notice details. And third, I made meticulous notes on my train ride back to St. Louis that night while everything was fresh and clear in my mind."

"And, from the sound of it, all you've done since then is memorize them."

"Objection!" Mr. Diamond said.

"Sustained," Judge Eiffel said.

Mr. Stilly continued to press Miss Jordan but gained no ground, so he gave up and sat down.

"Mr. Diamond, please call your next witness," the judge said.

"I have no more witnesses at this time, Your Honor. However, I would like to reserve the right to call additional witnesses later."

"Very well," Judge Eiffel said. "Mr. Stilly, call your first witness."

"Your Honor. I call Miss Gloria Galloway."

Miss Galloway rose and took the oath.

Under Mr. Stilly's guidance, she either denied or skirted every accusation Miss Jordan had made.

Then Mr. Diamond questioned her. "Miss Galloway, how can you deny everything Miss Jordan said? Don't you have a conscience or any integrity?"

"Objection!" Mr. Stilly said.

Mr. Diamond apologized and then continued.

Miss Galloway, Miss Jordan testified that you 'grabbed' Sarah, 'shoved' her to the sheriff, and told him to 'lock her in the car.' Why did you do that?"

"Well, first of all, I didn't 'shove' her to him. I guided her to him."

"But you did tell him to 'lock her in the car.' Why did you do that?"

"To keep her from escaping. She'd caused us a lot of trouble, and I wasn't about to let that happen again."

"Were you angry when you said that?"

"No, I may have been agitated, but I wasn't 'angry.'"

"Miss Jordan also testified that you said the Skaggs children were 'troublemakers,' who 'should be sent to reform school.' Why did you say that?"

"I don't remember saying that, exactly. I may have said something similar, but it has all been taken out of context."

"Well, out of context or not, those are pretty harsh words. Miss Jordan also warned you and the sheriff that she would file a complaint against you if you took hostile custody of the Skaggs children, so why did you go ahead and do it?"

"For the children's safety. Miss Jordan was unstable."

Mr. Diamond laughed. "Oh, so now, in addition to being a caseworker, you're also a psychiatrist? Just what made you think she was 'unstable?'"

"Her refusal to sign the form. There was no logical reason for her not to do it."

"Well, in her testimony, she gave a very logical reason why she didn't sign it–your belligerent treatment of Sarah and your general hostility toward the children."

"Objection," Mr. Stilly said. "It hasn't been proven that Miss Galloway was 'belligerent' or 'hostile.'"

"Sustained," Judge Eiffel said.

"Is that when you—and I again quote Miss Jordan's testimony—'snatched the document from [her] hands, signed it, shoved it back in [her] face, and told [her] to "Get the hell out of here?"'"

"No, that's when the sheriff told her I was authorized to take custody of the children, and I was going to do so whether she signed the document or not. So I signed it, but she didn't."

"And then that's when you said, and I quote her testimony again, 'See, Miss Jordan, we have law enforcement officers here who will do the right thing regardless of so-called proper procedures.' Is that correct?"

"Well, ah . . . ah . . ."

Mr. Stilly frowned and shook his head.

"Thank you, Miss Galloway. That's all I have for this witness," Mr. Diamond said and sat down.

"But I'm not finished!" Miss Galloway said. "He's taken everything out of context!"

"I'm sorry, Miss Galloway," the judge said, "but your testimony has ended."

She clenched her jaws and glared at the judge.

"Mr. Diamond, earlier, you reserved the right to call additional witnesses," the judge said. "If you still want to do that, this is the time."

"Yes, Your Honor. I would like to question the Skaggs children."

Elizabeth gasped and grabbed Miss Jordan's arm. "My babies are here?" she whispered.

"Yes," Miss Jordan said. "But, as I told you on the train, you may not get to talk to them until after the hearing."

"Trooper Johnson, please bring in the children." Judge Eiffel said.

Elizabeth turned and faced the door. As Trooper Johnson led the children into the room, time ticked by in slow motion.

For a moment, the kids paused and glanced around the room. Then they saw *her.*

"Mama!" Sarah shouted, and they dashed to her.

"My babies!" Elizabeth cried. She dropped to her knees and scooped them into her arms.

Tears gushed from their eyes, even Johnny's.

Sarah latched onto her mother and covered her face with kisses. "Oh, Mama, we been so lost without ya. I done my best, but I just couldn't take care of us like you can."

"We been tryin' to find ya, Mama!" Mark said. "We looked all over St. Louie for ya."

"Yeah, I know. I seen ya on the television news."

"We's on TV?" Mark said. "Like The *Long* Ranger?"

"Yeah, just like him," his mother said and kissed his cheek.

"Oh, my sweet Sarah, Johnny boy, and Marky! I missed y'all so much!"

Sarah opened her locket. "Look, Mama. I kept this with me all the time, so I could see your picture. You's with me ever'whur I went."

"Aww, baby, that's sweet."

"Whur's Hank, Mama?" Mark said.

Sarah gawked at Mark. She hadn't even thought about Hank.

"Okay, folks, let's continue the hearing," Judge Eiffel said.

Miss Jordan set three chairs between herself and Elizabeth, and the kids sat down.

Across the table from them sat Miss Galloway. Sarah glared at her and made the same hand gesture to her that the angry driver had made to them in St. Louis. She still didn't know its meaning, but it felt mean and made the sheriff laugh.

"Children, I want you all to look at me," Judge Eiffel said. "This is a hearing to find out what happened when Miss Jordan brought you back to Piggott, so you'll be asked a lot of questions. And the first one is: Mark, do you know what telling the truth means?"

Mark nodded. "Not lyin'."

"That's right," the judge said. "Everything you all say here must be the truth, okay?"

199

"Okay," the kids said. Then they took the oath.

With an occasional nudge from Mr. Diamond, Sarah laid the background for the August 6th events by telling how Hank had made their mother leave them. Then she came to the part she had never told anyone. "Two days later, I got sick."

Mr. Diamond squinted. "Sick? What was wrong with you?"

Sarah hung her head and clamped her eyes shut. "I don't wonna talk 'bout it."

"Why not?"

"'Cause it's bad. Really bad!"

Johnny glared at his sister and grunted. "What's so bad 'bout a little bellyache?"

Sarah glared back at Johnny. "It wudn't just a bellyache. I almost bled to death, so I set in the river all day."

Her mother burst into tears. "Oh, my precious little girl. You's becomin' a woman, and I wudn't there for you."

Mr. Diamond peered at Judge Eiffel. "Your Honor, may we take a short break?"

The judge nodded. "Yes, we'll recess for ten-minute. Miss Jordan, take Sarah and her mother to someplace private. The boys will stay here."

Miss Jordan led Sarah and her mother into an empty office and closed the door.

"Oh, Sarah, baby!" her mother said. "I'm so sorry I wudn't here to help you through your first period. I never thought about you bein' old enough for that."

"Whatcha talkin' 'bout, Mama? Whatcha mean by 'period?'"

"You mean nobody's told ya what was happenin' to ya?"

"No, Mama, I ain't never told nobody 'bout that till now. I's too embarrassed by whur the blood was comin' from."

"You didn't tell your school teacher nor none of your girl friends?"

"No, Mama."

"Bless your heart!" She cupped Sarah's face in her hands, gazed into her eyes, and brushed her cheeks with her thumbs. "Sarah, darlin', when a little girl becomes a woman and can start havin' babies, she starts bleedin' down there."

Sarah frowned, and tears filled her eyes. "But I don't wont no babies!"

"No, sweetheart," her mother said and hugged her. "You ain't gonna have no babies right now. But you will when you get married. Havin' periods is just part of it. It happens to ever woman. It ain't nothin' to be sceared of or ashamed of."

"You mean there ain't nothin' wrong with me? I ain't dyin'?"

"No, darlin'," her mother said and squeezed her. "You're fine. That's just how it works."

Tears poured from Sarah's eyes.

"But from now on, you're gonna have one ever month."

"On what day did that happen?" Miss Jordan said.

"Two days after Mama left."

"We left on July 14th," her mother said.

"Elizabeth, are your periods regular?" Miss Jordan said as she flipped the wall calendar back a month.

"Perty much."

"That was thirty days ago," Miss Jordan said. "You should have another one any time now."

Sarah burst into tears again. "But I don't wont another'n!"

"Aww, honey, don't worry," her mother said and kissed her. "It'll be all right. I'll be with you next time, and we'll get you through it like a breeze."

Sarah wrapped her arms around her mother. "I'm so glad you're back."

"And I'm so glad to be back."

Miss Jordan smiled. "Well, our time is up. Let's get back to the hearing."

Sarah resumed her story by telling about the whipping the Reverend gave her. Then she told about running away to St. Louis, being caught by the police, and being taken to the shelter by Miss Jordan.

Finally, she told about their return to Piggott and confirmed what Miss Jordan had said about the scuffle with Miss Galloway at the depot.

"Miss Jordan, were these children given physical examinations when you took them to the shelter?" Judge Eiffel said.

"Yes, Your Honor."

"Were any abnormalities found?"

"Nothing other than the cuts and bruises one might expect to find on homeless children."

"There were no marks on Sarah consistent with having been whipped?"

"Well, possibly," Miss Jordan said. "She had marks on her back, thighs, and legs, but the doctor thought she had gotten them while traveling since she was wearing a thin dress."

"While in your custody, did Sarah ever mention being whipped?"

"No, not until we got back to Piggott."

"Excuse me, Your Honor," Mr. Diamond said. "Sarah did mention being whipped in the interview I did with her and her brothers when they first arrived at the shelter, but Miss Jordan wasn't present for that, and she hasn't read the transcript."

"I see," Judge Eiffel said. "Miss Jordan, you testified earlier that you had no behavioral problems with these children and that no corporal punishment was administered while they were in your custody. Is that correct?"

"Yes, Your Honor. We never spank children at our facility. We use more humane methods of discipline."

"Miss Galloway, have these children been examined by a doctor since they returned?"

"No, Your Honor. We didn't see any need for it since they seemed healthy."

Judge Eiffel looked at the boys. "Have either of you been spanked since you returned from St. Louis?"

"No," they said.

"Sarah, have you been spanked since you returned?" the judge said.

"Yes, but they ain't just spankin's! They're whuppin's with the Reverend's ole strap!"

"Is Reverend Richter the only one who has spanked you since your return?"

"Yes," Sarah said.

Trooper Johnson raised his hand, and the judge acknowledged him. "Your Honor, that's not entirely true. Miss Galloway spanked Sarah today while we were picking her up at the Richters' house. And when we got back, I filed a report on the incident."

"You filed a report here today?" the judge said.

"Yes, I did, Your Honor."

"Mr. Collins, why wasn't I informed of this?"

"I wasn't aware of it either, Your Honor."

"Is this true, Miss Galloway? Did you spank Sarah today?"

"No, sir! I just swatted her. When she saw her brothers in the car, she ran and jumped in beside them. I was just trying to keep them apart."

"Keep them apart?" Judge Eiffel said. "Why?"

"So they couldn't share information that might be harmful to this hearing."

"What information could these children possibly share that would be 'harmful to this hearing?'"

Miss Galloway shrugged. "I don't know. I thought they might make up a lie to tell. So I figured it was best to keep them apart."

"And were you able to do so?"

"No, Trooper Johnson interfered. He got between us."

Once again, Johnson raised his hand, and the judge recognized him. "Your Honor, I'll go get the report if you'd like to read it."

"No, I'll go," Mr. Collins said. He rushed from the room, returned with the document, and handed it to Judge Eiffel.

"Miss Galloway, it says here you 'slapped' Sarah's legs. Is that true?"

She scowled. "No, sir, that's not true. Like I said before, I just swatted her."

"What's the difference?" Judge Eiffel said.

"Swatting is just to get someone's attention. It doesn't hurt them."

"Oh, I see," Judge Eiffel said. Then he looked at the state policeman. "Trooper Johnson, is it possible you've exaggerated Miss Galloway's actions in your report?"

"No, Your Honor. I had to pull Miss Galloway away from the girl."

"Miss Galloway, is this true? Did Trooper Johnson have to physically restrain you?"

"Your Honor," Miss Galloway's lawyer said. "May I confer with my client?"

"Mr. Hampton," Judge Eiffel said, "if this is so you can advise her not to testify against herself, let me remind you this is not a court of law. It's simply a hearing. However, I'll withdraw the question to respect Miss Galloway's 5th Amendment rights. Now, let's get on with it."

Sarah leaned forward, propped her arms on the table, and continued her story. "Mr. Bradford took Johnny and Mark somewhur else to live, and Miss Galloway and the sheriff took me back to the Richters' house. After they left, that old devil come after me again with his strap. He drug me upstairs, tied me to the bed, and tore off my dress. Then he whupped me till I fainted." Without thinking, she jumped up, lifted her skirt, and exposed the welts on her thigh, and her mother burst into tears again.

"And that ain't all he done neither!" Then Sarah frowned. She wished she hadn't said that. She flopped down into her chair, folded her arms on the table, and laid her head on them.

"Sarah," Mr. Diamond almost whispered, "what do you mean, 'that's not all he did?'"

"Nothin'!" Sarah said.

"Sarah," Judge Eiffel said, "I want you to look at me, okay?"

"No!" she whimpered.

The judge eased from his chair. "Miss Jordan, Mrs. Pinscher, bring Sarah and come with me. Everyone else stay here. Trooper Johnson, don't let anyone leave this room, not even to use the restroom."

Judge Eiffel led the three women into the same office where they had been before and closed the door. "Sarah, show us those marks."

She lifted her dress, exposed the still raw welts, and her mother sobbed.

"Miss Jordan, I want you to give Sarah a thorough inspection from head to toe," the judge said. "But don't treat anything, and don't clean anything. When you're done, come and get me."

"Yes, sir," Miss Jordan said, and the judge returned to the hearing room.

Miss Jordan kept her cool in front of Sarah and her mother, but once alone in the hallway, she slammed her fist against the wall. She wanted just one minute with this Richter guy.

When she stopped shaking, she called the judge into the hall. "I did not say anything to her mother, but Sarah has had very recent sex."

"I was afraid of that," Judge Eiffel said. "Let's get a doctor here ASAP to examine her and collect evidence."

"Yes, sir," Miss Jordan said and rushed to the receptionist who telephoned the hospital.

A half-hour later, there was a knock at Room 9.

"Good afternoon. I'm Dr. Leslie Parker," the man in the white coat said as Miss Jordan opened the door. "I was told I was needed here."

"Yes, Dr. Parker. I am Alexis Jordan. Please follow me, and Judge Eiffel will explain."

She led him to the hearing room, called the judge into the hall, and introduced the men.

"Doctor, we have a young girl whom we suspect has been molested and abused," Judge Eiffel said. "I want you to examine her, document everything you find, and include your opinions on what may have caused your findings."

"Yes, sir," Dr. Parker said. "I'll need a private place to do the exam."

"One has already been prepared," Miss Jordan said. "I will go get the patient."

"I don't wont no examination," Sarah said as her mother and Miss Jordan led her to the examination room.

"But your injuries need treatment," Miss Jordan said. "I promise it will not hurt."

Sarah's mother helped her undress and lay down on the examination table. Then Miss Jordan covered her with a sheet and called in the doctor.

When he touched Sarah, she shuddered and sat up. It was kind of like what the Reverend had done to her. "No! I ain't lettin' ya do that!" She said. She wrapped the sheet around herself and slid off the table.

"But you have to," Miss Jordan whispered and put her arm around her. "Your mother and I are here and will protect you."

Sarah frowned. "But I don't wonna be touched that way."

Her mother took hold of her hand. "He's a doctor, baby, and sometimes they hafta touch our private parts to find out what's wrong with us."

The women coaxed Sarah back onto the table, and while the doctor examined her, she covered her eyes and cried.

"It's okay, baby," her mother said. "It'll all be over in a minute."

The doctor finished the examination, packed his equipment, and left the room. Sarah stood up and hung her head. She felt humiliated and embarrassed.

While dressing, she listened to the muffled conversation between the doctor and the judge in the next room. After the doctor left, the judge made a serious-sounding phone call.

As Sarah, her mother, and Miss Jordan walked back to Room 9, Judge Eiffel and Miss Langston stepped in line behind them. While Judge Eiffel explained that Prosecuting Attorney Godfrey was coming to investigate what had happened to Sarah, Miss Langston set up her dictation machine in one corner of the room.

When the prosecutor arrived, Judge Eiffel returned to the hearing room.

Mr. Godfrey sat down facing Sarah and gently smiled at her. "I want you to know, Sarah, that you haven't done anything wrong. What has happened to you was not your fault, okay?"

"Okay," Sarah said, but she wasn't entirely sure what he meant.

"Now, I'm going to ask you some questions, and I'm sorry, many of them will be embarrassing, but you'll need to answer them anyway, okay?"

Sarah glanced at her mother.

"Do like he says, baby."

"Okay," Sarah said as she looked back at Mr. Godfrey.

"All right. Let's begin."

Mr. Godfrey had Sarah describe every whipping the Reverend gave her. Then he had her tell, in detail, about all the *other things* the Reverend had done to her, including what he had done earlier that day.

At the end of the session, Sarah looked at her mother, who had cried almost the whole time. Then she looked at Miss Jordan, who had the same look on her face that Bo Jesus always got just before he whaled the daylights out of somebody.

"Sarah, I'm sorry you had to tell us all of this," Mr. Godfrey said. "But the man who did this to you has to be stopped, and this is the only way we have of doing that. You're a brave young woman, and we want to ensure this never happens to you or anyone else again, okay?"

"Okay," Sarah said. Then she ran to her mother, threw her arms around her, and they bawled like babies. Afterward, Sarah felt better than she had felt since she was a little girl in her daddy's arms.

Before leaving, Prosecutor Godfrey briefed Judge Eiffel on his interview with Sarah and drafted a warrant for Gustav Richter's arrest. The judge signed the document and then called Trooper Johnson into the hallway. "When I signal you, I want you to take this warrant, serve it on Gustav Richter, and lock him in jail."

As Johnson stepped back into the hearing room, Miss Galloway bumped into him, and the document popped out of his hand. She caught the form in midair and handed it back to Johnson, who stuffed it into his coat pocket and returned to his post.

In the hearing room, Judge Eiffel whispered something to Mr. Collins and Mr. Frazier, and they followed him out of the room. A moment later, they returned, and the judge called the hearing back to order.

Sarah snuggled against her mother and stared at the judge as he spoke.

"Mr. Collins, Mr. Frazier, has all testimony and evidence been presented?" Judge Eiffel said.

"Yes, Your Honor," the men replied.

"Well then, Mr. Collins, have you reached a decision?" Judge Eiffel said.

"Yes, Your Honor, I have. From the evidence presented here, it is my ruling that the behavior of both Miss Galloway and Sheriff Crane *was* unethical while dealing with the return of the Skaggs children. Although I have no authority over Sheriff Crane, I do have authority over Miss Galloway. Therefore, I am suspending her from her job, without pay, for ninety days. And from now on, she is to have absolutely no contact with Mrs. Pinscher or her children." He peered at Miss Galloway. "Is that understood?"

"No, Mr. Collins, that is not understood!" Miss Galloway shouted as she jumped to her feet. "How am I supposed to earn a living for the next three months?"

Mr. Collins glared at the caseworker. "You should have thought of that before misbehaving at the depot."

Harry Hampton cupped his hand over his mouth and leaned toward his client. "If you wanna keep your job, Gloria, then sit down and shut up. This hearing's not over yet."

Miss Galloway flopped down into her chair and folded her arms. Sarah felt like laughing but didn't.

"Your counsel's right, Miss Galloway," Mr. Collins said. "Consider yourself lucky I'm not firing you. And in case you really don't understand why I'm suspending you, it's because you maliciously disregarded the welfare of the Skaggs children, especially Sarah's. And now that a criminal investigation is underway, that's all I'm at liberty to say."

Mr. Collins turned back toward Judge Eiffel. "Your Honor, I turn these proceedings back over to you."

"Does anyone have anything further to say?" the judge said, and no one answered. "If not, then this hearing is adjourned." He waved to Trooper Johnson. "Proceed with your orders."

Gloria Galloway stood up, picked up her purse, and turned to Harry Hampton. "Some damned lawyer you are! Ninety days suspension without pay! Your arrangement's canceled!"

"Oh no, honey! That ain't how it works!" Harry said. "Since you committed the act in front of eyewitnesses, I couldn't do anything about it. You hung yourself, so you still owe me."

"Well, you'll hafta take me to court to get it, you silly bastard! Come on, Charlie! Let's get outta here! I'm gettin' me drunk."

Charlie leaned over to Harry. "Don't even let me suspect ya of tryin' to collect," he whispered. Then he and Gloria hurried from the room.

Chapter 22

SERVING THE WARRANT

OUTSIDE THE WELFARE building, while Miss Jordan and her group headed to the boarding house for dinner, Trooper Johnson got into his car and headed to the Richters' to serve the warrant. As he passed the two-mile-turn east of Piggott, he saw a large cloud of black smoke high in the sky in front of him. At first, he thought it was a farmer burning brush, but then he saw it was the Richters' house and stomped the accelerator.

Along the highway in front of the house, a small crowd of onlookers stood beside their haphazardly parked cars gawking at the sight. Johnson swerved into the driveway, skidded to a stop, and jumped out of his car.

A bucket brigade passed anything that would hold water, including a pair of old rubber boots, from the yard pump to a big man at the end of the line who tossed the water onto the few flames that still existed. However, there wasn't much point to it since the structure had already disintegrated into ashes.

"Where are the Richters?" Johnson shouted as he ran to the brigade.

The man dumping the water pointed to the smoldering ruins. "We figure they're in there."

"They didn't get out?"

"Nobody's seen 'em."

Johnson glanced at the old garage that had escaped the flames. "Is their car still here?"

"They didn't have one. When they wanted to go anywhere, they got somebody from church to take 'em."

"Has the coroner been called?"

"Not that I know of. You're the first official to arrive."

Johnson marched back to his car and picked up the two-way's microphone. "Trooper Johnson to Clay County–over."

"This is Clay County–over."

"Gordon, I need the coroner sent out here to the Richters' place in Austin. Their house just burned down, and it looks like they may not've gotten out–over."

"Roger, Fred. I'll send him right out. Anything else–over?"

"Yeah, maybe. Hang on a second." Johnson laid down the microphone and rushed back to the bucket brigade. "Who was the first one here?"

A man in sooty overalls stepped from the line and ambled over to him. "I reckon I was." He pointed west to the house across the field. "That's my place over yonder. I seen the smoke and come a-runnin'."

"What time was that?"

"Just after five."

"Did ya hear any hollerin', screamin', or anything that made ya think somebody was still inside?"

"Nope, not a thang."

Johnson rushed back to the radio. "Gordon, I came here to serve a warrant on Richter, so he may be runnin'. Let's put out an APB on him and his wife. They'll probably be hitchhikin' to one of the bus stations or train depots. He's tall, skinny, and gray-haired. She's short, chubby, and round-faced. I figure they'll be carryin' suitcases–over."

"10-4, Fred. I'll broadcast it ASAP–over and out."

While Johnson waited for the coroner, he poked at the ruins. Since he didn't see or smell anything unusual, he was pretty sure Richter had run. Somehow, Gustav must have gotten word about the warrant and ducked out. But how? Gloria Galloway had seen the warrant, but the fire would have already been going by then, so someone else must have warned him.

If Richter got to Missouri before the Arkansas police caught him, he might never be caught. Johnson jumped into his car and sped to the state line but saw nothing. He turned around at the Brown's Ferry Bridge and picked up the microphone. "Johnson to Clay County–over."

"This is Clay County–over."

"Gordon, call those three lawyers at the boardinghouse and ask 'em to meet me here at the fire site–over."

"10-4, Fred–over and out."

Johnson wasn't about to let this guy escape on his watch.

As the coroner drove away, Billy, Franklin, and Ustus pulled into the driveway.

"Hey, guys," Johnson said as they approached him. "I came out here to serve a warrant and found this. Since the coroner didn't find anything, I figure I've got a runner on my hands. If he's already in Missouri, he's out of my jurisdiction, and that's a real problem."

"Well, let's go check it out," Franklin said. "Where's the nearest bus station?"

"Holcomb," Johnson said.

"Then let's get over there. And on the way, you can fill us in on the details," Franklin said.

Johnson removed his uniform hat and coat and locked them in the trunk of his car. "Can I borrow a jacket from one of you guys? I don't wanna go over there lookin' like a cop."

Ustus pulled off his coat, and Johnson put it on. Then they piled into Ustus's car and drove to the bus station.

"Let's not tip our hand here," Johnson said. "One of you go in first, and if ya think ya see 'em, then I'll take a look through the window."

"Okay," Billy said. "I'll go buy some cigarettes." He stepped out of the car, walked inside, and came right back out. "Yeah, there's a couple in there that's probably them. Trouble is, they're sittin' against the wall. Ya can't see 'em from the window. You'll have to look through the front door."

"Humm, that'll be tricky," Johnson said. "If I can see them, they can see me."

"Here, take my hat," Ustus said. "It'll help hide your face."

"And we'll cause a distraction, so they'll be looking the other way," Billy said. "I'll go in and have a seat. Then you come in, Frank, and we'll wrestle around like old buddies who haven't seen each other in a long time. We'll walk outside and come back here."

"Sounds like a plan," Johnson said.

Billy got out, walked inside, and sat down just past the couple. Then Frank strolled in, and while they acted out their skit, Johnson peered in through the front door.

"Yeah, that's them," he said when they met back at the car.

"Now we need to know if they're going north or south," Billy said.

"Gotta be north," Johnson said. "I don't think he'd risk goin' south. The bus crosses back into Arkansas."

"Well, I'll go find out." Billy ran back inside and immediately returned. "Yeah, you're right. It's north. There aren't any more south bounds tonight."

Johnson squinted at the lawyers. "Ya know, one of us needs to be on that bus with 'em."

Suddenly, a blinding bolt of lightning flashed, a deafening clap of thunder exploded, and the guys ducked as a giant sycamore tree crashed to the ground across the street.

"Gee whiz, that was close!" Ustus shouted. "Let's get back in the car!"

Within seconds, marble-sized hail pummeled the area. Then it turned into blowing sheets of rain.

"Hey, I got an idea," Johnson said. "I know the city marshal here. Maybe he can help us. Let's drive over to his office."

As Ustus started the engine, a police car pulled in beside them and shined its spotlight on them. Johnson rolled down his window, and the light focused on him.

"I just got a call 'bout some suspicious-lookin' characters hangin' 'round over here," the officer inside the cruiser yelled. "Who are you fellers, and what're ya up to?"

"Hey, Denny, it's me, Fred Johnson. We's just comin' over to see you."

"Well, howdy 'ere, Fred. Looks like I saved ye a trip. Ye're a little ways outta your territory, ain't ye?"

"Yeah, a little," Johnson said. "But it's for a good reason. There's a guy in the bus station I have a warrant for, and I need him back in Arkansas so I can serve it. What are my chances of gettin' the next bus reroute through Brown's Ferry?"

"Well, how 'bout that? This rain just warshed out a bridge 'tween here and Camel," Denny said.

Johnson grinned and nodded. "That works for me. So, how we gonna make that happen?"

"I'll tell the ticket agent, he'll tell the driver, and it'll just happen."

"Dang!" Johnson said and laughed. "Sounds like magic. Let's do it."

Denny drove to the depot door, got out, and ran inside. Then he came out and pulled back around beside Ustus. "Okay, Fred, it's all set. The bus leaves here at nine-thirty."

Johnson Boy Scout saluted Denny. "Thanks, bud. I owe ya one."

"Don't worry, Fred. I'll get ya back," Denny said and drove away.

"Who's gonna ride the bus?" Johnson said.

"I guess I will," Ustus said. "I'm the only one they haven't seen."

"Here, you'll need this." Johnson took off Ustus's jacket and handed it back to him.

"And I'll take the umbrella," Ustus said as he put on his hat and stepped out of the car into the rain. "If anything goes wrong, pick me up at Campbell. That's as far as I'm going."

"Don't worry," Johnson said. "Nothin'll go wrong. I'll nab Richter as soon as the bus crosses the state line. Then you can get back in your car with Billy and Frank. They'll be right behind me."

"Okay," Ustus said. "Good luck to all of us!"

When the bus arrived, the Richters picked up their bags and boarded. Then Ustus got on and sat down in the seat right behind them. A moment later, the driver boarded, and they drove away.

As the bus approached the Brown's Ferry Bridge, Gustav saw where they were and jumped to his feet. "Stop the bus!" he yelled.

The driver stomped the brake, the bus skidded, and several passengers fell to the floor.

"What in the hell's goin' on?" the driver shouted.

"My wife and I are getting off," Gustav said.

"Are you crazy? It's rainin' cows and horses out there. It's even hailin'."

"Well, here goes nothin'," Ustus muttered. He jumped up, took Gustav by the shoulders, and shoved him back down into his seat. "No, Papa! You don't wanna get off yet. We're goin' to St. Louis, remember? Go on, driver. He's just a confused old man."

Gustav glared at Ustus. "Take your hands off me, young man!" He stood up again and grabbed his bags. "Stop this bus, driver! Come on, Sister Richter! We're getting off here right now!"

Sister Richter looked at her husband and smiled. "Oh, sit down, Papa. You heard our sonny boy? It's not time to get off yet. We're going to St. Louis, remember?"

Ustus's eyebrows shot up, and he peered at the woman. That was strange, but he wasn't going to argue. He motioned for the driver to keep going, and the bus crossed the state line.

As Gustav glanced around nervously, a flashing red light came on behind the bus, and the driver stopped.

Trooper Johnson boarded the coach, showed his badge to the driver, and arrested Gustav. While he locked the prisoner in the police cruiser, Billy and Franklin retrieved the Richters' luggage, and Ustus helped Sister Richter into his car.

Then the bus continued its journey, and the cars drove to Piggott.

While Trooper Johnson booked Gustav into the county jail, the lawyers drove Sister Richter to the home of one of her friends.

As Johnson got into his car to leave the jail, the attorneys pulled up beside him. "Breakfast is on me in the mornin'," he said. "Seven o'clock at Hattie's."

"We'll be there," Ustus said, and they drove away.

Although it was almost midnight, Sarah, her mother, and her brothers were still awake when Miss Jordan knocked on their door.

"I thought you would like to know," she said with a big smile. "Gustav Richter has just been arrested."

Sarah burst into tears. She had been down in the dumps all evening because her second period had started. Even though her mother and Miss Jordan were helping her cope, she was still scared. But this news sent her spirit soaring again.

Chapter 23

THE TRIAL–PROSECUTION

MONDAY MORNING, SEPTEMBER 27th, most of the town's 2,600 residents, plus a thousand other area folks, flocked to the courthouse. No local preacher had ever been accused of a serious crime before, much less rape–and the rape of a child.

By eight-thirty, over 500 people had crowded into the court-room, with a maximum capacity of 400.

At nine o'clock, the judge's chamber door opened.

"All rise," the bailiff said as the judge strode to the bench and sat down. "Hear ye. Hear ye. Hear ye. Arkansas Second Judicial Circuit Court for Clay County is now in session. The Honorable Clarence Hunter presiding. Everyone having business before this court draw near, and ye shall be heard. God save the State of Arkansas and its honorable court."

Judge Hunter rapped his gavel on the bench and looked at the crowd. "Good morning, citizens. All but the jury may be seated."

The bailiff swore in the jury. Then the judge covered the trial preliminaries and had Prosecuting Attorney Vernon Godfrey and Defense Attorney Klaus Metzger introduce themselves.

"Okay, let's begin," Judge Hunter said. "Mr. Godfrey, present your opening statement."

Mr. Godfrey stood up, marched to the center of the room, and stopped in front of the jury. "Gentlemen, this case we are about to try involves one of the most loathsome, heinous, and abominable crimes one person can commit against another. It's called 'rape.'

"The victim, twelve-year-old Sarah Jane Skaggs, was placed by our child welfare system into the care of Reverend Gustav Richter and his wife, Edna, where she should have received love, care, and nurturing, but instead received verbal and mental abuse, numerous whippings, and multiple sexual assaults by the man who was supposed to be her father figure."

Mr. Godfrey paused and peered at the jury.

"It's a scary thing to have to sit in judgment over another person. But that's how our judicial system works. A person has a constitutional right to a trial by a jury of his peers. And through that process, justice is dispensed, allowing us to feel safe on our streets and in our homes. The process is not perfect, but it is effective and works most of the time. So, as a jury, it is your responsibility to return a fair and impartial verdict based on the testimony presented here.

"With that in mind, when we show beyond a reasonable doubt that Gustav Richter maliciously assaulted and raped Sarah Jane Skaggs, it will be your duty to find him guilty so that he will receive a just and proper punishment.

"Thank you!" Mr. Godfrey said and sat down.

"Sounds like 'ey're already throwin' a noose over a limb for ya, Reverend," a man shouted from the back of the room, and the gallery erupted with laughter and boos.

Judge Hunter hammered his gavel on the bench. "Order! Order in the court!" he shouted, and the noise subsided.

"Bailiff, escort that man from the room and don't let him back in," the judge said. "I want it understood right here and now. I'll not tolerate any bad behavior. No one's going to make a mockery of justice in my court. And anyone who tries will be held in contempt." The judge glanced around the room, and the gallery quieted.

"Mr. Metzger, present your opening statement."

The defense attorney stood and feigned a bow. "Thank you, Your Honor." He took hold of his lapels, wandered to the jury box, pursed his lips, and scanned their faces.

"Yes, gentlemen, the crime my client is accused of is horrible, but there is one thing you can be sure of: Reverend Gustav Richter did not commit it. So let's talk about justice. Just what is justice? The first word that often springs to my mind is fairness. The ability to make a decision based entirely on fairness, not on what one thinks is true or what one hopes is true, but on what is true.

"Too often in courts of law, juries let their emotions decide the verdict. When a terrible crime is committed, the public demands that someone be punished. And therefore, regardless of the evidence, juries often render a guilty verdict to appease the masses.

"Gentlemen, I want you to understand that emotions have no place in determining a verdict. There is no more horrible outcome to a trial than for an innocent person to be punished. Therefore, I plead with you to leave your emotions at home and only consider the facts. If you do that, it will lead you to the proper verdict of not guilty.

"Thank you!" Mr. Metzger said and strode back to his seat.

"Okay, let's proceed with testimony?" Judge Hunter said. "Mr. Godfrey, call your first witness."

"Your Honor, the prosecution calls Sarah Jane Skaggs to the stand."

"Bailiff, please bring Miss Skaggs to the courtroom," the judge said.

From the open, screenless, second-story window of the witness holding room, Sarah peered down at the curious crowd milling around the courtyard. What were they expecting to see and hear? They couldn't even get into the courtroom.

While Sarah pondered that question, there was a tap at the door, and the stocky, kind-eyed bailiff stuck his head into the room. "Miss Skaggs, the judge is ready for you now."

As Sarah and her mother followed the man into the courtroom, she gazed at the faces around her. She didn't like this. The whole town was there, and they looked like people at a moving picture show. Sarah couldn't tell who was on her side and who was on the Reverend's. She almost ran back out the door until she saw Miss Gibson and Miss Jordan smiling at her.

When they got to the women, her mother let go of her hand and sat down between them.

Sarah stiffened herself and marched through the gate that the bailiff held open for her. To her right sat Mr. Godfrey. She smiled as she passed him, then peered at the jurors. She couldn't tell whose side they were on, either. Their expressionless faces looked just like the people in the audience.

At the witness box, Sarah stopped like Mr. Godfrey had told her to do before the trial. And there, to her left, sat Reverend Richter, as clean and respectable as he ever looked from the pulpit. Vomit rose in Sarah's throat. She blinked and gagged it back down.

"Miss Skaggs, let's talk a moment about truth and honesty," the judge said. "Tell us, in your own words, what truth is."

"Somethin' that's 'real' and not 'false or fake,'" Sarah said.

"Okay," the judge said. "Now tell us what honesty is."

"Tellin' the truth. Not lyin.'"

Satisfied with her answers, the judge had her take the oath and sit down.

"For the record, Miss Skaggs, please state your full name and age," the judge said.

Sarah glanced around the room. Every eye was on her. "My name is Sarah Jane Skaggs, and I'm twelve."

"You may question the witness, Mr. Godfrey," Judge Hunter said.

The prosecutor stood up, buttoned his coat, and walked to the middle of the room. He smiled at Sarah, and she smiled back at him. He had told her all she had to do was tell the truth, and Reverend

Richter would get what was coming to him. So that was what she was going to do.

"Sarah, I know this is hard for you, but for justice to be served, I'm going to have to ask you some hard questions, and you'll have to answer them, okay?"

"Okay," she replied.

Then, question by question, Sarah told how she and her brothers had ended up at the Richters'.

"And what happened after Miss Galloway left," Mr. Godfrey said.

"The Reverend told us all of his rules, and when Marky got sceared and started cryin', he pulled his hair and slapped him. Then he locked the boys in their room and come after me in my room sayin' all kinds of mean thangs and callin' me bad names."

"What bad names?" Mr. Godfrey said.

"I don't know what it means, but he called me a 'har-lot.' Then he tied me to the bed, tore my dress open, and whupped me with that ole strap of his till I fainted."

Sarah glanced at her mother, who was crying.

"What happened when you came to?" Mr. Godfrey said.

Sarah slumped her shoulders and hung her head. "I cain't tell it in fronta all these people."

"But you have to," Mr. Godfrey said and peered into her eyes. "Forget about everyone else and just tell me. Did Gustav Richter put his hands on you?"

"Yes."

"Objection! Leading!" Mr. Metzger shouted.

"Sustained," the judge said.

Sarah closed her eyes, pinched her fingers, and tears trickled down her face.

Guided by Mr. Godfrey's questions and interrupted from time to time by Mr. Metzger's objections, she told what Reverend Richter had done to her.

"You're doing really well," Mr. Godfrey said. "Just stay with me a little longer, okay?"

"Objection!" Mr. Metzger said. "He's blatantly coaching the witness."

"Overruled," the judge said. "Since we're dealing with such a young witness, I will allow it. Please continue, Mr. Godfrey."

"Where was Mrs. Richter while Gustav was doing this to you?"

"In the kitchen."

"Objection!" Mr. Metzger said. "Speculation!"

"Your Honor, I can prove Sarah knew where the woman was," Mr. Godfrey said.

"Okay, Mr. Godfrey. Overruled."

"So, Sarah, how did you know Mrs. Richter was in the kitchen?"

"I could hear her warshin' dishes. And if I could hear her, she could hear me screamin'. And right after the Reverend whupped me, she cleaned me up and put salve on me."

"Okay, now let's talk about what happened when you returned from St. Louis," Mr. Godfrey said.

"Miss Galloway sent Johnny and Mark somewhur else to live and wouldn't tell me whur. Then her and Sheriff Crane took me back to the Richters'.

"When they left, the Reverend drug me upstairs, tied me to the bed, tore off my dress, and whupped me again. Then he done some really awful thangs," she said and burst into tears.

"It's okay, Sarah," Mr. Godfrey said. "What happened wasn't your fault."

"Objection!" Mr. Metzger said. "There he goes again, coaching."

"Overruled," the judge said.

"Sarah, I know this is painful for you, but we've got to hear you tell it in your own words. So then, what happened?"

Through tears, Sarah told everything the Reverend did to her. In the background, she could hear her mother whimpering. "Then Sister Richter warshed me and put salve on me again. She said God expected women to let men do them thangs to 'em. There wudn't nothin' I could do 'bout it. That's just how it was, and I'd get used to it."

"Has any more of that happened since then?"

"Yeah."

"How many times?"

"Three."

Mr. Godfrey gazed into Sarah's eyes. "You've done really well. I'm proud of you."

"Objection, Your Honor!" Mr. Metzger said. "You can't let him keep on doing that!"

The judge bristled. "Mr. Metzger, are you the judge here?"

"No, Your Honor."

"Well then, don't tell me what I can and can't do! Sit down and be quiet!"

Mr. Metzger plopped down into his chair, and Sarah almost grinned.

"That's all I have for the witness, Your Honor," Mr. Godfrey said, and he sat down.

"Okay, Mr. Metzger," the judge said. "You may cross-examine."

Mr. Metzger stood up and feigned another bow. He strutted across the room and peered at Sarah over the top of his glasses as he chewed on a toothpick. He removed the toothpick from his mouth and dropped his arms to his sides. "Miss Skaggs, do you really expect us to believe Reverend Richter, a man of God, actually did those vile and wicked things to you? Isn't it true you made up that story hoping to get back with your brothers?"

"Objection!" Mr. Godfrey shouted.

"Overruled," the judge said. "It's a fair question. Go ahead and answer it, Miss Skaggs."

Sarah frowned. "Ever'thang I said happened just like I said it did. I don't lie."

Mr. Metzger turned toward the jury and muttered something.

"Objection, Your Honor!" Mr. Godfrey said. "Mr. Metzger said something to the jury."

"Mr. Metzger, turn around here and look at me," Judge Hunter said. "From now on, anything you say will be said to the entire court. Is that understood?"

"Yes, Your Honor."

"Now, repeat what you just said so everyone can hear it."

"I'll be happy to, Your Honor. I said, 'But you don't exactly tell the truth either, do you?'"

"Objection sustained. The jury will disregard that remark," Judge Hunter said. Then he glared at the defense attorney. "Mr. Metzger, if you behave that way in my court, I'll hold you in contempt."

"Sorry, Your Honor. I beg the court's pardon." Mr. Metzger said. Then he turned back to Sarah. "Miss Skaggs, I don't doubt that something happened to you, but I can't believe Reverend Richter had anything to do with it. You must show us proof that he was the one who did those vile things to you. Did anyone see him?"

"My brothers heard him."

Mr. Metzger shook his head and smirked. "And just how did they do that? You testified that they had already moved before this alleged assault and rape happened."

"Yeah, but they heard him whup me the first time. They were still there then."

"I'm sorry, Miss Skaggs. All they heard was a Godly man administering reasonable punishment to an unruly child. Anything they could tell us would be hearsay. I have no further use of this witness, Your Honor," Mr. Metzger said and took his seat.

"You may step down, Miss Skaggs," the judge said.

As Sarah passed Reverend Richter, he scowled at her, and she scowled back at him. When the bailiff opened the gate for her, she shivered. There were all those faces again. Usually, folks didn't scare Sarah, but these people did. She squeezed in between her mother and Miss Jordan on the bench and snuggled up to them.

"Call your next witness, Mr. Godfrey," the judge said.

"Your Honor, the prosecution calls Dr. Leslie Parker as an expert witness."

Dr. Parker came forward, took the oath, and sat down.

"For the court record, please state your full name and occupation," the judge said.

"My name is Dr. Leslie Warren Parker. I took my degree from the University of Missouri School of Medicine at Columbia, and I practice internal medicine at Piggott Hospital."

"You may proceed with your questioning, Mr. Godfrey."

"Dr. Parker, were you called to the local welfare office on the afternoon of Thursday, August 12th, of this year?" Mr. Godfrey said.

"Yes, I was."

"And why were you called?"

"I was told a young girl needed to be examined."

"And did you perform that examination?"

"Yes, I did."

Mr. Godfrey took a folder from his briefcase. "Permission to approach the bench, Your Honor."

"Granted," the judge said.

"If it pleases the court," Mr. Godfrey said. "The State would like to mark this document for evidence identification as 'State's Exhibit One.'"

Judge Hunter inspected the document and motioned for Mr. Metzger to come to the bench. The defense attorney glanced through the papers and handed them back to the judge. "The defense objects to this document being admitted into evidence. It's irrelevant."

"Overruled," the judge said and handed the folder back to Mr. Godfrey.

"Thank you, Your Honor," Mr. Godfrey said. "May I approach the witness?"

"You may."

Mr. Godfrey passed the folder to Dr. Parker. "Do you recognize this document?"

"Yes, it's the report I wrote after examining Sarah."

"How do you know that?"

"It's the standard form I always use. It has the examination details, the date I performed it, and my signature at the bottom."

"Has it been altered since you last saw it?"

Dr. Parker scanned the document again. "No, it looks exactly as it did when I wrote it."

"Your Honor, the prosecution would like to file this exhibit," Mr. Godfrey said, handing it to the judge.

"This document will be admitted as evidence," Judge Hunter said. "Bailiff, let the jury look at it. Then give it to the clerk.

"Please continue, Mr. Godfrey."

"Dr. Parker, what did you find during your examination of Sarah Jane Skaggs?"

"I found live sperm and evidence of violent sexual intercourse–multiple contusions and tears in the tissue of the lining of the vaginal wall–that I estimated had occurred sometime within the previous ten hours."

Sarah scooted back in her seat and hid behind her mother and Mrs. Jordan.

"And at what time did you finish the examination?" Mr. Godfrey said.

"I signed the report at 5:15 p.m."

"So, considering Sarah had been at the hearing since three o'clock, within what timeframe would you place the rape?"

"Objection!" Mr. Metzger said. "Calling this a 'rape' is speculation. She may have injured herself for all we know."

"Overruled," the judge said. "Since the witness is a medical doctor, I'll let the term stand. Continue, Dr. Parker."

"I would say it occurred between 6:30 a.m. and 2:30 p.m."

Mr. Godfrey finished his questioning, and Mr. Metzger began cross-examination.

"So, Dr. Parker, how did you establish that time frame?"

"I prepared a slide of the fluids I found in Sarah and viewed it under a microscope."

"Do you usually carry a microscope with you?"

"No, not usually, but most examinations I perform at the welfare office involve microscopic evidence, so I took one with me."

"Oh, I see. You were expected to find sexual assault evidence, so you conveniently did so."

"Objection!" Mr. Godfrey shouted.

"Sustained," the judge said and glared at the defense attorney. "Mr. Metzger, you're beginning to annoy me. I'll not warn you again."

"Yes, Your Honor. I beg the court's pardon," Mr. Metzger said and turned back to the witness. "So, Dr. Parker, you based that timeframe solely on your opinion?"

"No, not 'solely.' It's based on my years of medical experience and information I've read in numerous medical journals. And even if we disregard that, Twelve-year-old girls don't ordinarily have sperm and tears in their vaginas, and Sarah Skaggs did."

Sarah closed her eyes and hid her face with her hands. She didn't understand what Dr. Parker said, but it sounded terrible.

"Dr. Parker, is there a test that can identify who the sperm came from?"

"No, sir, there isn't."

"Well then, this whole discussion about sperm is irrelevant, isn't it?"

"Objection," Mr. Godfrey said. "The fact that Dr. Parker found sperm is totally relevant."

"Sustained," Judge Hunter said.

"The defense has no further questions," Mr. Metzger said, and Dr. Parker stepped down.

"Mr. Godfrey, call your next witness," the judge said.

"Your Honor, the prosecution calls Miss Angela Billings."

Sarah's mouth gaped. Angela was here?

The bailiff escorted Angela into the room. When she passed Sarah, their eyes met like they had that day at church. They were foster sisters, and Sarah could see in Angela's eyes that the Reverend had used her, too.

As Angela walked through the gate, she glanced at the Reverend and smiled. Then she walked to the witness box, took the oath, and sat down.

"Your Honor," Mr. Godfrey said. "when we subpoenaed Miss Billings to testify, she refused to come. Since we had to send someone to Memphis to get her, at considerable expense, I would like permission to question her as a hostile witness."

"Very well, Mr. Godfrey," the judge said. "Let it be entered into the court record that Miss Billings is a hostile witness. You may begin questioning."

"Miss Billings, were you one of the Richters' foster children?"

"I still am one of their children," Angela said.

Mr. Godfrey smiled. "Okay, point taken. How old were you when you were placed in their home?"

"Thirteen."

"And at what age did you leave?"

"Nineteen."

"During that time, how did the Richters treat you?"

"Wonderfully."

"Did Gustav Richter ever physically discipline you?"

"Yes, when I was young, Daddy spanked me a time or two, and it did me good."

"By 'Daddy,' you mean Gustav Richter. Is that correct?"

"Yes."

"Were any of those spankings abusive?"

Angela shifted in her chair, glanced at Gustav, and looked back at Mr. Godfrey. "No, he only gave me what I deserved."

229

"And what had you done to 'deserve' those spankings?"

"I broke the rules."

"Which rules?"

"I don't remember. But Daddy is head of the family like God is head of the church, and he must be obeyed."

"Miss Billings, do you have children?"

Angela's eyes shot to Mr. Godfrey. "I'm single."

"Yes, I know, but I asked if you have children?"

Again, Angela shifted in her chair and glanced at Gustav. "I have a ten-month-old daughter."

"Who's your baby's father?"

"Objection!" Mr. Metzger said. "Irrelevant."

"Your Honor, please give me a minute, and the relevance of my question will become clear."

"Nonsense, Your Honor!" Mr. Metzger said. "This is getting out of hand. The baby's fatherhood is totally irrelevant to this case."

"On the contrary, Your Honor. It has great bearing on this case," Mr. Godfrey said. "Please let me continue."

The judge took off his glasses, rubbed his eyes, and then peered at the prosecutor. "Okay, Mr. Godfrey, but don't you be pulling any shenanigans. Objection overruled. Miss Billings, answer the question."

Angela burst into tears. "I don't know who he is."

"Your Honor, may I approach the witness?" Mr. Godfrey said.

"Okay, but behave yourself."

Mr. Godfrey pulled a handkerchief from his pocket and held it out to Angela. She hesitated, then took it, wiped her eyes, and laid the cloth in her lap.

"I'm sorry, Miss Billings, but I don't believe you. I think you know exactly who your baby's father is."

Angela glanced at Gustav again.

"Miss Billings, you keep looking at Gustav Richter. Is he your daughter's father?"

Mr. Metzger leaped from his chair as moans rose from the gallery. "Objection, Your Honor! That's preposterous!"

"Overruled," the judge said. "The witness will answer the question."

"No!" Angela said through her sobs.

"Miss Billings, I'm reminding you, you're under oath. How old were you the first time Gustav Richter raped you?"

Another murmur rose from the crowd, and again Mr. Metzger jumped to his feet. "Objection, Your Hon–"

"He's never raped me! Daddy loves me, and I love him."

"Are you saying you gave in willingly?"

Judge Hunter hammered his gavel on the bench. "Objection sustained. That's enough, Mr. Godfrey. I told you not to pull any shenanigans. Now, move away from the witness."

Mr. Godfrey backed away until Angela quit sobbing, then he continued. "So, Miss Billings, I ask you again. Is Gustav Richter your baby's father?"

Sarah stared at Angela. *Come on, sister! Tell us!*

"No, he's not! He'd never do anything to hurt me!" Angela said. Then she leaned back and folded her arms. "And that's all I'm gonna say!"

Mr. Godfrey grimaced and shook his head. "Okay, I'm done, Your Honor."

"Mr. Metzger, you may cross-examine," the judge said.

The defense attorney rose and folded his hands in front of him. "I have no questions for this poor young woman, Your Honor. Please excuse her."

"Very well," the judge said. "Miss Billings, you may step down."

As Angela approached the Reverend, he stood. Then they hugged. "You should be ashamed of yourself, Mr. Godfrey!" he shouted.

"Sit down, Reverend," the judge said and rapped his gavel on the bench. "Bailiff, escort Miss Billings from the room."

As Angela passed Sarah, she looked the other way. Sarah's eyes begged for the truth, but Angela wouldn't give it.

"Call your next witness, Mr. Godfrey," the judge said.

"Your Honor, since Mr. Metzger attacked the victim's character, I call Miss Elsie Gibson as a character witness."

Sarah smiled as Miss Gibson took the oath and sat down.

"Miss Gibson, how long have you known Sarah Skaggs?" Mr. Godfrey said.

"I met Sarah on her first day of first grade during summer split term in July 1948."

"So you've known her and been her school teacher for six years, correct?"

"Yes, that's correct."

"And how would you describe Sarah?"

"She's smart, friendly, honest, energetic, caring, happy, savvy, spirited, and rugged."

Sarah blushed and grinned.

"Well, that's quite a glowing description," Mr. Godfrey said. "Have you ever known Sarah to be dishonest or unruly?"

"No, those aren't words I'd use to describe her. I've never had any problems with Sarah. In general, she's well-behaved. But, she can be tough when she needs to be."

Sarah grinned again. That was true. A few times, she had been tough with Miss Gibson.

"What do you mean by 'tough?'" Mr. Godfrey said.

"She stands up for herself–doesn't allow anyone to bully her or her brothers. She's not a coward."

"So, overall, how would you rate Sarah's character?"

"In my opinion, she's an exemplary young woman. She has good sense and knows the difference between right and wrong."

"Thank you, Miss Gibson," Mr. Godfrey said.

He sat down, and Mr. Metzger stood up.

"So, Miss Gibson, Sarah has never been unruly at school? Is that what you're telling us?" Mr. Metzger said.

"Well, I can't say she's never misbehaved, but I can say she's never been 'unruly.'"

"Ahh, come now, Miss Gibson. It's the nature of children to be unruly?"

"Mr. Metzger, I've been a school teacher for over fifteen years and have dealt with dozens of unruly children, but Sarah Jane Skaggs is not one of them. She's never been disrespectful to me or anyone else. I know 'unruly' when I see it! So, don't you be trying to put words in my mouth!" she said, and the crowd laughed.

"Miss Gibson, you also said Sarah is honest. Does that mean she's never lied to you?"

"That's correct. She's never lied to me except for an innocent white lie."

"What do you mean by 'innocent, white lie?' Give us an example."

"Objection, Your Honor," Mr. Godfrey said. "More prejudicial than probative."

"Overruled," the judge said. "The defense has a right to try to impeach the witness's testimony. Answer the question, Miss Gibson."

"Well, on the day I discovered the Skaggs children's parents had left them, when I asked Sarah where they were, she told me they had gone to Piggott to take her uncle to catch his train."

"So you consider that 'a little white lie,' do you?"

"Yes, I do. Sarah thought she was protecting her brothers and herself by telling it."

"So she lied to keep from getting into trouble. Is that correct?"

"Well, she may have thought she–"

"Yes or no, Miss Gibson? Did Sarah lie to avoid getting into trouble?"

"Well, yes, but–"

"That's all, Miss Gibson. No further questions, Your Honor," Mr. Metzger said and sat down.

Miss Gibson glared at the defense attorney and marched to her seat.

"Call your next witness, Mr. Godfrey," Judge Hunter said.

"Your Honor, I call Miss Alexis Jordan as another character witness."

Sarah smiled again as Miss Jordan took the oath and sat down.

"Miss Jordan," Mr. Godfrey said, "how did you become acquainted with Sarah Skaggs?"

"I was the caseworker assigned to Sarah and her brothers when they were rescued from the streets of St. Louis by the City Police on August 2nd of this year."

Following some preliminary questions, Mr. Godfrey asked Miss Jordan the same questions he had asked Miss Gibson. She called Sarah "a perfect young lady."

Then Mr. Metzger cross-examined Miss Jordan. "So, you say you never saw any bad behavior from Sarah Skaggs. Is that right?"

"Yes, that is correct. She never exhibited inappropriate behavior."

"Oh, so now, you're changing your testimony from 'bad behavior' to 'inappropriate behavior.' What's the difference? They're both misconduct, aren't they?"

"Yes, that is true, but 'inappropriate behavior' is just unsuitable behavior for the circumstances at a particular time, while 'bad behavior' is never appropriate. It is true that Sarah expressed disappointment and cried sometimes, but she never misbehaved during those times."

"Aren't you bending the truth? What about Sarah's behavior at the depot when you brought her back to Piggott?"

"What about it? She did nothing wrong that day. It was Miss Galloway who misbehaved, which was confirmed by her 90-day job suspension. All Sarah did was defend herself. I consider that 'appropriate behavior.'"

Mr. Metzger scowled. "A child resisting authority? Really, Miss Jordan, how can that be deemed 'appropriate behavior?'"

Miss Jordan bristled. "If you want to talk about inappropriate behavior, let's talk about what that evil man sitting there did to that innocent young girl."

Judge Hunter struck his gavel on the bench and fought back a grin. "That's an *inappropriate* comment, Miss Jordan. The jury will disregard her remark."

"I'm done with this witness," Mr. Metzger said.

Miss Jordan stepped down and took her seat.

"Call your next witness, Mr. Godfrey," the judge said.

"I have no further witnesses, Your Honor. The prosecution rests."

"Very well," Judge Hunter said and glanced at his watch. "In that case, we'll take an hour-and-a-quarter lunch break. It's eleven forty-five. Court will reconvene at one o'clock," he said and whacked his gavel on the bench.

A few people hurried from the room to the nearby cafes, but most kept their seats. Many had brought lunches. Others purchased food from the vendors who swarmed into the room.

That morning, Miss Gibson had stowed a picnic basket filled with fried chicken and all the fixings in the cooler of a friend's nearby grocery store. While she fetched the food, Miss Jordan escorted Sarah and her mother into the shade of a large oak tree on a secluded corner of the court square. When Miss Gibson rejoined them, they spread their picnic on a blanket.

As they ate, Sarah talked about some of the interesting things she and her brothers had experienced while their mother was away. Several times, she had the ladies almost in tears as she told about eluding the railroad bulls, fighting the street gang, and eating out of garbage cans. But by the end of the story, she had them laughing as she told about eating dog stew with Bo Jesus, their encounter with Downtown Beulah Brown, and Johnny being snakebit by a red wasp.

Chapter 24

THE TRIAL–DEFENSE

SARAH AND THE ladies finished lunch, took a restroom break at the grocery store, and returned to their seats in the courtroom.

At one o'clock, Judge Hunter reconvened the court. "You may call your first witness, Mr. Metzger."

"Your Honor, the defense calls Dr. Walter Muller as an expert witness."

The doctor marched to the witness box, took the oath, and sat down.

"Please state your full name and profession for the court record," Judge Hunter said.

"I am Dr. Walter Günter Muller, and I took my degree from Heidelberg University Medical School. My speciality is gynecology, and I have a private practice in Chicago, Illinois."

"Proceed with questioning, Mr. Metzger," the judge said.

"Dr. Muller, how long have you been practicing medicine in the United States?"

"This is my twenty-sixth year. I came to this country in 1927 and began practice in 1928."

"You said your specialty is gynecology. Exactly what is that?"

"It's the medical branch dealing with the functions and diseases of the female reproductive system."

"Dr. Muller, Dr. Parker testified that he found live sperm in Sarah Skaggs's vagina and that it had been deposited there within the previous ten hours. Is it possible to determine how long semen has been in a woman's vagina?"

"No," Dr. Muller said, "there's no way to determine that. Sperm can live for five days after intercourse. If he found live sperm, it could have been there a long time."

"Dr. Parker also said there were 'tears in the tissue of Sarah's vaginal wall lining consistent with a forced entry.' Could there be another explanation for those tears?"

"Yes, young girls often engage in masturbation for sexual gratification, and that kind of vigorous stimulation can cause tears and bruises to the tissue."

"Objection!" Mr. Godfrey said. "Speculation!"

"Overruled," the judge said.

"So Sarah could have caused those injuries to herself?"

"Yes, that's correct."

Sarah peered at her mother. "What's 'masturbation?'" she whispered.

Her mother gawked, at a loss for words.

"We will explain later," Miss Jordan said.

Sarah frowned. The doctor thought she had hurt herself.

Mr. Metzger asked Dr. Muller a half dozen more questions. Then he bowed to the physician, thanked him, and sat down.

"Okay, Mr. Godfrey," Judge Hunter said, "you may cross-examine."

"Dr. Muller, are you saying Dr. Parker's explanation for what he found is wrong?"

"No, all I'm saying is that there could be other interpretations."

"So Dr. Parker's explanation could be valid, correct?"

"Yes, his opinion offers one possible explanation for what he found, but there are other possibilities."

"One final question, Dr. Muller. Was Gustav Richter your sponsor when you immigrated to this country?"

"Objection!" Mr. Metzger said. "Irrelevant!"

"On the contrary, Your Honor. Dr. Muller is paying off a debt he owes Gustav Richter by testifying here. Therefore, it's a conflict of interest."

"It's no such thing!" Mr. Metzger shouted. "Dr. Muller was chosen only because of his medical expertise."

"Yes, I agree with Mr. Metzger," Judge Hunter said. "I see no conflict of interest. Objection sustained. The jury will disregard the prosecutor's comments."

Mr. Godfrey scowled. "No further question, Your Honor," he said and headed to his seat.

Dr. Muller stepped down, and Mr. Metzger stood up.

"Your Honor, since one of the prosecution's witnesses attacked Reverend Richter's character, the defense calls Mr. Melvin Waters to the stand as a character witness."

Mr. Waters, a church deacon, called Reverend Richter 'a great man of God.' Then a half dozen other church members took the stand and praised him even more.

When the defense attorney attempted to call yet another character witness from church, Judge Hunter stopped him. "Mr. Metzger, this court doesn't have time for you to call the entire River Church congregation to the stand. We've already heard from an adequate number, so call your next relevant witness."

"Yes, Your Honor," Mr. Metzger said. Then he peered at Reverend Richter, who nodded to him. "May I take a moment to confer with my client?"

"Okay, but be brief."

Mr. Metzger sat down beside Reverend Richter, and they whispered to each other. Then he stood back up. "Your Honor, the defense calls Reverend Gustav Richter to the stand."

Judge Hunter paused and looked at the defendant. "Reverend Richter, by law, I'm required to inform you of your 5th Amendment Rights regarding self-incrimination. You do not have to testify in this trial. However, if you waive those rights, you cannot reclaim them later. Is my explanation of your rights clear to you?"

"Yes, Your Honor, but since I'm innocent and know Almighty God will deliver me from this ordeal, I have no fear of testifying before this court."

"Okay," the judge said. "Come forward."

Sarah's flesh crawled as the Reverend strode to the witness box. He might look holy, but he wasn't. She and God knew what he was.

The Reverend took the oath and sat down.

"Please state your full name and occupation for the record," Judge Hunter said.

"My name is Reverend Gustav Niclas Richter, and I am the pastor of the River Community Church."

"Proceed with questioning, Mr. Metzger," Judge Hunter said.

"Reverend Richter, how long have you and your wife, Edna, been foster parents?"

"We moved here in 1933 during The Great Depression and were immediately asked to take four children into our home. We've been doing it ever since."

"That's twenty-one years, and how many children have you cared for during that time?"

"We've only been without children three times since then. The last time we counted, thirty-one children had passed through our home."

"Does that number include the Skaggs children?"

"No, their stay was too chaotic and brief."

"How was it 'chaotic?'"

"They disobeyed rules and were belligerent. They attacked Sister Richter and myself with umbrellas and numerous other weapons."

The hair bristled on Sarah's neck, and she almost stood up. She had never heard such lying. The Reverend had attacked them, not the other way around, and now he was trying to lie his way out of it.

Sarah's mother tugged her back into the seat.

Mr. Metzger asked more questions, and the Reverend spat out more lies. He said Sarah had made up her story, and none of it had ever happened. But the worst thing was Mr. Godfrey didn't stop him.

Sarah looked at Miss Jordan and frowned. "Why don't Mr. Godfrey do somethin'?" she whispered.

"He will. When it is his turn to speak again," Miss Jordan whispered back.

"So, Reverend, how did you deal with the situation?" Mr. Metzger said.

"I separated Sarah from her brothers and locked them in their rooms."

"Did that help?"

"Yes, until they broke out and ran away."

Sarah covered her mouth and snickered. She was still proud of how well her escape plan had worked.

"Now tell us what happened when Sarah was brought to you the second time."

"She persisted in being hostile, so I obeyed God's command and did not 'spare the rod.'"

Sarah rubbed her legs where the marks had been. He hadn't just spanked her. He had beaten her. She wished all those people could have seen the bruises and welts he put on her and how much he enjoyed doing it.

"Did that cure her disobedience?"

"Yes, she submitted after that."

"Now, Reverend, I hate to ask you this, but it's necessary for your defense. Did you ever sexually molest Sarah Skaggs?"

The Reverend's face flushed, and he scowled. "Certainly not! I would never do such a thing!"

Sarah glared at him. "Liar, liar, go to hellfire!" she whispered.

"No! of course not!" Mr. Metzger said. "Thank you, Reverend. No further questions, Your Honor."

Then Mr. Godfrey cross-examined the Reverend.

"Mr. Richter–"

"My title is 'Reverend,' sir, and I demand you use it."

Mr. Godfrey snickered and shook his head. "That's absurd. You're on trial for rape."

Laughs and boos rose from the gallery, and Judge Hunter rapped his gavel on the bench.

"Objection!" Mr. Metzger shouted. "The prosecutor's acting like my client has already been convicted."

"Sustained," Judge Hunter said. "Mr. Godfrey, you will treat the Reverend with respect."

"Yes, Your Honor," the prosecutor said and turned back to the defendant. "All right, then, 'Rev-er-end Richter–'"

Sarah giggled. Mr. Godfrey made it sound like an insult.

"–have you ever seen Sarah Skaggs naked?"

Sarah snuggled against her mother and hid again.

The Reverend shifted in his seat and frowned. "No, never!"

Sarah peeked at the jury. Some of them had funny looks on their faces.

"Have you ever touched Sarah Skaggs sexually?"

Sarah snuggled even tighter against her mother.

"Objection, Your Honor!" Mr. Metzger said. "I've already asked these questions."

"Your Honor, the defendant has not been asked these particular questions, and the jury needs to hear his answers."

"Very well, Mr. Godfrey. Overruled. Answer the question, Reverend."

"No, sir, I have not."

"Reverend Richter, do you understand that perjury is a felony and carries a prison sentence?"

"So does rape, Mr. Godfrey, and I'm guilty of neither."

Several members of the Reverend's church clapped and cheered. Judge Hunter picked up his gavel, and the noise subsided.

"Reverend Richter," Mr. Godfrey said, "why did you and your wife suddenly leave home the day your house burned?"

"Objection!" Mr. Metzger said. "Irrelevant!"

"I beg the court's indulgence, Your Honor," Mr. Godfrey said. "Please let me continue, and the question's relevance will be revealed."

Judge Hunter glared at the prosecutor. "Mr. Godfrey, you're beginning to make a habit of this tactic, and it's getting tiresome. This is the last time I'm going to allow it. Overruled," he said and looked at the witness. "Answer the question, Reverend."

"When we realized we couldn't extinguish the fire, we gathered what belongings we could and left for my brother's home in St. Louis."

"The house was on fire, but you still had time to pack?"

"Well, we saved what we could."

"And then you just left . . . without a word to anyone?"

"We were in shock."

"You were in such deep shock that you walked eight miles to the Holcomb bus depot in the August heat?"

"Well, actually, we only walked about a mile. Then a kind young man stopped and gave us a ride the rest of the way."

Mr. Godfrey glared at the Reverend. "So, you're telling us that some 'kind young man' drove right past a house fire without stopping to help put it out and gave you a ride to the Holcomb bus depot?"

"Yes, that's correct. He said enough people were already fighting the fire, and he didn't want to get in the way."

"Did he ask if you had any connection to the fire?"

"No, he only asked where we were going. I suppose, to him, we were just hitchhikers?"

Mr. Godfrey stared at Reverend Richter. "When you left that day, did you know a warrant had been issued for your arrest?"

"No, I did not."

"Well, I don't believe you. Isn't it true that someone tipped you off about the warrant, so you set fire to the house, hoping people would think you and your wife had died in the blaze because you knew 'your sins [were about to] find you out?'"

Sarah grinned. She loved it when Mr. Godfrey made Reverend Richter squirm.

"No, the fire was simply an accident, and we were escaping it."

"You were escaping, all right. Escaping your crimes," Mr. Godfrey said. "Gustav Richter, how many girls have you raped during your years as a foster parent?"

"Objection, Your Honor!" Mr. Metzger shouted as he leapt to his feet.

"None!" Reverend Richter shouted. "All of my girls are good girls!"

"Sustained," Judge Hunter said and scowled. "The jury will disregard the prosecutor's remarks."

"No further questions," Mr. Godfrey said.

Sarah's grin faded as Mr. Godfrey sat down. Was that it? Why didn't the judge make Reverend Richter answer the question? That would have nailed him.

"Call your next witness, Mr. Metzger," Judge Hunter said.

"I have no further witnesses, Your Honor. The defense rests."

"Very well then. The court stands in recess until tomorrow morning at nine o'clock when we'll hear closing arguments." Judge Hunter struck his gavel on the bench and marched from the room.

Chapter 25

ADAM ZIMMERMAN

BECAUSE THE TRIAL affected everyone in the community around Adam Zimmerman's store, he closely followed its progress. He wanted to observe the American legal system in action and be able to discuss the proceedings intelligently with customers who brought up the subject. In his opinion, not only were those two things good business, they were also good citizenship, and Adam Zimmerman was all about good citizenship.

In 1939 when the Nazis occupied Poland, he fled to New York and became a naturalized citizen. Then, with hard work and help from a wealthy sponsor, he was awarded a business grant, which allowed him to move to Austin Community in 1947 and open his store.

Adam felt blessed to live where his neighbors accepted him without prejudice, and he was always looking for ways to thank them. He loved his new country and its freedoms and wanted everyone to know just how important it was never to take those freedoms for granted.

When Adam heard that Elizabeth Pinscher and her children needed money, he sent five hundred dollars to them through their attorney, Ustus Harlow. Along with the check, he included a letter telling them to let him know what else they needed.

That evening, as Adam stood on the store's porch watching a customer leave, Elizabeth and Ustus arrived.

"How may I help you, folks?" Adam said as they approached him.

Elizabeth pulled the check from her purse and peered at Mr. Zimmerman. "I wonted to come and thank you for offerin' to help my kids and me, but I cain't take this. I'd never be able to pay ya back," she said and held the check out to him.

Adam cupped his hands around hers and folded the check back into it. "This isn't a loan, Mrs. Pinscher. It's a gift. My reward is knowing you and your children are being cared for. I'm just glad I can help, and I'll keep helping until you don't need it anymore. You look after your family, and I'll cover your expenses."

Elizabeth looked at the check and then looked at Mr. Zimmerman. "Are you sure? It's a awful lotta money."

"I'm absolutely sure. You take it and use it however you see fit."

He released her hand, and she tucked the check back into her purse.

For a moment, they stood awkwardly gazing at each other. Then Adam got his voice back. "Wait here a minute! I'll be right back!"

He hurried into the store and returned with a bottle of nice hand lotion and a paper bag filled with licorice and sassafras candy. "Just something for you and your children," he said as he handed them to her.

Elizabeth blushed and took the gifts. "My goodness! Money and presents, too!"

While Adam helped Elizabeth into the car, Ustus got into the driver's seat.

"Anytime you're out this way, Mrs. Pinscher, be sure to stop in and see me."

"Okay, I will, Mr. Zimmerman," she said as they looked at each other.

While the car pulled away, Adam and Elizabeth waved to each other.

"I think that man likes you," Ustus said.

Elizabeth smiled and peered down at the gifts in her lap. "I like him, too."

Chapter 26

THE VERDICT

ON TUESDAY MORNING, Sarah, her mother, and Miss Jordan returned to their front-row seats in the courtroom. Miss Gibson had pre-term work to do at the schoolhouse.

Sarah bounced in her seat. Today, Reverend Richter was finally going to get what was coming to him.

At nine o'clock, Judge Hunter called the court to order, and closing arguments began.

Mr. Godfrey marched to the jury box and peered at the men. "Gentlemen, during this trial, we have presented evidence clearly linking Gustav Richter to the assault and rape of Sarah Jane Skaggs.

"That brave little girl sat here and told us, in her own words, how that despicable man sitting there," Mr. Godfrey said and wagged his finger at Reverend Richter, "brutally whipped and raped her.

"Then Dr. Parker described the physical evidence he found when he examined Sarah, which supported her testimony and proved the crimes had been committed.

"Although Reverend Richter and his lawyer have done everything in their power to cast doubt on Sarah's story, including trying to make her out to be the liar, they have failed to do so. They even called numerous members of the Reverend's congregation who testified that he is a 'holy man,' hoping to persuade you of his innocence, but that proved nothing. Why? Because those church members have only seen him thundering down from the pulpit about the wrath of

God. They've never seen him behind closed doors, but Sarah Skaggs has. And we all know how a man acts in public can be totally different from how he acts in private, especially in the bedroom.

"Then you heard Angela Billings, another one of the Richters' foster daughters, testify that the Reverend had also whipped her. And despite being raised in the Reverend's supposéd holy realm, she is the unwed mother of a ten-month-old child whose fatherhood is questionable.

"Now, against all logic, the defense is asking you to believe these witnesses have cast reasonable doubt on the Reverend's guilt. But how can you trust the words of a former foster child over whom he still has complete control? And how can the people who only see him in church really know him?" Mr. Godfrey fanned the air with his hand. "That's totally ridiculous!

"Then, on the other hand, there is Sarah Skaggs, whose face you have looked into and whose testimony you've heard about the vile things she's suffered at the hands of this evil man. Sarah, an innocent little girl who knows nothing of the adult world, told the truth about what's happened to her, and you can see that for yourselves.

"So, I put it to you, gentlemen. Are these so-called doubts about Gustav Richter's guilt reasonable? No, they're not! Why? Because we have proven, beyond any reasonable doubt, that Gustav Richter was the only man with whom Sarah had contact during the times in which these crimes were committed. Therefore, you must find him guilty so he will receive a just punishment.

"Thank you."

Sarah had sat like a granite statue during Mr. Godfrey's entire speech. How could anybody believe Reverend Richter after that?

Then it was Mr. Metzger's turn. He took hold of his lapels, strolled to the jury box, and peered over his glasses at the group. "Gentlemen, although a mountain of false and misleading evidence has been presented against my client, the fact remains that he is an innocent man.

"Reverend Gustav Richter is by no means a perfect man. But he is certainly not the demon the prosecutor has made him out to be. He is simply a good man, a just man, and being a member of the clergy, a God-fearing man. And as you have heard repeatedly from his parishioners, he is a respected community leader.

"You have also heard testimony from one of his adoring children, who said he's nothing like the figure Sarah Skaggs painted. And though the prosecutor has tried to present this as something dark and nefarious, it is not. The Richters are a kind, loving couple who have opened their home to numerous needy children without the slightest thought of their own sacrifice.

"Then, on the other side, there's the story of a disrespectful young girl–a runaway–who fled the Richters' care, which the prosecutor tried to convince us was due to yet another crime committed against the so-called 'victim,' when in fact, Miss Skaggs deliberately planned the event to humiliate the Richters.

"However, the prosecutor was right about one thing. You have heard the testimony of Reverend Richter, and you have heard the testimony of Sarah Skaggs. Therefore, you can either believe an undisciplined girl who says this revered man of God is secretly a sexual pervert and an open liar, or you can believe a host of other folks, including one of his loving and devoted daughters, who say that Sarah Skaggs is the liar.

"And if you hesitate–even for a moment–to believe Miss Skaggs's story, well then, that in and of itself constitutes reasonable doubt.

"So, God leaves the decision in your hands."

Mr. Metzger nodded to the jury and took his seat.

Once again, Sarah sat like a granite statue during the speech. In fact, she had sat so still that she found it hard to breathe again.

"Okay, gentlemen," Judge Hunter said as he turned to the jury, "you're about to be sequestered to render a verdict in this case. While doing so, there are three things to keep in mind: common sense, credibility, and the burden of proof. Common sense means using sound judgment. If something seems right, then it usually is right. If, on the other hand, something seems wrong, then it probably is wrong. Credibility is about the witnesses. Were they trustworthy and believable? Did their words ring true? And finally, there's the burden of proof. Until proven guilty, the defendant is innocent, and proof of guilt is the burden of the prosecution. Was the presented evidence sufficient enough to prove guilt?

"In addition to these three things, there is also the question of statutory rape. In Arkansas, the age of consent is sixteen. 'If you believe that the defendant had sexual intercourse with Sarah Jane Skaggs at a time when she was under sixteen years of age and at any time before the filing of the information in this case, then it is immaterial whether she consented to the act or not, and it is also immaterial as to whether it occurred on the 12th day of August, or on some other day.'

"If, beyond a reasonable doubt, you believe that the defendant did not commit this crime, then you must find him not guilty. However, if, beyond a reasonable doubt, you believe that the defendant did commit this crime, then you must find him guilty. You must make the best decision you can."

Sarah didn't understand most of what the judge said. She just hoped the jury believed her. The only thing she had done was protect herself and her brothers. It was the grownups who had done wrong, and the Reverend had done the most wrong of all.

The jury filed out of the room, the judge recessed the court, and Sarah looked at Miss Jordan. "So, what do we do now?"

"We wait for the jury to return, and that may be a while."

Miss Jordan led Sarah and her mother downstairs and outside onto the courtyard. Suddenly, a man ran up to Sarah and spat on her. As Miss Jordan and Sarah's mother sandwiched her between them, a group of church women surrounded them and made rude comments. Miss Jordan grabbed Sarah and her mother and literally dragged them upstairs to the holding room.

A half-hour later, word circulated that the jury had reached a verdict, and they returned to a standing-room-only courtroom.

"Gentlemen, have you reached a verdict?" Judge Hunter said.

The jury foreman rose and looked at the judge. "Yes, Your Honor, we have."

Judge Hunter peered at Reverend Richter. "The defendant will rise and face the jury."

Sarah gripped her mother's arm and stared at the foreman.

"In the matter of the State of Arkansas vs. Reverend Gustav Niclas Richter, how do you find?" Judge Hunter said.

Sarah's heart pounded, and she held her breath.

"Your Honor, we find the defendant not guilty."

The gallery erupted with cheers, whistles, and groans. Several people leaped from their seats and punched their fists into the air.

Sarah gasped and peered blankly into space. The blood drained from her face, tears gushed from her eyes, and she fell into her mother's arms. "They believed the Reverend," she blubbered. "They looked at him, and they looked at me, and they believed him."

The judge hammered his gavel on the bench. "Order!" he shouted, and the noise subsided.

As Sarah bawled, she looked at Judge Hunter, and he stared back at her with sad eyes.

"Bailiff, release the defendant. This case is closed. The jury's dismissed, and the court's adjourned." The judge rapped his gavel on the bench. Then he hurried to his chamber and closed the door.

Once again, cheers erupted, and a large group of people rushed to the Reverend. Sister Richter waddled to him and kissed his cheek.

"Let's go home, Sister Richter, and put this nonsense behind us," the Reverend said.

As they passed Sarah, she grabbed hold of Sister Richter's arm. The Reverend tried to push her away, but Sarah held fast.

"You know what he does, and ya just let him keep on doin' it! You're as guilty as him!" Miss Jordan tried to pull Sarah back, but she tightened her grip on Sister Richter. "I know you're sceared of him, and so was I, but if a little girl like me can stand up to him, so can you!"

The Reverend broke Sarah's grip and nudged his wife forward.

"You know who else knows!" Sarah shouted. "God knows! And ya cain't lie your way past Him!"

"Get her out of here!" the Reverend yelled.

As the parishioners shoved Sarah away, she saw sorrow in Sister Richter's eyes for the first time.

The Richters hurried from the room, and for a moment, Sarah stared into the empty space they had left behind. Then she looked at her mother, Miss Jordan, and Mr. Godfrey, the only ones left in the room with her.

"What happened? Why'd they let him go?"

"I guess they didn't want to convict one of their own," Mr. Godfrey said.

Sarah burst into tears again. "But I told 'em! Didn't they believe me?"

"I'm sure some of them did," Mr. Godfrey said. "But no one actually saw him do anything."

"Sister Richter knows. Why didn't she tell 'em?"

"She couldn't," Mr. Godfrey said. "The law doesn't allow husbands and wives to testify against each other in this kind of trial."

"But she knows he done it!" Sarah cried.

"Baby," her mother said, "when Hank forced me to leave you and your brothers, I didn't wonna do it, but if I hadn't, he might've hurt us. I ain't sayin' that Sister Richter's keepin' the Reverend's secret is right because it ain't. What I'm sayin' is maybe she didn't have no choice. Sometimes women don't."

"But they coulda stopped him, and they didn't!" Sarah said. "Now he's got away with it and will do it again! It ain't fair!"

"No, it's not fair," Mr. Godfrey said. "Justice doesn't always prevail, and we don't always win. I know that's a hard lesson for a young person like you, but that's how life works."

Sarah frowned. "That's the kinda thang Sister Richter says, and I'm tarda hearin' it. There's gotta be a way of stoppin' him."

Sarah's mother took hold of her hand. "Come on, baby, let's go. You'll feel better after ya eat and take a nap."

At the courtroom door, Mr. Zimmerman walked up to them. "Mrs. Pinscher, my car's outside, and I'd be honored to take you and your children wherever you want to go."

Elizabeth blushed. "Thank you, Mr. Zimmerman. That's mighty nice of ya, but Miss Jordan's lookin' after us today."

"Well now, Elizabeth, if you had rather go with Mr. Zimmerman, that is quite all right," Miss Jordan said. "You are not obligated to go with Ustus and I."

Elizabeth smiled. "Well, okay, then we'll go with Mr. Zimmerman."

When the group stepped outside onto the courtyard, Johnny, Mark, and Ustus joined them. As they walked to the cars, several people booed. Sarah picked up a rock and hurled it at the tormentors. "Get outta here, ya lamebrains!"

Her mother grabbed her and pulled her back into the group.

"Right now, Mom, Sarah needs your full attention," Miss Jordan said. "Ustus, Mr. Godfrey, and I will take the boys with us."

As the cars pulled away from the court square, a small group of angry church members chased them. While Mr. Zimmerman sped away from the harasser, Sarah laid her head on her mother's shoulder and closed her eyes.

"Mrs. Pinscher, I know this may not be the best time to ask you this," Mr. Zimmerman said, "but you're going to need a job, and I need someone to help me at my store. Would you consider working for me? I can only pay you a dollar an hour, but I'd be honored to have you working there with me."

Elizabeth peered at Mr. Zimmerman. "My goodness. That's a high wage for somebody like me who's never done nothin' but cook and clean house."

"Well, it may seem that way right now, but it's a fair wage for the work you'd be doing."

"How many hours a week?"

"About forty, and you can set your own schedule. It's mostly stocking and cleaning."

"You mean I'd be makin' forty dollars a week?"

"Even more if you can work some overtime."

"Well, with my kids to take care of, I ain't sure how much time I'd have for workin'. I'll hafta thank about it."

"Oh, Mama," Sarah said. "You don't need to thank 'bout it. Just take it. You'll have plentya time for us kids and work, too. Whur else ya gonna make that kinda money? We gotta buy groceries and pay rent."

"Yeah, we do," her mother said. She took a deep breath and let it out. "Okay, I'll try it."

Mr. Zimmerman smiled. "Good! Now I can stop worrying about that."

The men parked the cars at the boardinghouse, and the group walked inside, where Miss Esther Evans, the owner, met them in the parlor.

"We would like lunch for eight," Miss Jordan said.

"Sorry, my dining room's full," Miss Evans said.

Miss Jordan pulled off her gloves and peeked around the corner. "It does not look full to me. I only see three people."

Sarah grinned. She loved it when Miss Jordan did things like that.

"The others just haven't arrived yet. They'll be here any minute now," Miss Evans said. "And they also want all of my rooms, so I've moved you all out."

"But we have already registered and paid," Miss Jordan said.

"So take me to court, why don't ya? Your bags are by the front door. Take 'em and get out. You're no longer welcome here. This is a respectable place, and I intend to keep it that way."

"Oh-h-h, now I get it!" Miss Jordan said. "This is about the outcome of the trial. Okay then, refund our money, and we will go."

Miss Evans pointed to the sign on the wall. "See that? 'No Refunds!'"

"But that is for people who make reservations and then do not show up, is it not?"

"It's for whoever I say it's for, and right now, it's for you."

Ustus pulled his business card from his pocket and stepped forward. "Never invite a lawyer to take you to court, Miss Evans, because that's exactly what I'll do if you don't refund our money right now. I'm sure town gossip about your involvement in a lawsuit will add tremendously to the respectability of this place and attract tons of business for you."

Miss Evans read the card and huffed. Then she scurried away to her office, returned with a wad of cash, and handed it to Ustus. "Now, sign this receipt and get out!"

As they picked up their suitcases to leave, Sarah ran back to Miss Evans. "You silly old cow!" she said and kicked her.

"That does it!" Miss Evans screamed and picked up the telephone. "I'm callin' the law!"

Sarah's mother grabbed her and pulled her outside. "What'd ya do that for?"

"Because she deserved it. I'm tarda people gettin' away with thangs. It feels good to get justice. And from now on, I'm always gonna get justice. I ain't never gonna let nobody hurt me again. And if they try, I'm gonna kill 'em!"

Her mother slapped her—hard, across the face. "That's a terrible thang to say!"

Sarah rubbed her cheek. She had never seen her mother so riled up.

They threw their arms around each other and bawled.

"I know ya been hurt, baby, and it breaks my heart. But it hurts me even more to see you actin' hateful like this. I'm losin' my sweet little girl, and it's tearin' me apart."

"I'm sorry, Mama, but nothin' seems to go right anymore. People do all sortsa bad thangs, and nobody stops 'em. They just get away with it."

"Yes, baby, I know it seems that way, but there's still lotsa good people in the world. Just look at what all Mr. Zimmerman's doin' for us."

"Yeah," Sarah said, "but him, Miss Gibson, Miss Jordan, Mr. Jake, and Bo Jesus are the only ones left."

After they dried their eyes, Sarah took hold of her mother's hand, and they walked to the cars.

"Is everything all right?" Miss Jordan said.

"Yes," Elizabeth said. "We just needed a mother-daughter talk."

"Okay, are we ready to go eat?" Mr. Zimmerman said. "I'll buy everyone's lunch at Hunt's Log Cabin. We know Fleta's nice. She was even nice to Ernest Hemingway when he lived here."

As they piled into the cars to leave, a police car pulled into the boardinghouse parking lot. "Ah, don't worry about him," Ustus said. "I'll deal with that later."

Hunt's was a cozy little cafe that specialized in sandwiches. Fleta Hunt and her mother ran the place alone, except for busy times when they hired a helper.

For the next hour, the group relaxed and enjoyed their meal. Then Mr. Godfrey said goodbye and went home.

"Well, now that our stomachs are full, all we have to do is find rooms," Miss Jordan said.

"I've got just the place," Mr. Zimmerman said. "I own a small furnished house next to my store, and right now, it's vacant. Mrs. Pinscher, I want you and your children to move into it. That way, if anyone tries to bother you or if you need anything, I'll be close by to help. It'll also be convenient for you to get to and from work. Miss Jordan can spend tonight there with you and the children, and Ustus can camp out with me in the back of the store. What do you say?"

Miss Jordan peered at Sarah and her mother. "Sounds good to me. What do you ladies think?"

"We'll take it," Sarah said.

"Well, if we do, Mr. Zimmerman's gotta agree to take the rent outta my pay."

Miss Jordan smiled. "So, Elizabeth, you are going to work at the store, are you?"

"Yes, Mr. Zimmerman's made me a offer too good for Sarah to refuse," she said, and everyone laughed.

"I'm just thinking of your welfare," Mr. Zimmerman said. "Some folks around here don't like you very much right now. You and your children need a safe place to live, and I have one."

"But there'll be gossip," Elizabeth said.

"So, let them gossip," Mr. Zimmerman said. "I'm still going to help you."

"He is right," Miss Jordan said. "Ignore the talk. There is no disgrace in taking help when you need it."

"I reckon not," Elizabeth said. "And if anybody does try'n hurt us, I'll gonna need all the help I can get to stop 'em."

Sarah grinned. After seeing her mother's reaction to her behavior at the boardinghouse that afternoon, she dared anybody to try to harm them. Her mother had become a fighter.

"Good!" Mr. Zimmerman said. "Now let's go get the place ready to live in."

On the way to the house, they stopped at the store and got everything needed to make it comfortable. Then while Johnny and Mark gathered firewood for the cookstove, the women made the beds, and the men stocked the cabinets.

Just before sunset, Mr. Zimmerman and Ustus returned to the store, made sandwiches, and brought them to the house along with potato chips, pork and beans, and cold sodas.

At dusk, Elizabeth lit the coal oil lamps and called everyone to the kitchen, where they filled their plates and returned to the front porch to eat.

After the meal, the kids chased lightning bugs while the adults sat and talked.

"How come there ain't no moskeeters here?" Elizabeth said.

"Because it's dry," Mr. Zimmerman said. "They're still thick over by the river."

"You know, it's funny. They don't bother the kids much, but they just eat me up."

"That's because you're so sweet," Mr. Zimmerman said, and everyone laughed.

Elizabeth knew Mr. Zimmerman was attracted to her and wasn't quite sure how she felt about that. But at least he wasn't pressing for anything–not yet, anyhow.

"What time y'all wont breakfast in the mornin'?" Elizabeth said.

Mr. Zimmerman looked at Miss Jordan. "What time does your train leave?"

"At ten-thirty. Ustus is taking me to the depot at ten."

"And I open the store at eight. How long will it take to fix it?"

"About forty-five minutes," Elizabeth said.

"Okay then, how about seven-thirty? Ustus and I'll bring the groceries over at six-thirty?"

"Yes, that'll work," Elizabeth said. Then she peered at her kids in the yard. "Sarah, Johnny, Marky, y'all come in now. It's bedtime."

"Ahh, Mama! Cain't we play just a little bit longer?" Mark said.

"No, it's gettin' late, and we gotta get up early in the mornin'." She ushered the kids inside, helped them wash, and put them to bed.

Tears filled Sarah's eyes as she kissed her mother's hand. "I'm sorry I's so hateful today. I's mad because they let Reverend Richter go."

"I know, baby," her mother said. "I'm sorry they let him go, too. Go to sleep now, and tomorra, you'll feel better." She closed the bedroom door and walked back to the front porch.

"Is everything okay?" Mr. Zimmerman said.

"Ever'thang's wonderful," Elizabeth said. Then she eased to his side, folded her arms, and gazed up at the stars.

When Mr. Zimmerman accidentally brushed against her, he flinched. "Oh, sorry! I didn't know I was so close."

"That's okay," Elizabeth said and smiled. He was a kind, gentle man like Ralph had been. And she felt good being around a nice man again.

"Well, I guess we'd better go," Mr. Zimmerman said. "Morning will get here before we know it."

"Yeah," Ustus said as he stood up and stretched. "Nights are always too short to suit me." Then he and Miss Jordan's strolled to his car.

Mr. Zimmerman gazed into Elizabeth's eyes. "You got everything you need?"

"Yeah, I thank so. I really appreciate ever'thang you're doin' for us."

"I'm glad I can help," he said and took hold of Elizabeth's hand. "If you need anything before morning, just holler, and we'll come running."

"Okay, I will."

He squeezed her hand and released it. "Goodnight."

"G'night."

The ladies watched from the porch as the car drove away. Then they walked inside, and Elizabeth locked the door.

While Miss Jordan got ready for bed, Elizabeth peeked in on her kids.

"Mama?" Sarah said when she saw her.

"Yes, baby?" her mother said and sat down on the edge of the bed.

"Why'd they let Reverend Richter go?"

"I don't know, baby."

"Did they thank I's lyin'?"

"No, they didn't thank that."

"Then why didn't they put him back in jail?"

"I don't know, baby, but you don't need to be thankin' about that. It's been a long day, and ya need to rest. Go to sleep now and have sweet dreams. If ya need me, I'll be right here."

While her mother hummed a lullaby, Sarah drifted off to sleep. In the early morning hours, she dreamed Reverend Richter had been convicted, and she saw him in prison. He looked old and haggard, and she felt sorry for him. Even though he had done those horrible things to her, Sarah forgave him. Then she slept peacefully for the rest of the night.

Chapter 27

AT HOME WITH MAMA

THE FOLLOWING MORNING, right on time, Mr. Zimmerman knocked on the front door.

"G'mornin'," Elizabeth said as she opened it.

"Good morning," he replied and stepped inside carrying a box of groceries, with Ustus right behind him carrying a block of ice in iron tongs.

While Mr. Zimmerman set the groceries on the cabinet counter, Elizabeth opened the icebox, and Ustus chunked the ice block inside.

"Whew!" Ustus said. "I'm not used to such hard work, especially early in the morning."

"Who wonts coffee?" Elizabeth said as the men rested.

"I'll have some," Mr. Zimmerman said.

"Yes, me too," Ustus said.

Elizabeth took three mugs from the cabinet and set them on the table. She wrapped a dish towel around the hot pot handle and poured the aromatic liquid into the cups. "Who wonts cream and sugar?"

"None for me," Ustus said.

"Yes, I'll take a little sugar," Mr. Zimmerman said.

Elizabeth puckered her lips like she intended to kiss him, then set the sugar bowl on the table, and the men laughed.

"Did you rest well, Mrs. Pinscher?" Mr. Zimmerman said.

"I rested great," Elizabeth said. "Since I got back to my kids, I been sleepin' like a baby. Maybe now, these dark circles under my eyes will go away. I didn't useta have 'em."

Mr. Zimmerman smiled. "Well, you've certainly gotten prettier since you've been back. And you smile a lot more now than you did at first."

"That's because I ain't worried nomore. I feel like ever'thang's gonna be okay again, except maybe for Sarah. That might take a while."

As Elizabeth refilled the men's coffee cups, Miss Jordan entered the room.

"Well, good morning there, Miss Lazy Bones," Ustus said. "How are you today?"

"Wonderful!" she said and yawned. "How are 'y'all?'"

"My goodness!" Ustus said. "Listen to her! She's become a Southern gal!"

Miss Jordan pulled the newspaper from Ustus's back pocket, plopped it into his hand, and pushed him into the living room. "You guys go sit down and read. Elizabeth and I need room to work in here."

As Miss Jordan set the last bowl of food on the table, the kids shuffled into the kitchen. Mark looked at the meal and grinned.

"What do you think, Mark?" Miss Jordan said. "Did your mother do a good job?"

"Yeah, she sure did. I want some of ever'thang."

Elizabeth seated the kids on the wall bench and the men at the ends of the table. Then Miss Jordan sat next to Ustus, and Elizabeth sat next to Mr. Zimmerman.

While Elizabeth filled Mark's plate, everyone else helped themselves.

When the boy's plates were ready, they started eating.

"Wait!" Sarah said. "We ain't said grace yet."

"We ain't said grace since we's at Miss Gibson's," Johnny said.

"Yeah, I know," Sarah said. "But we're a family again, now, and we need to start sayin' it."

"Yes, you're right," her mother said. "Would one of you gentlemen like to do that for us?"

The men gawked at each other.

"Well, Sarah, since this is your home," Miss Jordan said, "perhaps you should do the honors."

"Okay, let's all hold hands," Sarah said, and when the circle was connected, she began. "Dear God, Thank you and Mr. Zimmerman for all this wonderful food. And thank you for givin' us back our Mama to fix it for us. We love her very much. And thank you for all our new friends who are helpin' us and for all our old friends like Bo Jesus and Mr. Jake who helped us while Mama was gone. Bless them whurever they are. And bless all the people who are eatin' outta garbage cans. Help them find somethin' good to eat, so they won't go hungry. And bless us, so we won't ever hafta do that again. Oh, and God, please bless Reverend Richter, and make him a good man, so he won't ever hurt nobody again. Amen."

Everyone, including Mark, sat silently for a moment, then Elizabeth spoke. "That was beautiful, baby!" she said and wiped her tears on her apron. Then she gazed at Sarah and smiled. Maybe she wasn't going to have to worry about her little girl after all.

Miss Jordan looked at Ustus, took a deep breath, and blew it out like a whistle. "'Out of the mouths of babes!'"

After eating, the kids played outside while the adults talked and drank more coffee.

"Well, I guess I'd better go open the store," Mr. Zimmerman said, and everyone stood up. "Have a good trip home, Miss Jordan, and thanks for everything. You have a good trip, too, Ustus," he said, and the men shook hands. "Anytime you're up this way, drop in and see me."

"You can count on it," Ustus said.

Mr. Zimmerman joined Elizabeth, and they strolled to the front porch. "And thank you, Mrs. Pinscher, for that wonderful breakfast."

"Well, you brung me the stuff to make it with. All I done was cook it." Then Elizabeth paused and gazed at him. "Mr. Zimmerman, I don't wonna be called 'Mrs. Pinscher,' nomore. Please call me 'Elizabeth.'"

He gazed back at her and smiled. "Okay, then, 'Elizabeth.' I want you to call me 'Adam.'"

"Okay, 'Adam,'" she said and then chuckled.

"What's the matter?" Adam said.

"That sounds so strange to me after all these years of callin' you 'Mr. Zimmerman'. It's gonna take me some gettin' used to."

"Yes, I know what you mean. It'll take me a while to get used to calling you 'Elizabeth,' too.

"Well, I need to go. Somebody will be waiting for me to unlock the door. It's always like that, but that means I'm making money."

Elizabeth leaned over and kissed Adam on the cheek. "I'll be along in a little bit."

He looked at her and smiled. "No hurry," he said. Then he trotted down the steps and waved goodbye as he headed to the store.

While Elizabeth cleaned the kitchen, Miss Jordan and Sarah made the beds. Just before ten, Ustus loaded Miss Jordan's luggage into his car. Then they all gathered on the front porch.

"I'm gonna miss you, Miss Jordan," Sarah said as they hugged.

"I am going to miss you too, Sarah. Your mother has my address, so write to me."

"Oh, I will. I'll write to you today."

Then Elizabeth and Miss Jordan hugged. "I wish I had somethin' special to give ya. You been a real blessin' to us. I don't know what we'd done without ya. We're already lookin' forward to your next visit."

"So am I," Miss Jordan said.

As they drove away, everyone waved.

Then Elizabeth locked the house, and she and the kids walked to the store. It was her first day of work.

When people learned that Mr. Zimmerman had befriended Sarah and her family, his business dropped by more than half. Then, one night, someone threw a brick through the store's front window. Life was changing again.

Chapter 28

THE UNEXPECTED

ON SUNDAY FOLLOWING the trial, the church welcomed Reverend Richter back with open arms and celebrated his court victory with a dinner on the ground. In a special ceremony, the congregation presented the Richters with keys to the new parsonage built on the exact spot where the old one had stood.

Over the next few weeks, the community settled back into its daily routine as though nothing unusual had happened.

Then, on October 31st, when Cecil and Helen Mitchell arrived, as usual, to take the Richters to Sunday morning worship, they found Sister Richter sitting alone on the front porch in her rocking chair.

Puzzled by her behavior, they walked onto the porch, and Sister Richter invited them inside for coffee.

"Where's the Reverend?" Cecil said as he and Helen sat down at the kitchen table.

"Oh, he's-on-the-back-porch, in-the-bath-tub," Sister Richter said in her sing-song voice as she poured coffee into their cups.

"But this is Sunday," Cecil said. "Isn't he going to church?"

"No, he won't be going."

"Is he sick?" Cecil said.

"No, his mind's gone bad," Sister Richter said. "All he's been talking about lately is taking in another girl child."

"Ah, surely not," Cecil said, "after what happened with that Sarah girl."

"Yes, that's how I feel, too. I tried to tell him, but he scolded me–reminded me he was head of the household–and said it was his decision."

Helen cleared her throat. "Well, I'm sure he–"

Sister Richter turned away, opened the kitchen door, waddled onto the back porch, and left the door open. There sat the Reverend in the bathtub with his back to them and slumped as if taking a nap.

Cecil and Helen gawked at each other.

"What's she doing?" Helen whispered.

"Beats me," Cecil said, and they looked at the Reverend again.

"Pink soapsuds?" Helen said.

Cecil stood up, eased onto the porch, and peered around at the Reverend's face. Suddenly, he covered his eyes and sprang backward. "Oh, My Lord! His throat's been cut!"

Helen screamed and jumped to her feet.

"God told me to send him home, so I did," Sister Richter said. "Now, he's in the arms of Jesus." She smiled, sipped her coffee, and wandered back into the kitchen.

While the women sat at the table, Cecil telephoned the Sheriff.

That evening as Sarah and her brothers sat on the front porch of their little house watching the sunset, an old coupe rattled into the driveway. A few seconds later, three more cars clattered out of the twilight and parked along the road in front of the house.

"Mama, you'd better come out here! I thank there's gonna be trouble!" Sarah shouted as she and her brothers stood up.

Their mother walked outside behind the kids and laid her hands on Sarah's shoulders as they watched the people get out of the vehicles. A moment later, Mr. Zimmerman eased onto the porch carrying an ax handle.

While the people huddled behind the cars and spoke in whispers, a woman Sarah recognized from church passed out candles, and a man followed her, lighting them with his Zippo.

With their faces aglow in the candlelight, the people marched single file into the yard, singing "Amazing Grace."

Sarah peered down at them as they lined up in rows in front of the house. She sure hadn't expected this.

When the song ended, a church elder and his wife walked onto the porch.

"Sarah, we're here to apologize," he said. "I'm sure you've heard–"

"About Reverend Richter?" Sarah said. "Yes, we heard, and we're sorry."

"Sister Richter has been taken to the State Hospital in Little Rock," the elder said. "But before she left, she told about five other girls the Reverend molested, and that's why we're here."

The elder's wife handed Sarah a bouquet of red roses, and hugged her. "Please, forgive us for not believing you."

Sarah gazed into the woman's eyes, took the roses, and clutched them to her chest. Then she looked at the glowing faces. "There ain't nothin' left to forgive. I already done it."

"We have a lot of making up to do," the elder said, "and we want to start by inviting you and your family to begin attending church with us."

Sarah smiled and stepped to the edge of the porch. "We'd love to," she said. Then she sang: "Je-sus loves-me, this-I-know . . ." and everyone joined in: "For-the Bi-ble tells-me-so . . ." When the song ended, the people blew out their candles, returned to their cars, and drove away.

"Well, I was wrong," Sarah said. "People are still good after all."

Chapter 29

A NEW BEGINNING

WHEN THE TRUTH about Reverend Richter's crimes circulated, all the taunts and threats toward Sarah's family and Mr. Zimmerman stopped. Immediately, the store's business rebounded, making record profits. Then someone slipped an envelope full of cash under the front door with a note saying it was to pay for the smashed window. Never had Mr. Zimmerman nor Sarah and her family been so prosperous and happy.

True to Sarah's word, they all began attending the River Church, and at that year's Christmas party, Mr. Zimmerman and Mr. Peterson announced their engagements to Elizabeth and Miss Gibson.

Then, on New Year's Day, 1955, with all the Austin Community in attendance, Reverend Elmo Hawkins, the new River Church minister, conducted a double wedding ceremony.

The reception that followed is still talked about today. Someone spiked the punch, and everyone, including the children, got tipsy. They never found out who did it, but Belladonna Hemlock accused Al Peterson.

Over the next few months, Sarah and her family settled into a pleasant routine. Elizabeth even reconnected by mail with her St. Louis friend, Kate Carson.

Then on a Saturday evening in May, while the kids sat on the store steps eating strawberries, a movement down the highway caught Sarah's attention. "Who's that?" she said as she shaded her eyes and peered at the figures backlit by the hazy sunset.

"Who's who?" Johnny said.

"Who's that man with a dog comin' up the road?"

Johnny and Mark also shaded their eyes and peered at the silhouettes.

Suddenly, Sarah sprang to her feet and flung her half-eaten strawberry to the ground. "It's Mr. Jake and Houdini!"

The kids launched from the porch, and Sarah ran head-on into Jake, who scooped her into his arms while the boys and Houdini danced around them.

The commotion brought Adam and Elizabeth out onto the porch.

"Hey, Mr. Zimmerman, look who's here! "Sarah shouted as she pulled Jake toward the store. "It's Mr. Jake and Houdini!"

"Is that the 'Mr. Jake' the kids have told me so many stories about?" Elizabeth said.

"Yes, that's him," Adam said. Then he hugged Elizabeth and smiled. "How would you like to spend more time at home?"

"I'd love to! But I got work to do here."

"Well, I may have a solution for that."

Mr. Zimmerman rushed down the steps and shook Jake's hand. "Mr. Dooley, how would you like a full-time job?"

"Full-time?" Jake said as he squinted and scratched his chin whiskers. "What's it pay?"

"A dollar-and-a-quarter an hour."

Jake's eyebrows shot up. "Why so much?"

"Because my wife, these kids' mother, wants to spend more time with them at home. And for that to happen, I'll need someone to take over her store work."

"Ya mean 'ese kids ain't orphans no more?"

"No, they're not. When their stepfather got killed in St. Louis, their mother returned to them, and I married her, so they're hers and mine now."

"Well, I'll be dog!" Jake said and grinned. "I'm mighty glad to hear that! I been wonderin' what happened to 'em ever since that day the schoolmarm come and took 'em away. So, I fig'red I'd swang by here and see if'n I could find out somethin.'"

Sarah put on her most serious grown-up face and swaggered into step with the men. "Well, sir, I tell ya, Mr. Jake, we had us some perdy rough ole times there for a spell after that, but now, thangs is okay again. Mama and Mr. Zimmerman's, takin' real good care of us. And now that you and Houdini's back, thangs'll be even better."

"So, how about it, Mr. Dooley?" Mr. Zimmerman said, "Will you take the job?"

Jake paused and looked at the kids. "Well, sir, me and Houdini's kinda been thankin' 'bout settlin' down and gettin' off the road. The older we get, the tougher it is to always be on the move. So maybe it *is* time for us to plant some roots, if'n I can find somewhur cheap to live."

"I've got just the place," Mr. Zimmerman said, "and it won't cost you a cent. Since I've moved in with Elizabeth and the kids, you can have my old room in the back of the store."

Adam and the kids escorted Jake to the room, and he gave it a "looking-over."

"So, what do you think, Mr. Dooley?" Mr. Zimmerman said.

"Well, okay. I'll give her a whirl and see how she works out."

"That's great," Adam said and hurried away to tell Elizabeth the news.

Over the next few weeks, Jake and Houdini settled into their new living quarters and got used to their new lifestyle. Jake liked no longer having to hunt for food or find places to spend the night. But most of all, he enjoyed the company of the kids. Every day he told them stories about his travels around the country and the interesting people he had met. He even claimed to have spent some time with their friend, Bo Jesus, which made Mark giggle. But as good as Jake's stories were, some of Sarah's were even better. Whether true or not, they caused Jake's hair to stand on end. And that took some doing.

Chapter 30

THE MARBLE GAME

ON MONDAY MORNING, July 11, 1955, the first day of summer split-term, Sarah, Johnny, and Mark strolled the quarter-mile from home to Austin School.

Inside Johnny's jeans pocket, he tumbled the new marbles Mr. Zimmerman had given him. He pulled out one, closed his left eye, and looked at it against the sky.

"Whatsamatter? Don't ya like 'em?" Sarah said as she stared at him.

"Yeah, I like 'em just fine. But there's only one marble I really care 'bout, and that's the agate Daddy give me–the one I traded to Brewster Holland last year for Marky's lunch."

"Well, ya said you'd get it back."

"I am gettin' it back! I'm winnin' it back today, and I cain't hardly wait."

Sarah glared at Johnny. "Well, you'd better, or you'll hafta fig're out some other way to get it."

At morning recess, Johnny raced outside, challenged Brewster to a game of keeps, and he accepted. They marched to the marble pad and spent the rest of recess preparing it for the game.

At lunch break, they both dropped six marbles into the ring. Johnny's eyes sparkled as Brewster pulled out his shooter. It was the agate he had to win back.

Brewster drew a lagging line in the dirt, and the boys stepped back ten feet. Johnny shot his taw toward the mark, and it stopped two inches short. Then Brewster shot the agate, and it stopped an inch closer.

Brewster knuckled down just outside the ring, aimed at an easy target near its edge, and knocked it out. He pocketed his prize and then took position where his agate had stopped. Again he targeted a marble on the edge of the cluster. This time, both the target and his agate rolled out of the circle.

Brewster knuckled down again and shot, but only his agate exited the ring this time.

Johnny pulled out his shooter and also targeted the marbles closest to the circle's edge. He knocked out three, then missed his fourth shot, and his taw stayed in the ring.

Brewster shot at Johnny's taw, which was shielded by other marbles, so he didn't knock it out. But he did win another marble, so it was still his turn. Then Brewster claimed three more orbs with deadly accuracy, clearing a straight shot at Johnny's taw.

Johnny's heart pounded as he watched Brewster's agate knock his taw within a half-inch of the border. When Brewster's agate rolled outside the ring, Johnny breathed a sigh of relief and took shooting position. He knocked out one marble, then missed his second shot, and his taw stayed in the circle.

As the other kids finished lunch, they gathered around to watch the game, which was now down to only two marbles.

Brewster aimed at Johnny's taw and shot. As the agate rolled toward its target, Johnny held his breath. Suddenly, the agate hit a bump and veered to the side. It deflected Johnny's taw, but both marbles stayed in the ring.

Johnny knelt down, carefully aimed, and shot at Brewster's agate. In what seemed like slow motion, his taw hit the agate and spun both marbles from the ring.

Johnny leaped to his feet and shot his arms into the air. "Yes!"

Brewster flopped backward onto the ground and moaned. Then he picked up his agate, handed it to Johnny, and the boys shook hands.

Johnny held his prize agate up to the sun and rolled it back and forth between his thumb and forefinger. "I'll never lose you again," he said. Then he tucked the orb into his pocket.

On September 26, 2020, with Sarah, Mark, and his wife, Kim, by his side, Johnny died of stomach cancer at his home in Mountain Home, Arkansas.

At his funeral in Piggott, just before they closed his casket for the last time, Sarah tucked Johnny's precious agate into his coat pocket and kissed him on the forehead. "You'll need that for your marble games in heaven," she whispered.

- THE END -

Epilogue

SARAH

SARAH TURNED EIGHTEEN in 1960 and moved to St. Louis, where Miss Jordan helped her get a job at a department store.

In 1962, she became a member of the first class to attend St. Louis Community College.

In 1964, she enrolled in the Political Science Program at the University of Missouri in St. Louis, where she graduated two years later with high honors.

In 1967, she married a lawyer named Thomas Truman, who was four years her senior and had grown up in Kansas City, Missouri. That fall, they moved to Columbia, Missouri, where Thomas had joined a law firm.

Over the next four years, they had two children, Timothy Ray in 1969 and Judith Faye in 1971. During those years, Sarah worked as a Child Advocate for Boone County Social Services in Columbia.

At thirty-three, Sarah entered state politics and was elected to the Missouri House of Representatives. She remained politically active for the next 30 years, focusing much of her attention on helping children.

At 63, Sarah and Thomas moved back to Kansas City, Missouri.

Timothy Ray remained single all of his life and taught college English in Seattle, Washington.

Judith Faye married a struggling hillbilly musician and spent the rest of her life in Nashville, Tennessee, working to pay the bills. They never had children.

JOHNNY

In 1963, at 18, Johnny joined the United States Army and made it his career.

In 1966, at 21, he served a tour in Vietnam.

In 1968, at 23, he was ordered to South Korea, where he met a beautiful Korean woman named Kim Chong, and they married in 1969.

Over the next three years, they had two daughters, Young-hee in 1970 and In-sook in 1972.

In 1993, at 49, E-9, Sergeant Major John H. Skaggs retired from the military, and he and Kim moved to Mountain Home, Arkansas, where he became a part-time fishing guide.

Young-hee married a United States Air Force 1st Lieutenant, and they had four children, three sons, and a daughter.

In-sook married a professor of medicine in Atlanta, and they had two daughters.

On September 26, 2020, Johnny died of stomach cancer at his home in Mountain Home, Arkansas. He was buried at Piggott Cemetery beside his parents, Ralph and Elizabeth Skaggs, with a space next to him for Kim.

MARK

After graduating from Piggott High School in 1966, Mark tried to join the United States Air Force but was rejected due to impaired hearing. He stayed in Austin, became a farmer, and ten years later, owned 600 acres of rich Saint Francis River delta land.

In 1969, at 21, he married 19-year-old Sheila Sarver, one of his Austin schoolmates, and over the next four years, they had two sets of twins. Ralph Louis and Edward Thomas were born in 1971, and Sarah Jane II and Mary Elizabeth II were born in 1974.

Mark and his sons spent much of their free time hunting and fishing along the St. Francis River.

When Mark retired, Ralph and Elizabeth II's husband, Bert Massey, took over the farm. Edward and his wife moved to Williams, Arizona, where he worked at the Grand Canyon. Sarah Jane II and her husband, Lanton Paxton, moved to Boise, Idaho, where he worked as a Payette River Ranger in the Boise National Forest.

ELIZABETH AND ADAM ZIMMERMAN

Elizabeth Hood Skaggs Pinscher Zimmerman, born in 1921, and Adam Zimmerman, born in 1918, ran their store until 1985, when they sold it and retired. When Adam died of a stroke in 1995 at 77, Elizabeth moved in with Mark and his family. She died in her sleep at 79 in 2000. Adam is buried in the Piggott Cemetery next to Ralph and Elizabeth.

JAKE DOOLEY

Buford "Jake" Dooley was born sometime around 1900. After he and Houdini retired from life on the road, Jake worked and lived at Mr. Zimmerman's store until Houdini got old and died in 1965. Then Jake moved to an Old Soldier's Home in Little Rock and was never heard from again.

BO JESUS

In the summer of 1966, a major United States picture magazine published an extensive article on American Hoboes, and Sarah bought a copy. Featured in one of the pictures was Bo Jesus, holding up an old church key and smiling.

Author's Notes

Because farm children had to help with the crops, their school year was split. The following chart shows when their school terms were in and out of session in 1954.

NORTHEAST ARKANSAS SPLIT SCHOOL TERM 1954:
School In: January 4, 1954–May 7, 1954
School Out: May 10, 1954–July 9, 1954
School In: July 12, 1954–August 20, 1954
School Out: August 23, 1954–October 1, 1954
School In: October 4, 1954–December 17, 1954

The Bible

There are several "so-called" Bible quotes in this book commonly quoted by people as Bible scriptures but are not actually found in the Bible.

CH 9:–Miss Gibson says, "Because the Bible says, "Cleanliness is next to Godliness," but this is actually an old Babylonian and Hebrew proverb and not a passage from the Bible. Sir Francis Bacon is said to have used it in 1605.

CH 9:–Reverend Richter says, "Well done, my good and faithful servant: enter thee into the kingdom of heaven." This is probably a paraphrase of Matthew 25:21 in the King James Version, which says, "Well done, thou good and faithful servant: thou hast been faithful over a few things, I will make thee ruler over many things: enter thou into the joy of thy lord."

CH 10:–Reverend Richter says, "The Holy Scripture says, 'He who does not work, neither shall he eat,' and that, 'idle hands and idle minds are the devil's workshop.'"

Concerning: "He who does not work, neither shall he eat," the King James Version says in 2nd Thessalonians 3:10: "...if any would not work, neither shall he eat."

Concerning: "Idle hands and idle minds are the devil's workshop," the King James Version says in Proverbs 16:27: "An ungodly man diggeth up evil: and in his lips there is as a burning fire."

The Bible does not actually say, "Idle hands and idle minds are the devil's workshop." That saying was traced back to Chaucer in the 12th Century. St. Jerome is also credited with a similar quote between 347 and 420 A.D.

CH 10:–Reverend Richter says, "'Spare the rod and spoil the child,' sayeth the holy scripture!" This saying was also often credited to the Bible but is actually from a 17th Century poem titled Hudibras by Samuel Butler.

> "What medicine else can cure the fits
> Of lovers when they lose their wits?
> Love is a boy by poets styled
> Then spare the rod and spoil the child."

CH 24:–Mr. Godfrey says, "Well, I don't believe you. Isn't it true that someone tipped you off about the warrant, so you set fire to the house hoping that people would think you and your wife had died in the blaze because you knew 'your sins [were about to] find you out?'" This quote is taken from Numbers 32:23 of the King James Version: "But if ye will not do so, behold, ye have sinned against the LORD: and be sure your sin will find you out."

CH 27:–"Miss Jordan peered over at Ustus. She took a deep breath and blew it out like a whistle. 'Out of the mouths of babes!'"

King James Version–Psalm 8:2–"Out of the mouth of babes and sucklings has thou ordained strength because of thine enemies, that thou mightest still the enemy and the avenger."

Matthew 21:16–"And said unto him, Hearest thou what these say? And Jesus said unto him, Yea; have ye never read, Out of the mouth of babes and sucklings thou hast perfected praise?"

ACKNOWLEDGEMENTS

THANKS TO MY daughter, Amy Hitt, for all her support, suggestions, and inspiration.

Thanks to my journalist friend, Bill Bowden, who always knows what "Lou" is up to.

Thanks to Jackie Stites and Robert Laurence for guiding me to helpful contacts.

Thanks to my editors, Dave King, John Abernathy, and Dave Edmark, for their guidance and corrections.

Thanks to my legal advisors, Kim Smith and Tim Tarvin, who helped make the court scenes believable and who gave me other legal guidance.

Thanks to my late friend and first reader, Patricia May, who urged me to finish the story.

Thanks to my late Beta Reader, Jim Fuller, who still makes me laugh every day. And yes, Jim, when I asked you to read it, I knew you weren't part of my target audience. Thanks for doing it anyway.

Thanks to all of my other Beta Readers. Your feedback was invaluable. When you reread this story, you will recognize your contributions. In alphabetical order by first names: Dale Parsons, Dave Edmark, Glenna Cates, Janna Fry, Judy Christian, Judy Kelley, Mary Jo Schneider, Steve White, Mary Catherine (Sherraden) White, Terry Parker, and Vicky May.

A special thanks to Beta Reader Mary Jane Van Horne. Advice from people whom authors don't personally know is often some of the most valuable.

Thanks to all the publishing staff who put this novel out there for others to read and enjoy.

And finally, thanks to every person who reads this book. I hope you enjoy it. If you have comments, questions, etc., please email me at my website, <carlhitt.com>.

CPSIA information can be obtained
at www.ICGtesting.com
Printed in the USA
JSHW082029210623
43507JS00009B/10